FIVE
CARD
MURDER

A SMILEY AND MCBLYTHE MYSTERY

Five Card Murder
© 2021 Bruce Hammack
All rights reserved.

Published by Jubilee Publishing, LLC
ISBN 978-1-7350302-9-6

Cover design: Joyce Hammack
Editor: Teresa Lynn, Tranquility Press

FIVE CARD MURDER

A SMILEY AND McBLYTHE MYSTERY

BRUCE HAMMACK

BOOKS BY BRUCE HAMMACK

The Smiley and McBlythe Mystery Series
Exercise Is Murder, Prequel
Jingle Bells, Rifle Shells
Pistols and Poinsettias
Five Card Murder
Murder In The Dunes
The Name Game Murder
Murder Down The Line
Vision Of Murder

The Star of Justice Series
Long Road to Justice
A Murder Redeemed
A Grave Secret
Justice On A Midnight Clear

Want to know how Steve Smiley got his start in homicide? Sign up for my newsletter on brucehammack.com and get a free copy of *Seeing Red*!

1

H eather's gaze lifted from the mound of documents on her desk. "I hope you brought us a nice juicy murder to solve."

"How did you know?" asked Steve with a hint of mischief in his voice. "It just hasn't happened yet."

She watched as Steve swept his white cane before him until he reached her. He extended a hand holding a registered letter.

"I received a phone call Monday morning from a rancher I haven't spoken to in fifteen years. He bent my ear for half an hour. I didn't know Charley could string that many words together in one conversation. He asked me to be the executor of his will and said he'd mail me the original. I assume that's what I signed for this morning."

"Why didn't you tell me about this? It's Thursday afternoon."

Steve settled in a chair in front of her desk, hooked an ankle over a knee and leaned back. "Monday you jetted off to Florida. Tuesday you were in Raleigh buying a pharmaceutical testing company, and last night you sounded preoccupied. From the volume coming through the cat door between our dining rooms, I surmised you and Jack needed to hash things out. Besides, I was busy."

A snicker escaped before she could stop it. What he said wouldn't make sense to someone not familiar with their unique living situation and the fact they share a Maine Coon cat named Max. Hence, the cat door between their separate condos. "Sorry you had to experience the domestic disturbance." Heather turned to look out the window. Nothing blocked early June's afternoon sun, but all she could see was a cloudy future. "We had a spat."

"Is that what you call it? Maggie and I used to call those knock-down, drag-outs."

Her gaze shot back to her business partner. "It was nothing more than two attorneys defending their positions." Even to her, the words had a hollow, tinny ring to them.

Steve unhooked his foot. "I've heard worse, but not without someone going to the hospital."

With chin cupped in her hands, she sighed. "Jack's a great guy, but he's smothering me. He said we need to spend more time together and I work too much."

"He only spoke the truth. A week off is what you need."

Heather stuck her tongue out at the man who couldn't see her.

Steve blocked the tacky response she'd planned by getting back to his purpose in coming to the office. "Open the letter. I'm interested in knowing how big of a mess I got myself into."

"We'll get to that later. You mentioned a murder that hasn't happened yet. What did you mean?"

Steve flicked his hand as if shooing away a fly. "Only an old man's ramblings. He rattled on about what a poor job he'd done raising his children and how they couldn't wait until he died so they could sell the ranch. He didn't hold back on how they hated him."

"Enough to kill him?"

"Killing a parent is rare." Steve tilted his head as he reminisced. "Although I once worked a case where a daughter killed her father by adding minced oysters to his bowl of soup. Anaphylactic shock closed his airway."

"And the motive? It must have been something awful."

Steve answered with a straight face. "He refused to shell out for a destination wedding to Hawaii."

He chuckled as she groaned. "That pun deserves the electric chair."

"I'm shocked you said that."

"Enough!" said Heather as she tried to choke back a giggle. "I'll read the will if it will keep you quiet."

She reached in her desk drawer for a silver letter opener while Steve's phone, equipped with an app for the blind, announced in a mechanical voice, "Call from Marvin Goodnight."

Steve told the phone to disconnect the call. "I don't know anyone by that name. He can leave a message if it's legit. Open the letter."

Heather pulled out a single page of hand-printed scrawl, dated May 20.

This is my last will and testament. I name Steve Smiley the executor of my estate.

I want that lawyer you work with to read this to the children I list below.

It's done rite and legal—dated, signed by two witnesses and notarized.

I give Ester Mae, Leroy, Sue Ann and Rance five days to come up with a plan on how to divvy up everything. They have to be 100% in agreement on what to do with every head of cattle, every acre of land, the houses, barns, life insurance money and anything else I might have missed.

If they can't agree, there's a second part of the will that you'll get five days after the reading of this one.

One more thing. Steve Smiley is to run the meetings as he sees fit.

Heather puffed out her cheeks and let a breath escape. "This is the strangest will I've ever seen."

Steve's frozen expression reminded her of a bronze statue until he reanimated and asked, "Is it legal?"

"Do you want the long answer or the short one?"

"Short."

"It satisfies all legal requirements."

Steve shifted in his chair. "Well, unless he's terminally ill, which he didn't mention in our phone conversation, it may be a while before I have to worry about this. I don't think he's old enough to have one foot in the grave. On the other hand, maybe he has suspicions that one of his kids is tired of waiting on their inheritance."

"You just said a child murdering a parent was rare."

Steve shrugged. "Rare, yes, but not unheard of. All joking aside, I have seen cases where the child killed the parent. And almost anything is possible in Llano County. There's still a little of the wild, wild west down there."

"Llano County?" With two-hundred and fifty-four counties in Texas, Heather hadn't committed their names to memory. "Where is it?"

Steve curled his fingers inward but left his thumb sticking out. "Take a road map of Texas and put your fist square in the middle. Your thumbnail should be over Llano County."

"Sounds desolate."

Steve didn't have time to respond as his phone announced, "Call from Sheriff Stony Blake."

Heather listened to the one-sided conversation.

"This is Steve Smiley... Yes, Sheriff, I remember you... Oh, sorry. I didn't know Marvin Goodnight was your chief deputy... You don't say. Hold on, I'm putting you on speaker."

"Like I was sayin', we found Charley Voss by his barn this morning. He's been dead for several days."

The voice reminded Heather of a weathered barn, seasoned by sun and wind, and capable of standing up to harsh weather. She sat upright and turned her head, ensuring she wouldn't miss a word.

"Charley called me Monday and asked me to be executor of his estate. I received his will by registered mail today. My partner and I were reading over it when you called. I'm guessing he left a message or told someone to call me if something happened to him. Was he terminally ill?"

Steve paused. "Or was it murder?"

The voice on the phone hesitated. "Why would you ask a question like that?"

"Just a hunch. From what Charley said Monday, his relationships with his children were strained, to say the least."

"Let's just say, I have some strong suspicions. He's on his way to Austin for an autopsy."

The meaning of the sheriff's last statement told Heather homicide was not out of the question.

"Who found the body?" asked Steve.

"The ranch foreman, Hector DeLeon."

"He's still working at the Rocking V? Is he a suspect?"

"I've got him in an interview room and he's cooperating. If his alibi checks out, I'll cut him loose."

"Any idea when the funeral might be?"

"Not yet, but it'll be a closed casket. Buzzards and coyotes had at least two days with him."

Steve grimaced.

Heather's mind turned to consider the killer. The trail was days old, plenty of time for the murderer to get away or establish an alibi.

Steve continued, "I'll need to give you a formal statement. If you call the Montgomery County Sheriff's office, I can take care of it before I come. They'll e-mail it to you."

The sheriff issued a raspy cough and spoke in short bursts. "Thanks. I'll keep you informed concerning the funeral." He paused. "I remember you were a bright kid. Too bad you can't tell a goat from a deer."

Laughter broke out on both ends of the phone. "Thanks for reminding me. I guess I'll never live that down," said Steve.

He signed off and Heather didn't wait. "I want to hear about the goat."

Steve pushed up from his chair. "What happens at a deer lease, stays there. Besides, I was thirteen and the statute of limitations ran out years ago." He made for his desk. "It will be at least five days before the funeral and another day or two before reading the will. Can you arrange your schedule to take a week off or do I need to find someone else?"

Heather's gaze took in the stacks of documents and yellow legal pads ready to waterfall off her desk. Despite the mounds, Steve was right about her needing time off. "The other attorneys in the office can take up my slack. Are we driving?"

"We don't have to. That jet you got for Christmas will do nicely, and there's an airport big enough to handle it." A smile that relayed secret knowledge crossed Steve's face. "Leave the arrangements to me."

2

Heather slid her Mercedes SUV into a parking spot at Conroe-North Houston Regional Airport and turned to Steve. "I'm sorry. I didn't mean to say you looked funny."

Steve didn't respond, which was worse than if he'd chewed her out.

"It's not a big deal," she said. "You can change into a white shirt on the plane."

He snapped back, "I can't believe you let me walk out wearing a pink shirt and olive pants."

She rubbed eyes that felt as if someone had spooned sand into them. "I didn't go to sleep until three-thirty. It was still dark when Max woke me demanding breakfast."

"By the time you got up, I'd fed him," countered Steve. "He wasn't asking for his breakfast; Max thought you were missing your Thursday morning workout." He let out a huff and lowered his voice. "Heather, you're working yourself to death. You can't keep up this pace."

She closed her eyes. Steve was right. She'd heard the same words a hundred times from Jack. Well, not a hundred, but enough to where the repetition had worn thin. Life hadn't always been so hectic. When did she climb on the treadmill of mergers and acquisitions? And more important, how could she get off?

A knock on the window startled her back to reality. A man dressed in black slacks, a white shirt and black tie smiled at her. She opened the door and addressed the co-pilot of her plane. "Good morning, Tim. Are we ready?"

He cut a handsome, albeit young, figure with gelled black hair and aviator sunglasses. "Yes, Ms. McBlythe. Johnathan's doing his walk-around. Pop open the back and I'll get your luggage."

Steve's door opened as she stepped to the rear of the vehicle. "I'll need everything. Sorry there's so much."

Steve expressed his displeasure about her bringing so much work by first issuing a loud moan. He followed it with, "I thought you were going to delegate to the other attorneys."

"I did delegate. There are just some things I have to do myself."

"Try not to get a hernia, Tim. I'm surprised she didn't bring her desk and chair."

Heather pointed to a box. "Put this one in the cabin with us and I'll take my briefcase."

"Hand me my garment bag," said Steve. "She didn't realize pink and olive don't blend until she stopped for a double espresso."

"Pink shirts are in these days, Mr. Smiley," said Tim.

"They might be for you, but for an old codger, people will think I'm chasing the glory days of youth. Once you hit fifty, your fashion tastes simplify. It also saves money if I don't have so many choices."

Steve dragged his hand down the front of his shirt. "Could I interest you in a gently worn, pink, button-down Oxford?"

Tim's smile collided with Heather's scowl. He lowered his head, grabbed bags and said, "This will take several trips. The plane's ready to board whenever you are."

Heather's phone chirped with an incoming call. She retrieved it and listened to the concerned voice of an attorney from her office regarding a merger Heather had been working on for several months. Out of the corner of her eye, she saw Steve shake his head and speak to Tim. The attorney chattered on about being unable to get a current spreadsheet on the company McBlythe Enterprises was considering acquiring. Meanwhile, Tim picked up a box and placed Steve's hand on his shoulder and walked him to the plane.

It took Tim three more trips to ferry the luggage and boxes of files to the twin–engine Cessna Citation M2, a Christmas present from her father. With the phone pressed to her ear, Heather looped the straps of her briefcase and purse over her shoulder, grabbed her extra-large coffee and locked the car. She acknowledged Johnathan, the pilot, with a nod as she boarded.

Configured to seat five passengers in beige leather chairs, the corporate jet made Heather feel like she'd made it to the big leagues. One seat, facing the cabin door, was seldom used, but Steve sat there, a sign he was still stewing over his mismatched clothes. Or was it that she'd been working sixteen-hour days? Either way, Steve's display of passive-aggressive behavior didn't escape her. That left Heather to distribute her bags, purse and a box of files in the remaining three seats, with one for her to occupy. She dug through a box, produced the missing spreadsheet and continued her phone conversation while buckling her seat belt.

Steve, seated nearest the cockpit, instructed the pilot to take off. The high-pitched cry of jet engines coming to life preceded a catapult-like ride down the runway and sucked Heather back in her seat. If it had been any other day, she would have loved the exhilaration of thrust, a steep ascent, and a hard bank to the right. Not today; she had problems to solve.

Once airborne, she pulled a fold-down table top from the wall and settled in to make changes to a contract and field two more calls. Her gaze shifted in time to see Steve insert ear buds and relax with feet outstretched and eyes closed. Not until the sound of the landing gear being deployed did she glance out the window. A shimmering body of water snaked its way through hills covered with stunted trees. By the time she returned the papers to their proper boxes, the wheels kissed the runway. She looked at her watch. Fifty-five minutes had elapsed since the engines came to life.

Tim unlatched the door and unfolded steps. He made sure Steve negotiated his way to the tarmac. Heather followed once she grabbed her purse and briefcase containing the papers that needed her immediate attention. Her breath caught as she stood in the cabin's door. They'd landed on a plateau over-looking a body of water and what appeared to be a miniature city, something like an elaborate model train set. She'd been around the world and seen awe-inspiring sights. This panoramic view had a quality all its own. Perhaps it was the contrast between the harshness of the terrain and the shimmering water of the lake that caused her mouth to hinge open.

The pilot spoke from behind her and broke the spell. "Welcome to Horseshoe Bay Resort. This is their private jet airport. Quite a view, isn't it?"

"I had no idea this existed in Texas. It's gorgeous. What lake is it?"

"It used to be called Granite Shoals Lake, but they renamed it after President Johnson. Everyone calls it Lake LBJ."

Further historical facts had to wait as a young woman wearing a uniform of sorts exited a black limousine and approached Steve. Heather joined them as the pilot and co-pilot retrieved luggage and Heather's boxes.

Heather eased beside Steve and placed his hand on her shoulder. "I can't believe this place."

He gave his head a single nod. "Wait till you see the resort and the golf courses."

"You've been here before?"

Steve swallowed hard. "I surprised Maggie with a weekend here to celebrate our fifteenth wedding anniversary."

Heather reached and squeezed his hand. His only response was to say, "Let's get to our rooms. I didn't sleep well last night."

She wanted to say something more, but Steve didn't give her a chance. "I scheduled the reading for five o'clock this afternoon. You brought the will, didn't you?"

A moan answered the question. She stopped and circled back to the captain as he exited the plane carrying her boxes. "I left an important document back at my office. I need you to return to Conroe ASAP and fly back with it. Someone from my office will meet you at the airport."

"No problem. Do you want us to stay here after we return? Just in case you need us again."

"That won't be necessary, but keep your phone on. I've got a lot going on right now."

Heather looked at Steve standing on the tarmac. What memories of his deceased wife must haunt him? She searched for something pithy to say, but only managed to scrape up a lame apology. "Steve, I'm so sorry I forgot the—"

He yelled, "Tim. Look in my garment bag and see if there's a white shirt. I need to change."

Heather slapped her forehead. Words of apology weren't welcome, so she walked around the limo and opened her door while Steve changed shirts.

A Ford Explorer with an emblem on the side came toward them.

"Did you expect the sheriff to meet us?" asked Heather.

Steve raised his chin as he buttoned his shirt and stuffed the tail in his pants. The thrusting out of his chin gave him the appearance of a hunting dog trying to catch a scent. "No, but it doesn't surprise me."

3

The man exiting the patrol vehicle didn't meet Heather's expectations of a sheriff named Stoney Blake. She'd pictured the sheriff as a sixty-something year old, leather-faced part-time rancher with a tin of snuff in his back pocket. A simple explanation became apparent as she read the name tag of the man in his thirties wearing a khaki shirt. GOODNIGHT. From the top down the deputy wore a straw cowboy hat whose brim looked a half-size too big, wrap-around sunglasses, a uniform shirt with a sheriff's department patch on one sleeve and an American flag on the other. A brown hand-tooled belt held two speed loading cylinders of extra shells. A Colt Python .357 magnum rested in a brown holster on his hip. Blue jeans and scuffed square-toed cowboy boots completed the ensemble.

Heather's first assessment of Deputy Goodnight was that, despite his relatively young age, he'd gone back in time forty years. The six-shot double-action pistol, a much-loved standard of Texas lawmen in bygone days, made way for the fourteen-plus shot 9mm and .40 caliber semi-automatics that officers carry today. She had to admit, the retro-look fit the rugged terrain. The only thing missing was a horse.

The deputy nodded a greeting to Heather and looked at Steve. "Are you Mr. Smiley?"

"Sheriff Blake couldn't make it?"

The man hooked his thumbs in the gun belt. "I'm Chief Deputy Marvin Goodnight. I'm in charge of the Voss murder investigation."

Was it the emphasis on "I'm" that rubbed Heather the wrong way? Perhaps it was the lack of sleep that caused her first impression to be a bad one. Whatever it was, she dismissed it and took a step toward the deputy with her right hand extended. "Heather McBlythe. I'm Mr. Smiley's partner."

He shook her hand. "Ma'am. Sheriff Blake asked that I get a copy of the will."

"Uh... it will be here this afternoon or I could have someone fax you a copy."

Steve interrupted. "Follow us to the hotel. I scanned it to my computer. We can get a copy made in the business center."

Heather grimaced. Steve hadn't trusted her to come prepared, so he made sure he was. It was time to get her mind on the case enough to do a good job. She also needed to tell the pilots not to worry about returning with the will.

"Goodnight?" asked Steve. "Are you a descendant of Charles Goodnight?"

The man raised his chin and straightened his posture. "That's right. I see you know Texas history."

"Some, but not as much as I'd like to. Tell me about your great-grandpa."

"You're close. My great-great-grandpa."

Steve had primed the pump. Deputy Goodnight's chest swelled. "The Goodnight-Loving cattle drives gathered longhorns from all over south Texas." He waved an extended hand to the east, south and west. "My great-great-grandpa and Mr.

Loving took two-thousand head of free-range longhorns to Fort Sumner, New Mexico in 1866. They traveled west until they hit the Pecos River and then followed it north by west."

The lesson continued as Heather looked on. Steve encouraged him by asking questions and speaking in a Texas drawl thick as mud. Was Steve protecting her from additional embarassment, or was this his way of getting back at her for not focusing when they had a murder to investigate? It could have something to do with a pink shirt.

The pilot motioned for Heather to join him. They met at a point beyond Steve's hearing.

"Everything you brought is in ground transportation." He looked at his watch. "You better call your office and have someone meet us at the airport. Cruising at four-hundred and sixty miles an hour means we might be there before they can fight their way through traffic."

"No need. Steve brought what we need, but keep your phone on all the same."

"We're paid to fly whenever you need us." He gave her a slack salute and boarded the stairs, followed by Tim, who nodded. She wondered how many girlfriends Tim had around the country.

She took Steve's hand and placed it on her shoulder. With as much western twang as she could place over her Boston accent, she said, "We'd best mosey down the trail. That fancy plane needs to head east." Her attempt at humor fell flat.

"Follow us to the hotel," said Steve to Deputy Goodnight. "We'll get a cup of coffee and you can tell me about the cattle drive to Denver."

Heather placed Steve in the front seat so he could chat with the driver. They exited the airport property and descended a steep hill past homes and clusters of condos with swimming pools and professional landscaping. She noted how spread apart they were, with natural flora and fauna looking for a chance to retake smaller verdant lawns. The contrast between the areas graced with abundant water and care, and that of the dull, dangerous, natural landscape of varieties of cacti brought to mind one of her trips to Africa. What a difference water made.

Names of streets caught her eye as the roads wound downward. Signs reading High Stirrup, Bull Whip, Out Yonder and Branding Iron passed by her window. A steep drop gave way to undulating land and a dramatic entrance announcing Horseshoe Bay Resort. The closer to Lake LBJ the road took them, the more impressive the real estate became. A resort hotel rose above hundreds of swanky condos, duplexes, and single-family homes. Scrub land inhabited by wild cattle making their way to drink from the Colorado River, had been transformed into a playground for wealthy visitors, all within driving distance of Austin, the state capital.

Hotel bell hops sprang into action as soon as the limo came to rest under the hotel's awning. Heather took care of checking in and getting a copy of the will from Steve's computer while Deputy Goodnight continued to bend Steve's ears. After handing Steve a key to his room, she announced, "I'll take care of putting Steve's things away and make some phone calls."

Steve nodded. "Marvin and I will grab lunch at one the restaurants. It's not every day I get to learn the history of a real Texas legend."

"I've plenty to keep me busy, so I'll call for room service." Heather's words may have been those of agreement, but her thoughts traveled in a different direction. What was Steve after? Unless she missed her guess, he'd pump every drop of information about suspects out of Deputy Goodnight.

Her thoughts shifted to the reading of the will. Just as fast, they drifted to the acquisition of a gold mine. A lot of work remained to bring in the deal.

HEATHER ROSE TO ANSWER THE KNOCK ON HER DOOR WITH HER phone pressed against an ear. After putting an attorney from her office on hold, she threw open the door and looked at Steve. "You're early."

"I'm on time and we need to talk."

Heather led him to a chair and moved a small mountain of files by placing them on the uncovered portion of her king-size bed. She answered a final question and ended the conversation by stating she wasn't taking calls for the next two hours.

Heather laid her phone down and looked at Steve. He hadn't contacted her all day. When he didn't like something, his first reaction was to keep quiet. She ran her fingers through her hair and cleared off the second chair that sat at an angle to his and opened with, "I know, I'm working too hard and I need to get up to speed on this case. What did you get from Deputy Goodbye?"

"It's Goodnight. Marvin Goodnight."

She wanted to slap her forehead again, but covered up her mistake with a white lie. "Don't be so snippy. I was testing to see if you still had a sense of humor."

"Ah."

That meant she didn't fool him for a minute. Time to raise her voice and sound cheerful. "Did you discover any juicy family secrets? What are you expecting? Are any of Charley's four children a suspect?"

She noticed Steve's chest expand and then slowly return to normal. "Marvin and I talked about cattle drives most of the time."

Heather tilted her head. "What about Charley's murder? I thought that's why we're here."

Steve shook his head. "I came here to read a will and coach four mourning children through a difficult week of deciding how to divide an estate of nine thousand acres, cattle, and substantial life insurance settlements."

"What about the murder case?"

"We're not invited."

Heather stared at the man she thought she knew so well. He had a way of surprising her.

"It's not wise for us to get involved. At least not yet. I offered our help, but Marvin made it clear he doesn't want or need it." He allowed the words to sink in. "One more thing. No one has hired us to investigate the crime."

Heather stood. "So that's it? You're just going to walk away?" She began to pace. "Then why am I here?"

"Because I asked you to come and you need a break."

The words came like a punch in the gut. He followed them with, "It's a little plan I cooked up to save you from yourself. You can work here on your merger and enjoy the amenities of the resort. There's a first-class fitness center, yoga, swimming, tennis courts and plenty of places to walk. You can even rent a boat at the marina. Maggie talked about the spa for the rest of her life, so I'm sure it will meet your expectations. Of course, you're more than welcome to sit in on the sessions I'll conduct with the heirs if you want to."

He walked toward the door with his cane leading the way. "Grab the will. If you're coming with me, we need to get going. If not, give it to me and I'll handle the meeting."

"Just a minute," said Heather with a lump in her throat. "I appreciate what you're trying to do, but this merger means so much to me."

"Why?"

"Huh?"

"Why does this merger mean so much to you?"

"Well... it just does. Father handed it off to me before Christmas and I promised I wouldn't let him down."

"Ah."

Heather sensed her Irish blood begin to warm. "What's that 'Ah' supposed to mean?"

Steve stopped and turned around. "It means you've changed since Christmas, and not for the better." He took a step toward her. "By the way, did you call Jack and let him know you were leaving town for a week?"

She groaned.

"Don't worry. I told him last night."

She jerked her briefcase from the bed, sending stacks of papers cascading to the floor. "Let's go."

4

The Live Oak conference room boasted a long table with sixteen plush executive chairs set at precise intervals around the rectangle. Two of the heirs sat on Steve's immediate right while a younger one faced them. A sheepish looking couple came in and took their places. Marvin skipped three seats and viewed from a distance. Heather closed the door and returned to her seat beside Steve at the head of the table.

"Who are you people?" asked the woman to Steve's immediate right.

"Thank you for asking, and that's the first order of business. I'm Steve Smiley and beside me is Heather McBlythe, Attorney at Law and my business partner. You probably don't remember me, but my father and I used to hunt on the Rocking V. We're here because your father asked me to be executor of his estate and he specified that Ms. McBlythe could accompany me."

"When did this happen? Why wasn't I told?" The accusatory voice came from the same woman.

"Monday, a week ago," said Steve. "Before we continue, I need each of you to state your name so I can get a read on where you're sitting."

A man's voice interrupted. "I remember you. You're the one that shot the goat." A laugh exploded from the man, but he laughed alone.

"You must be LeRoy," said Steve. "If memory serves me right, we suspected you of tying antlers on that goat and staking it in front of my deer stand."

LeRoy continued to grin. "I go by Roy and nobody proved it was me."

"That didn't save you from your mother taking a limb from a peach tree to you."

"Can we dispense with the trip down memory lane?" asked the sharp-tongued woman with streaked blond hair.

"Let me guess," said Steve. "You're Ester Mae, the eldest."

"It's Mae. Mae Richards. Like Roy, I dropped the country bumpkin first name as soon as I left that God-forsaken ranch."

Steve turned to his left. "Sue Ann, do you still go by both names?"

A tiny voice answered from the first seat on Heather's left. Her blouse and slacks were clean, but threadbare. "I do, and my husband Grant is here with me, Mr. Smiley."

"Then that leaves Rance, the youngest."

"Over here, beside Grant."

Roy pointed toward the only person in the room that had not spoken. "Why's Dudley Do-Right here?"

Marvin narrowed his eyes, but Steve spoke before the deputy could. "It's standard for law enforcement to be present at the reading of the will when the death of the testator is ruled a homicide."

Heather noticed that Grant Blankenship's eyebrows knitted together when Steve used the word *testator*. She spoke for everyone's benefit so as not to embarrass Sue Ann's husband. "Testator is the person who made the will."

Roy spoke again. "Sue Ann, we all know that big words give Grant trouble. Tell him that means our loving father."

Grant's right fist formed into a meaty club.

Steve kept talking. "Now that I know where everyone's sitting, Ms. McBlythe will pass out copies of the will and read it."

Heather stood and read at a slow, deliberate pace. It didn't take long for Mae to come uncorked. "Is this a joke? It can't be legal. I'm the oldest and I should be the executor, not some man who can't even see. By the way, how much are you being paid? What deal did you make with our father?"

Steve didn't respond.

Roy broke the silence. "My older, and, might I add, rude and bossy sister, alluded to one pertinent point in her rant. Is this legal?"

Heather held up the document. "This is what's known as a holographic will. It's written in the testator's own hand, nothing typed, nothing in any other color ink, and nothing written by another person. The basic requirements for a will to be valid in Texas are that the testator must have achieved eighteen years of age and be of full mental capacity at the time of writing the will." She lowered the sheet. "It's legal."

"How can it be?" asked Mae. "What man in his right mind would make such a stupid will? Everyone knows the first child in the bloodline should be the executor."

Heather nodded, but only in partial agreement. "The testator has great latitude in assigning the executor. Sometimes it's the oldest sibling, but not always. If the estate is left intestate, a judge will assign an executor." She looked around and found a couple of blank stares. "Intestate means without leaving a will. Here, there's a will that exceeds the legal requirements."

"Explain," said Mae.

"Two reputable men witnessed the document, and it's notarized."

Steve spoke next. "I contacted both witnesses. The first is a local physician and the other's a rancher who knew your father for fifty years. They're both willing to testify that your father was in complete control of his faculties when he wrote this will."

The room fell silent. As was fast becoming her custom, Mae broke the calm. "I don't believe you. I'm going to have an attorney I know and trust look at this before I accept what you're saying."

Roy clapped his hands and laughed. "Bravo, Mae. You play the part of a fool better than anyone I know." He leaned forward with palms flat on the table and stared at his elder sister. "I'll bet you ten-to-one you'll be back tomorrow with your liposuctioned tail tucked between your legs."

Mae rose as Steve held up a hand. "Mae, you need to remember that you only have five days to come to an agreement with your siblings. This is your chance to work out an equitable division of the property without taking a chance on what the second part of the will might say."

Heather added, "I advise you to—"

Mae had already headed for the door as she overrode Heather's advice. "You're not my attorney and I wish to God they weren't my brothers and sister. I won't be cheated out of what's rightfully mine."

The door slammed.

Up to now, Rance, a rangy young man who looked to be in his late twenties, had not said a word. He folded rough hands together on the table in front of him. "Mr. Smiley, how do you suggest we proceed?"

"I'll let Heather take this one."

Heather concentrated on Rance's gray eyes hooded by long black lashes. "The first thing we need is a full accounting of all assets. That means everything. You won't get a fair distribution without it."

Rance nodded. "I'll get a count on the livestock."

Roy spoke up. "I don't mind getting property valuations, but I don't have a clue how much land there is."

Steve came to his rescue. "I have legal descriptions of the ranch properties on my computer and made copies for everyone. They're quite extensive and cover multiple tracts of land."

Roy laughed. "That's because great-grandpa kept winning at poker. He'd add eight hundred acres one week and take off six hundred the next, just to make it look like he wasn't cheating. He won a lot more than he lost. I guess that's where I got the gene that makes me a good gambler."

The small voice of Sue Ann sounded next. "The kids and I can go to the ranch house and make a list of everything."

Roy piped up. "That won't take long. Dad squeezed a dollar until it screamed."

Sue Ann dabbed her eyes as her husband glared at Roy.

"It's a good start," said Steve. "We'll meet here tomorrow afternoon at five to see what progress you've made."

Rance pushed away from the table and stood. "I might be late. There's a heifer springing heavy, and I'm not sure she can drop the calf without help." He held his straw cowboy hat in his hand and took sure strides to the door.

Roy stood and looked Heather up and down. "Ms. McBlythe, what's the chance of you having a drink with me this evening?"

Heather inspected the man wearing his shirt with one too many buttons undone. "I have plans, Mr. Voss."

His hands went over his heart like he'd been shot. Then he shrugged. "I rolled the dice, and they came up snake eyes. Oh well, if one table's cold, there's always another game. See you two tomorrow."

Sue Ann and her husband, Grant, left with heads down, not saying a word. That left Marvin. He approached as Heather stuffed the will in her satchel.

Steve must have heard his footsteps on the carpet. "Did anything they say help you, Marvin?"

He shook his head. Heather mimed that he needed to speak to answer Steve's question.

"I know one of them did it, but which one? They all have keys to the gate and the ranch house. Any of them could have killed him. The coroner says the death occurred last Monday, a short time after he called you. That means all four were within driving distance of the ranch, even Roy."

"He doesn't live nearby?" asked Heather.

"Las Vegas. He's a professional gambler. He came to Austin for a private poker tournament, or at least that's what the people at the table said."

"Not much of an alibi," said Heather.

Steve yawned. "I don't know about you two, but I'm bushed. I think I'll lie down before supper."

"Do you need me to help you to your room?" asked Heather.

"I counted the steps on my way here. I can manage."

Steve unfurled his cane, followed it out the door and turned left.

Marvin shook his head. "He's quite a man. How did he lose his sight?"

"Street thugs attacked him and his wife in Houston. Maggie died and Steve... well... you're right. He's quite a man."

"Was he as good a cop as Sheriff Blake says?"

Heather looked toward the open door. "Better." Her phone vibrated in the pocket of her blazer. "Hello, Father. No, I've been busy for the last hour. What do you mean they're getting cold feet?"

Fifteen minutes later, Heather finished the call. She sat alone in the room.

5

The hotel's fitness center lived up to its advertising and Heather's expectations. After forty-five minutes on state-of-the-art exercise equipment, she mopped sweat from her face and arms. An attendant brought her a complementary bottle of spring water and made sure she knew about the yoga classes and the spa. Heather thanked the eager young woman and gave a non-committal response to the low-pressure sales pitch.

She stopped at Steve's room and knocked. No response. It wasn't unusual they went their separate ways while at home, but this was different. When traveling, they kept each other informed of their location. But then, she hadn't told him of her plans to have an early morning workout.

A pang of guilt competed with a hint of resentment toward her father. Yesterday's phone call had not gone well. He said the acquisition had to take place. Rumors were circulating that another company was interested in the same mining company, and a bidding war loomed on the horizon. She'd lose the opportunity of the decade if she didn't ink the deal.

Instead of grabbing a shower, Heather made for the elevator. Once downstairs, she approached the desk clerk. "What would you recommend if I wanted to get an American-style breakfast?"

The desk clerk looked over the top of her half-framed glasses. "I have two recommendations. The first is J's Restaurant, here in the hotel. The second is the Slick Rock Bar and Grill, which overlooks the twelfth fairway at the Slick Rock Golf Course."

"Is that nearby?"

"It's off High Stirrup, about a mile from here." The clerk handed her a map and pointed with a pen.

"Let me make a call before I drive that far," said Heather.

Steve answered on the second ring. "Good morning. You're missing a great breakfast."

"Where are you?"

"At the Slick Rock Bar and Grill."

"How did you get there?"

"I hitchhiked."

Heather heard a muffled female laugh in the background.

"Stay where you are. I'll come for you."

"Take your time. Remember, this trip is part business, part vacation." Her phone went dead.

She returned to the desk. "I understand there's a shuttle that services the golf courses. Do I catch it out front?"

"Yes, ma'am." She pointed to a black SUV.

Something told Heather she needed to have more immediate transportation. "Is the concierge handy?"

The woman took off her glasses. "She's assisting another guest at the moment. How can I be of service?"

"I'll need a rental while I'm here. Something in an SUV would be preferable. The name's Heather McBlythe."

"I'll have one delivered this morning."

It didn't take long before a black shuttle bus ferried her to the Slick Rock golf course and its restaurant. The drive gave her time to wonder if the laughing female voice might have been someone at another table.

Like everything at the resort, the clubhouse, gift shop, and restaurant held a charm that enticed guests to relax and unwind from hectic schedules. The view out the windows of the sports bar and grill made her slow her pace and enjoy the scenery of rolling hills and a foursome of golfers enjoying the relative cool of an early morning round. After asking the hostess if she'd seen a blind man, she motioned her to follow and deposited her in front of Steve and a brassy blond about the same age as Steve. She took another look at the surgeon-augmented visage and added eight years to her original estimate.

"Have a seat, Heather. This is Bridget Callahan. We met last night, and she's been showing me around."

Heather didn't need to ask how Steve knew it was her. One of his heightened senses was that of smell, especially when a woman's sweat mingled with her perfume. "Excuse my appearance. As you can see, I've just come from the gym."

The woman brushed off the apology with a flip of the wrist that set two inches of bracelets jangling. "Honey, wear that tight yoga outfit as long as you can. Believe me, gravity will someday be your worst enemy."

Bridget made a point of fingering a necklace with a gold nugget suspended well down the deep cut of a loud floral blouse. "Heather. You don't mind if I call you Heather, do you? Steve's told me so much about you, I feel like I've known you forever."

A tight-lipped smile gave enough of a positive reply that Bridget careened on. "Isn't Steve a dear?"

Bridgett's face lined with worry as she dropped the smile to something more natural. With concern accentuating the wrinkles on her sun-damaged face, she leaned toward Heather. "I know men, and this one's worried about you. He says you've lost your ability to relax."

Heather's gaze never left Bridget's face. With teeth clenched, she forced a smile. Under the table, she located Steve's leg and gave it a kick.

He responded with a chuckle, which caused Heather's anger to rise even more.

Without warning, Bridget rose. "Now that you're here, I can go to the spa. I have a hot date tonight and I want to do all I can to please him. Tootles until tonight, Steve."

Heather waited until Bridget strutted out of sight before she looked at Steve. "Tootles? Who says *tootles* anymore?"

"I can only name one person. What does she look like?"

It was time to have fun at Steve's expense. "Picture a geriatric Barbie trying to look like she and Ken are on their first date in fifty years."

"I was afraid of that. The clanging bracelets were giving me a headache. She must have taken a bath in perfume this morning."

Heather found it hard not to giggle.

Steve continued on. "And speaking of bathing, how was the gym and why didn't you take time to shower?"

"I was looking for a partner that went AWOL."

Steve took a sip of coffee. "I must admit, I was glad to get your call and even more glad when you showed up. She was trying to rope me into a massage. I'm not sure she meant for it to take place at the spa."

Heather kept covering her grin but couldn't contain a snicker.

Head down, Steve said, "She ambushed me last night. Before I knew it, she'd arranged breakfast and planned a secret outing for us tonight." He scratched his chin. "What's a good excuse? The flu? A stomach bug? Leprosy?"

"Face it, you're the main course for a cougar tonight if you don't come up with something more convincing than that."

The server arrived to take Heather's order.

"What did you have, Steve?"

"The hungry golfer. Eggs, bacon, pancakes and tasty fried potatoes."

Heather thought about the calories and threw caution to the wind. "Same for me, and coffee."

The two sat in silence as they nursed their coffee. A full minute of silence passed before Steve made an observation. "You're too quiet. What's wrong?"

She scrunched the cloth napkin on her lap. "My father called yesterday afternoon. He's convinced someone is after the mining company we're trying to buy. He told me to wrap up the deal by Monday or he'd do it himself."

Steve folded his hands. "What's your gut telling you?"

Heather filled her cheeks with air and let it out. "My gut is making more acid than a battery manufacturer. Something's not right, but I can't find it in any of the spreadsheets or financial statements. I've gone over the numbers dozens of times. The mine's produced solid results and the latest test holes show potential for ten times the production."

"Where is this mine?"

"Montana."

"Have you seen it?"

"I have photos and a promotional video."

"Ah."

Heather crossed her arms. "There you go again with another 'Ah.' What does this one mean?"

"Did you rely on photos when you were a detective in Boston, or did you visit the crime scene?"

Heather's eyes opened wide. "A good detective always goes to where the crime took place."

She pulled her phone out of a small pocket in her workout

top and punched a name. "It's Heather. Call Tim and get to Horseshoe Bay as quick as you can. Pack for several days. We're going to Montana."

Heather's breakfast arrived and she all but inhaled it. With her mouth half-full she asked, "Sure you don't need my help this afternoon with the Voss clan?"

Steve settled his cup. "Nothing important is going to happen today. If the natives get rowdy, Marvin will be there to make sure they don't get out of hand. You have a lot to do if you're going to Montana. Let's get back to our rooms."

The shuttle eased to a stop at the hotel. Steve waited until they were on the elevator before he said, "I've got it!"

"Got what?"

"We'll trade rooms. I didn't give Bridget my phone number, but she called me this morning on the phone in the room. That means she knows what room I'm in."

"Coward."

"I'll have enough trouble playing referee to the Voss children. I don't need Senior Citizen Barbie picking out a new dream home for me."

6

Steve waited until the last minute to arrive at the Live Oak conference room. Angry voices spilled into the hallway and grew louder as he approached. Marvin Goodnight's voice rose above the others. "Sit down. He's coming down the hall now."

Assuming his position at the head of the table, Steve pulled out his cell phone and placed it on the table. "I'll be recording this session and any subsequent sessions. You're welcome to do the same. I only ask that you speak loud enough for the phone to pick up what you say." He folded his cane and pulled his chair under him. "Is everyone here?"

Deputy Goodnight, sitting next to Steve, responded for the group. "Everyone that was here yesterday is here again today, plus one."

"Oh? And who might that be?"

The sound of chair wheels rolling preceded a baritone voice that came from Steve's right. "I'm Patrick Shaw of the law firm of Walsh and Walsh. I'm here to represent Ms. Richards in these proceedings."

Steve nodded. "Is it your intention to challenge the validity of the will?"

"At this point, we believe the will to be valid. Mae wants it clarified that she's only interested in a fair division of the property. It's our intention to present the siblings with a thorough accounting of the estate and recommend a prudent course of action."

"Ha! That's a laugh," said Roy. "How much of a cut are you planning on taking from each of us for coming up with a plan that will leave Mae sitting pretty?"

"Shut up, Roy," said Mae. "It will be worth every penny, and it's only fair that we share the expense of professional representation."

Roy looked to his other siblings. "Did you hear that? She wants us to pay for Pat cheating us." He shifted his gaze to Mae. "This latest paramour won't get a penny out of me."

"Let's move on," said Steve. He folded his hands together and placed them on the table. "Roy, how are you coming with the land valuations?"

Mae shouted, "What land valuations?"

The attorney interrupted. "Mr. Smiley, I must protest. Mr. Voss is neither trained nor qualified to give accurate valuations to such a large estate. To allow him to do so would be a severe dereliction of your duties as executor."

Steve ignored the protest. "Roy, you didn't answer my question. Did you make progress?"

"I hired a local attorney to go over all the documents you gave me. He spent the day double checking mineral rights, but he's nowhere near finished."

Mae's voice remained at a high decibel level. "What documents? Why didn't I receive them?" She stood. "I see what's going on. You three have formed some sort of pact, just like when we were kids. I won't stand for it this time around. Tell them, Pat."

Roy's voice cut across the table. "Ah-ha. So, it's Pat, not Patrick. Be careful, Pat, you might be the fifth notch on Mae's marital bedpost. She's always been partial to attorneys and real estate brokers. They improve her commissions on condo sales."

Steve stood to keep the scene from deteriorating. "Mae, you didn't receive the documents because you walked out of yesterday's meeting. I brought you a list of all the properties." He turned to Marvin Goodnight. "Would you look in my briefcase and give the folder on top to Mae?"

The sound of Marvin delivering the file and returning to his seat on Steve's left gave him his cue to proceed. "Sue Ann, how is your inventory of the ranch house progressing?"

For once, Mae didn't object.

"I made it through the bedrooms," said Sue Ann. "I started going through old pictures that Mama took before she died and lost track of time. I'll go back tomorrow, and Sunday if I need to."

Mae made a noise that sounded like a mule snorting. "There's nothing of value there. That house needs to be torn down and the land by the lake developed by professionals."

"Let me guess," said Roy. "You expect to get the lakefront property."

"It's only right since I'm the oldest and the only one with a real estate background."

Patrick Shaw followed with, "To get the most potential out of lakefront, we should leave it as one tract. Mae will get the property by the lake. The bulk of the land will be divided between the other siblings. She'll make no claim on that land, other than for ingress and egress easements on the roads we'll build leading to the lake."

Roy slapped the table. "Mae, this guy may be the slimiest one yet. Rance, you and Sue Ann count your fingers if you shake hands with him. You might not get them all back."

"Now, wait a minute," said the attorney.

That's all he got out before Roy let out a cackle of a laugh. "What's wrong, Pat? Can't take a joke?" His voice lowered and he gave a piercing stare. "Neither can I."

Roy's voice once again shifted in tone and direction. "Sue Ann and Rance, listen to me. This shyster and Mae will try to bluff us. They'll say anything to get us to agree to their plans. So far, I haven't heard one word out of Pat or Mae that I'm willing to consider. Remember, we all have to agree."

Steve nodded. "Roy's correct. All four must agree, and at this pace, you're not getting any closer. Rance, did you make progress on counting the livestock?"

Rance's voice came from well down the table. He must have decided to avoid the fray by putting distance between himself and his siblings. "As my brother and sisters know, Dad wasn't much to keep records. I spoke with Hector this morning. He has the most accurate count we're likely to get, but to be truthful, it will only be an estimate. There're places on the properties that are so rough and thick I won't take a horse through them."

Mae spoke up. "That ignorant old Mexican can't count past ten in English."

Rance stood and thrust his hands in his pockets. "I don't have time for this. I've been in the saddle since dawn after staying up most of the night pulling a dead calf out a heifer that didn't make it either. Hector just sent me a text saying some of our cattle are grazing in the bar ditch on Highway 71. While you're eating supper, I'll be fixing fences."

Attorney Patrick Shaw spoke next. "Mr. Voss, I hope you realize how important it is that we have an accurate count of the cattle and not an estimate."

Rance settled his hat on his head and glared at the attorney. "Mr. Shaw, if you want to come with me and count cattle, I'll saddle a horse for you and I'll even loan you a flashlight. It shouldn't take us more than two weeks to round them up if we don't eat or sleep."

The attorney didn't accept the invitation.

Roy's roar of a laugh ushered his little brother toward the door. "Little Rance don't say much, but when he does, it's priceless. What do you say, Pat? Are you ready to plow through thousands of acres of mesquite, cactus, rattle snakes, tarantulas, coyotes and the occasional bobcat?"

"Your humor escapes me, Mr. Voss."

It was easy for Steve to pick up on Rance's footsteps heading to the door. The cowboy had failed to remove his spurs. Steve pushed his chair away from the table. "Hold up, Rance. When you come tomorrow, could you bring us a rough estimate of the livestock?"

"Hector's been on the ranch longer than any of us, including Mae. I'd wager his numbers against mine any day."

Roy affirmed Rance's opinion. "That's a bet I wouldn't take. Hector might not know how to read or speak much English, but he knows cattle. His numbers will be good enough for me."

Hope for agreement, at least on a minor issue, rose when Steve asked Sue Ann if she had any objection to Rance's suggestion that they use Hector's estimate of livestock. After a muffled conversation with her husband, Sue Ann said, "Grant says we're okay with Rance's idea."

Another conversation of muted voices occurred between Mae and her attorney. Mae followed Sue Ann's agreement with a terse, "We'll consider the proposal and let you know tomorrow. It sounds slip-shod, but what can one expect from this family?"

"If you don't like his plan," said Roy, "I'm sure Rance would be glad to put both you and Mr. Fancy-Pants on horseback." He followed the goad with another laugh that no one responded to.

"If there's nothing else," said Steve.

Patrick Shaw interrupted. "Tomorrow afternoon I'll come with a map showing the proposed division of the land, and I'll answer questions. I'm sure after you hear how this plan will benefit everyone we'll come to an agreement."

Roy chuckled. "Will it be equitable?"

"Of course. The numbers will tell the story for me."

This brought a laugh from Roy. "I'm reminded of an old saying: 'Figures don't lie, but liars figure.' There's as much chance of an ice storm tomorrow as you bringing us a fair proposal."

Roy's next question came to Steve. "Mr. Smiley. Why is Pat the pick-pocket allowed in the meetings? I thought the will called for the heirs to decide how to split the sheets. It said nothing about lawyers."

Steve leaned back in his chair and tapped his lips with an index finger. "You're half right, Roy. The will mentions the children, but leaves it to me to decide who else may attend."

"I object," said the attorney.

"Object all you want," said Steve. "This isn't a court of law."

"That's where it's headed if you bar me from these discussions."

Steve remained quiet as he considered what course of action he would take. It would be easier to eliminate Mae's attorney. On the other hand, he'd allowed Pat to sit in on this session and the objection to his presence wasn't raised beforehand. Besides, the heirs weren't any closer to agreement than when they started. Roy could hold his own, and even Rance stood up to Pat when it counted. Sue Ann, however, didn't seem to possess a backbone. Her husband was a wild card. He didn't have a read on Grant yet.

"Mr. Shaw," said Steve. "I'll give you thirty minutes to present your proposal tomorrow afternoon at five. You'll be the first to speak. After that, I'll invite you to leave."

The sound of Mae's chair flying backward and hitting a wall preceded her shout of, "You can't tell me who I can and can't have in this room."

"I can." The voice belonged to Marvin Goodnight. "Mr. Smiley rented this room. It's his to use as he sees fit. If he tells me no one but family can be here, then that's the way it's going to be."

The sound of papers being gathered drifted Steve's way.

Roy spoke next. "There she goes again, with another future ex-husband trailing behind." He raised his voice. "This is two days in a row you've walked out, Mae. I'm betting you'll make it three tomorrow."

More sounds of chairs and people rising. The soft voice of Sue Ann came near. "I'm sorry, Mr. Smiley. Things weren't ever good between us kids, but after Momma died, it was extra hard."

"Quit yakking, Sue Ann," said Grant. "This is two days in a row I've had to take off work early and pay someone to watch the kids."

Quiet filled the room after Roy chuckled his way into the hall. Steve sat back down and took in a deep breath. He allowed the quiet to wash over him and then said, "Marvin. Describe Grant Blankenship to me."

"He's a tough man who grew up poor. Works at the granite quarry. He and Sue Ann have four stair-step kids. Grant's been arrested a half dozen times for domestic violence after he got drunk. Loves to fish."

"Any recent domestic violence?"

"Not in a while. Why?"

Steve rose from his seat. "I could hear his teeth grinding several times today. He's going to be tested in the next few days. Be sure to keep an eye on him."

"What's going to happen tomorrow?"

"Mae's attorney will look for an advantage. He'll try to drive a wedge between Sue Ann and her husband by seeking to have him excluded from the meeting. Spouses weren't named in the will and Roy doesn't think much of Grant, either."

Marvin released a slow whistle. "What will you do?"

After grabbing his brief case, Steve took a step. "I'm calling Heather for legal advice."

The two walked side by side into the hall. Steve caught the scent of a familiar perfume. He stopped and whispered. "I need help. There's a woman after me and I'd rather run through stinging nettle barefoot than have to spend the evening with her. Can we go to town? There has to be a good chicken-fried steak in Marble Falls."

7

S teve tried to clear his throat before he answered his phone, but his words squeaked with the telltale sound of an interrupted nap. "What time is it?"

"It's two o'clock on a sunny day in Montana," said Heather. Her words came fast, laced with purpose and excitement. "Why are you sleeping in the middle of the day?"

He grabbed pillows, stuffed them behind his shoulders and raised himself to a sitting position. "I slept lousy last night." He didn't need to tell her that memories of Maggie came calling, as they sometimes did.

"Oh. Sorry. Did you take the Melatonin I packed for you?"

"I forgot, but before you chew me out, I promise to take it tonight." Steve yawned and stretched life into his legs.

"Tell me about yesterday's meeting."

"No blood but I need some advice. Mae brought her attorney, a fellow named Patrick Shaw. There's more to them being together than legal briefs."

Heather chuckled at the inuendo. "Did anyone else show up with a mouthpiece?"

"Only Mae. I think Pat's intentions toward her aren't honorable." Steve reconsidered his last statement. "He and Mae seem to be cut from the same bolt of cloth. To hear Roy talk, there's not much chance that either could sully the other's reputation. Pat's presenting their idea of a fair division of property to the rest of the siblings today. Roy's taking odds that the plan will be less than equitable."

"Don't take the bet. Roy may be obnoxious, but he's a shrewd gambler. I checked his finances on the flight yesterday. He's doing well for himself."

"And the others?"

"Mae spends more than she makes. Sue Ann and Grant have credit card debt beyond their ability to pay. Rance is at the tail end of paying off student loans. Two years at A & M set him back a pretty penny, but that's all he owes."

Steve took in the information and placed it in mental files. One sibling needs money to keep her children fed, one wants wealth to obtain a lifestyle, one works hard to earn his way in life, and the other makes big money by counting cards and distracting opponents until they make mistakes.

"Back to the attorney," said Heather. "Did others object to him being there?"

"Roy expressed his opinion."

"I bet he did."

"Even quiet Rance found his voice when Pat tried to bull-doze him. There's more to that young man than meets the eye."

"If you could see him through the eyes of a woman, you'd double that opinion. He's a tall, dark-skinned cowboy with lonely-looking eyes. The type some sweet girl would love to walk into church with and walk out as Mrs. Rance Voss."

"Have you been reading western romance novels again?"

Heather's laugh was a good sign. She must be on the right track for finding information on the mine. But first, he needed to finish telling her the rest of the story of yesterday's meeting and get her advice. "I'm giving Patrick thirty minutes to make

41

his pitch. After that, I told him he'd have to leave. Marvin made it clear he'd enforce my decision to limit attendance to those mentioned in the will."

"Perfect," said Heather. "Is that all?"

"It hasn't come up yet, but I'm expecting Mae and Roy to challenge Grant's right to be in the meeting. What do you think?"

Several seconds passed. "You can decide either way. The will gives you sole discretion on how to interpret Charley Voss's intentions. It gets complicated because of the state's community property laws. It's the old, 'and the two shall become one' argument."

"What would you do?"

Heather exhaled a full breath. "I'd let him stay. He's already sat through two sessions and didn't cause any problems."

"That's what I thought, too. Now tell me what you've found out about the mine."

"Not much, but enough to make me suspicious. I checked with the power company that services the mine and discovered their use of electricity started dropping a little every month last year. I spoke with property managers and real estate agents who serve the areas that house mine workers. They report a slow, steady rise in vacancies."

Steve knew that both might be signs of a work slowdown, but they could have other logical explanations. He didn't want to interrupt Heather when she was hot on a trail.

"I should know soon if this is a huge con-job or if the mine is for real. Last night Tim and I went to a bar on the same side of town as the mine. I tried to pump some guys that worked at the mine for information. They were tight-lipped, like they'd been warned not to talk."

Steve stood and stretched as Heather continued.

"Tim had better luck. He plied a girl with drinks and spent the night twirling her around a tiny dance floor. She explained to him that a gold mine runs on diesel. If you want to know the health of a producing gold mine, see if the diesel usage is going up or down."

"Well? Which is it?"

"She didn't know. She confirmed there's been a slowdown, but the quality of the ore is as good as it's ever been. She operates some sort of machine in the mine. I'll find out this evening about the diesel usage when I wine and dine the fuel supplier and his wife. Either way, I'll fly back tonight. Are you still in my room?"

"Still here and with no cougar bites."

Heather's laugh caused a smile to part Steve's lips. She ended with, "Good luck at today's meeting."

"Thanks. I'll need it."

ROY'S BRAY OF A LAUGH CUT THROUGH THE ROOM FIVE SECONDS after Patrick Shaw finished his twenty-five-minute presentation of what he considered a fair division of property. Roy followed his hysterics with a question. "Why didn't you use your red crayon and color in all the property for Mae?"

"It's equitable for all parties," said the attorney in his smooth-as-silk voice.

"If you think that, I'll take the four miles of lakefront with adjoining property and Mae can have my land you colored in yellow."

Mae didn't disappoint as she barked out, "Shut up, Roy. Pat has the floor for thirty minutes. Listen to all he has to say."

Steve leaned back and tried to appear as an impartial spectator. In fact, that's what he hoped he would be at the Saturday afternoon edition of battling siblings. Everyone had listened quietly to a polished attorney make an impassioned plea for the waterfront land to remain intact, along with a mile and a half setback to accommodate a marina, luxury waterfront homes and tall condominiums with views of the lake. The carrot the lawyer offered was a promise to give the remaining siblings a ten percent share of the profits from the sale of the developed properties.

It came as a surprise that Roy sat in silence as Patrick made his pitch. What didn't surprise Steve were the challenges he now sprayed like confetti.

"Pat, I have to hand it to you; that was an impressive presentation. I liked the pictures of multi-million-dollar homes and the smiling women sunbathing. Let me see if I have this right. Mae gets all the best land. Everything touching the lake, everything a mile and half back from the lake, and land for new roads, each with a generous easement. Is that right?"

"The land on either side of the roads will only be a hundred and fifty yards deep. That will allow for future commercial development, which will profit everyone."

"Profit. Now there's an interesting word. If I heard right, Sue Ann, Rance and I will someday get ten percent of the profit from this deal, once you recoup your investment. Right?"

"We take all the risk and front all the capital," said Patrick.

Roy left his seat and paced on the opposite side of the table from Mae and the attorney. "That means Mae gets seventy percent of the profits."

"But you'll have your sections of land to sell or keep or develop."

"What's the valuation of the land Mae will receive as compared to ours?"

"It's a fair deal. You'd be foolish not to agree."

Roy stopped pacing. "You're bluffing with a deuce and a five as your hole cards. You spent your time working on a slick presentation instead of doing research." Roy paused. His words slid out on a laugh. "That's not right. You did both. That's the largest remaining tract of undeveloped lakefront property in the state. You know how much it's worth and so do I."

Roy seemed to enjoy himself. His pacing stopped. "Tell you what, Pat. I'm a gambler. I'm going to write a number and give it to you. If you agree to my price, I'll fold and let you fight it out with Rance and Sue Ann. But first, I'm going to write them a brief note, too. I've been in contact with local real estate brokers. They gave me their estimate of land valuations. Let's see how your numbers stack up against theirs."

A hush fell on the room as Roy settled in his chair. The sound of a pencil scratching paper reached Steve. Rance and Sue Ann both thanked him then Roy's footsteps circled the table.

It didn't take Mae long to react. "This is ridiculous. It's a hundred times more than what that property's worth."

Roy countered with, "Not when you consider all the future profits you're promising. In fact, it's less than the windfall Patrick said we'll get in his presentation."

"I promised nothing," said Patrick. "Those were projections."

"Take it or leave it," said Roy. "By the way, Pat, your thirty minutes is up. Hit the road."

Marvin Goodnight stood. "Unless Mr. Smiley's changed his mind, only family members are to be here."

"If he leaves," said Mae, "Grant has to leave, too. He's not mentioned in the will. All he's added to these meetings is a nasty smell. Sue Ann, what did you ever see in this oaf? He can't even support you and the children."

No response came from Sue Ann or Grant.

This was the moment Steve had dreaded. He leaned forward and allowed seconds to pass as he reconsidered his decision. He folded his hands together like he was praying, which in fact he was. "I thought this might happen, so I consulted Ms. McBlythe to make sure I wasn't making a legal error. She said I could decide on allowing Grant to stay or leave.

I've decided he can stay as long as he isn't disruptive. I've also decided that he can't address the group. He and Sue Ann can converse, but only she can speak."

Whispers floated from Sue Ann and Grant followed by her saying, "We're fine with that, Mr. Smiley."

"Well, it's not with me," shouted Mae. "You're all too stupid to know what's good for you. I'll wait and take my chances with the second part of the will. That old buzzard might have left everything to the eldest child like he should have."

She stormed out of the room. Rance asked her to wait, but she didn't respond.

As expected, Roy laughed when Patrick followed Mae and Rance out the door. "I told you she'd leave before the meeting was over. At least everyone knew better than to bet against me. I'm on a winning streak and I have a feeling it's about to get better."

Rance returned after only a brief absence. "I gave Mr. Shaw my estimates on the number of cattle. He said he'd try to calm Mae down and get her back tomorrow."

"Mr. Smiley," said Rance. "I'm laying a sheet of paper in front of you. It's a tally of the livestock divided into groups of bulls, steers, cow/calf pairs, heifers, slaughter cows and a few orphaned calves. I calculated the value of the livestock by what the latest sale prices are. Everyone has a copy."

"Thanks, Rance. I appreciate your diligence." Steve faced the spot where Sue Ann and Grant were sitting. "Did you finish your inventory of the ranch house?"

"Huh?" said Sue Ann. "Were you talking to me?"

Grant's voice sounded as hard as the granite he mined at the quarry. "Answer the man. Tell him you finished at the ranch."

"Oh. Yes. I made copies for everyone. There weren't much anything of value. I didn't go in Rance's room. Some things in the living room and the clothes in the laundry room are his."

Roy piped up, "There's nothing in that house I want. You and Rance and Mae can do whatever you want. My suggestion is you burn it down."

"Grant says we ain't interested in anything in the house," said Sue Ann. "Can we leave, Mr. Smiley?"

"Let's hope we make better progress tomorrow afternoon," said Steve. The room cleared and he wondered if Mae might be right. Perhaps the second part of the will would clarify the division of the estate and get him off the hook.

The voice of Bridget Callahan tumbled through the door, floating on wafts of perfume. "Yoo-hoo. Steve-e. You're not getting away from me tonight. I made reservations for us at the Yacht Club Restaurant, and after that we're playing a round of golf."

"In the dark?"

HEATHER RAN HER HAND OVER THE LEATHER SEAT OF HER Citation M2 and thought about how much she loved its comfort and being able to fly anywhere at a moment's notice. Muted lights and the opulence of the cabin gave her a mixed sense of belonging and being somewhere foreign. A look out the window reinforced her thoughts. The plane cut through rarefied air, which reminded her of the wealth she'd been born into. She'd taken a ten-year break to become a policewoman and had come full circle back to extreme wealth. Well, almost full circle. Working murder cases with Steve kept her grounded and allowed her to right wrongs in a way she found satisfying. The red light on the tip of the plane's wing, however, seemed to blink a warning that great wealth came with great responsibility.

She sipped a cup of coffee and stared into the open door of the cockpit, where instruments cast a fluorescent green aura in front of the pilot, Johnathan, and co-pilot, Tim. Their training equipped them to make decisions that could affect three lives tonight. She also had a decision to make that might affect the lives of hundreds or even thousands of people. She picked up the phone from its recessed holder by the seat and placed the call.

"Father, it's Heather."

A stiff voice answered. "Do you know what time it is?"

"It's almost 1 a.m. in Boston. That means you've already slept three hours and you're in your robe checking the Asian markets. You'll be awake until two and then you'll go back to bed until six."

He didn't disagree. "To what do I owe this unexpected pleasure? I know it's too late for you to be calling to say you've obtained the signatures on the acquisition."

"No, but the mine is the reason for my call. I've been in Montana the last two days doing research on the company and their operations."

"Why would you duplicate work?"

Heather closed her eyes. She'd expected resistance, and the tenor of his voice bore aggravation.

"I've had suspicions for quite some time that something is amiss."

His response came back with too much speed. "Successful businesses don't run on suspicions. I've gone over the reports you sent and this is a golden opportunity."

"Nice pun, father, but something's not right."

"I see you're still flippant. Why are you really calling?"

Heather knew she needed to be firm and decisive. "I'm putting off the acquisition until we can have new sample holes dug."

"That's not possible. We'll lose out to Apex."

"It would be a mistake to go forward."

She could tell by his tone her father was digging in his

heels. "Perhaps I made a mistake in giving you such responsibility."

"Perhaps, but I'm not willing to do something we'll regret."

"Right now, the only thing I regret is taking the acquisition from Webster and giving it to you."

This wasn't the conversation she intended to have. Her Irish anger rose, but she knew she couldn't back down. "When you give it back to Webster, ask him why he didn't discover the electricity use at the mine has been going down for the last year. While you're at it, ask him why the housing vacancies in the towns around the mine are going up. See if good-old-Webster can explain why sales of diesel fuel to the mine are half of what they were this time last year."

"Logical explanations exist for each of those things. In fact, Webster and I have already discussed some of them. He assures me the slowdown is temporary and the drill holes show a new deposit twice as large as what they have mined up to now. I've seen the projections and the assays."

"Like I said, I'm suspicious. They look too good to be true."

Her father's voice had that ring of steel to it that always infuriated her. "This is a rare opportunity, child."

She cringed at the use of the patronizing replacement for her name but kept talking. "If that's true, why are they selling?"

The phone went silent for several seconds, followed by, "I've decided, Heather. I'm giving the job to Webster."

Something like a limb breaking from under her took place in Heather's soul. She straightened her back. "So be it. I resign from McBlythe Enterprises. I'll have my attorneys contact yours and work out the details. Since this airplane is in the company's name, I'll return it to you or purchase it from you with funds from the inheritance I received from Grandfather."

His voice cracked. "That was a Christmas present. I wanted you to have it."

"Then you should have given it to me yourself and not put it in the company's name. Give Mother my love."

She crammed the phone back in its holder and stared out the window. The blinking red light on the plane's wingtip hadn't lied.

8

The car wheeled into a parking space and stopped. "Are we there?" asked Steve.

"The sign on the building says Bluebonnet Cafe," said Heather. "Is this where you and Marvin dined while I was in Montana?"

Steve reached for his door handle. "You'll like it. Great food and the best pie I've had in years."

Heather unlatched her seat belt and took stock of a white stucco building that looked like a series of shoe boxes joined together, evidence that the business had expanded over the years. "Not much to look at."

"We're not here to look. It's almost three in the afternoon and I missed breakfast and lunch."

She placed Steve's hand on her shoulder and led him across an ample parking lot. They entered the building through what looked like a back door. Their trip into the dining area took them past a tall refrigerated pie case with layer after layer of decadent meringue-topped diet destroyers.

"Ya'll sit wherever you want," said a middle-aged server in

casual dress. "You're a tad early if you came for the pie happy hour. It don't start 'til four."

Heather chose a booth with a view of a sidewalk running the length of the cafe and a very busy Highway 281, a main artery that led to San Antonio.

After she settled Steve, Heather said, "Let me guess. You had a chicken-fried steak here on Friday night."

"I needed comfort food after the session with the Voss clan."

The woman took drink orders and Steve launched into a recitation of the most recent meeting and the lack of progress. By the time he gave a synopsis of the contentious gathering, the server stood with pen in hand, ready to take their order.

"Are you still serving breakfast?" asked Steve.

"We serve it all day, hon. How hungry are you?"

"The buttons on my shirt are scratching my backbone."

"You need a three-egg omelet. You want Spanish or western?"

"I like it spicy."

She spoke as she wrote. "One Spanish omelet. That comes with a choice of hash browns or grits."

"Hash browns and add a side of grits."

"It also comes with your choice of Texas toast, regular toast or biscuits."

"Biscuits with gravy," said Steve. "That should leave room for pie."

Heather shook her head. "I'll have the grilled chicken Caesar salad."

She noticed a trio of knobby-kneed men wearing loud shorts and knit shirts. They were close enough that their conversation made it to her ears. All old enough to be retired, they carried on about the shots they made and the ones missed that morning. With eighteen holes, lunch and a nap under their belts, they were early arrivals for the pie happy hour. Gray fringes protruded from baseball caps, each embroidered with the logo of a different golf course.

Turning to Steve, she asked, "I told you about the disaster with my father. It's your turn. Did you avoid Bridget the barracuda last night?"

"She caught me coming out of the meeting room. We had an excellent dinner at a restaurant on the lake and then we played eighteen holes of golf."

Heather was thankful she didn't have her mouth full of water. It would have sprayed all over Steve and the table. She gave him a squinted stare. "You're joking."

"Not at all. I had chicken-fried lobster, and she had a fillet. She drank wine, and I had iced tea. Boats pulled up to the dock, people unloaded and enjoyed a sunset and excellent food."

She expected a zinger punch line, but one didn't come. "I'm gullible enough to believe you had dinner with her, but not you playing golf."

He held up three fingers like a Boy Scout reciting his pledge. "Eighteen holes on the Whitewater Course not over a hundred steps from the hotel. It's awesome. You should play a round or two while we're here."

Heather shook her head. "I'm not buying this tall tale."

"I'll prove it." Steve slipped out of the booth and approached the golfers at the table. Two of the three came back with him.

"Tell her I played golf last night at the Whitewater Course."

They each nodded. The one wearing green shorts said, "We could see Steve and Bridget both needed help. I let Harry go ahead with Bridget while I told Steve the distance and set him up for the angle of the puts. Of course, I didn't let him hit out of the sand traps."

"Of course," said Heather in a mocking tone. "What about his shots off the tee or his iron play or chipping?"

The second man with a roll of belly over the white belt

holding up azure shorts joined the conversation. "There's no driving or iron play on the Whitewater. It's putting only."

"Are you telling me there's a putt putt golf course at the Horseshoe Bay Resort?"

"Not exactly," said Steve, "but the same idea."

Green pants began the lecture. "It a par 72 course with 56 sand traps, putting only. It covers one-hundred and forty-seven acres. The greens are Zoysia grass while they sow the roughs in Bermuda. It's a challenge for any professional, let alone us old duffers."

"Speak for yourself," said the man wearing the powder-blue shorts. "I'm not so old that I didn't get a date for tonight with Bridget." He uttered the deep purr of a cat.

"What time did this alleged golf game take place?" asked Heather, still not totally convinced.

Steve said, "We started around eight."

Green pants added, "They light the course. You need to try it. It's a blast. Steve said you need to find something to do besides work. We've been there, done that. Still recovering from time we spent on the corporate treadmill."

The arrival of their orders allowed for only a word of thanks from Heather as the men returned to their table and tales of triumphs and tragedies on the links.

"Biscuits and gravy at twelve o'clock. Your omelet runs all the way from three-o'clock to nine on the oblong plate. It's enough food to feed a foursome."

Heather leaned forward. "You sly old dog. You pawned Bridget off on a nice old man last night. How did you do it?"

"I told her I had leprosy."

Heather's cackle caused heads to turn. "Serves me right for asking."

"Bridget's an excellent match for Mac. They're both lonely."

"Aren't you?"

"Sometimes, but not as often as before. Kate and I talked for an hour after I got back to the room. She's encouraging me to finish the book and get it published. Writing is the hardest thing I ever tried to do. Give me a murder and I can usually solve it. Tell me to write about it in a way that doesn't sound like a police report, and the words get stuck in my brain."

"Did you tell her about what we're doing now?"

He stuffed a bite of omelet in his mouth and moaned, then chewed until he could speak again. "She said it would make a good short story if something unexpected happens at the end. Not enough twists and turns to make into a novel. She wants me to call her back after we read the second part of the will."

"You don't think the four Voss children can come to some sort of agreement?"

He loaded another bite onto his fork, but it fell off. "We'll be lucky if they don't kill each other."

"Was yesterday's meeting that bad?"

His empty fork hovered over his plate. "We need to make a rule. If it's the middle of the afternoon and I haven't eaten all day, I don't have to answer questions until I'm sure I won't pass out from starvation."

"Starvation and leprosy? We'd better get you to a hospital."

Heather looked up to see a white shirt with a badge on it. Her eyes traveled upward and beheld rosy cheeks and a serious scowl under the brim of a cowboy hat. A pudgy finger touched the brim of the hat and the man said, "Ma'am. Excuse me. I'm Sheriff Stony Blake. If you're Heather McBlythe, I need to talk to you and Steve."

She shifted herself and her plate, making room for the man. He yipped in pain as he sat down.

Steve put his fork beside his plate. "What's wrong, Sheriff?"

"Rance Voss found Hector DeLeon's body today around noon. Somebody shot him. I understand the Voss children are to meet today at five. Is that right?"

Steve answered with a tight-lipped nod.

"I want to be there to see how they react to the news."

"I do too," said Heather.

"Good enough. This is getting out of hand and I'm not sure Marvin is up to the challenge of two homicides."

9

By now Steve had the layout of the meeting room memorized. He'd been quiet since they left the café. Heather knew his silence didn't stem from being satisfied after an amazing meal since he left most of it uneaten. She bought him a cup of coffee at the Starbucks in the hotel to go along with a cinnamon roll she purchased on their way out of the cafe. Wayward specks of glaze dotted his shirt, showing he'd at least put some fuel in his tank.

Being thirty minutes early to the daily meeting meant they had time to talk before the Voss children and Sheriff Blake arrived. Heather placed her satchel on the table and walked to a bank of windows overlooking a patio that led to a swimming pool swarming with adults and children. She turned. "Are we working this case or not?"

He pulled a hand down his face. "I'm sure the sheriff wants our help, but he never came out and asked. Reading between the lines, I'd say he wants Marvin to find the answers, but for us to point him toward them. Remember, we still don't have a client."

"So, we're to look into it, but not too hard. Is that what you're saying?"

"Something like that. If we find something useful, we'll drop breadcrumbs for Marvin to follow that keep him on the right track."

"I don't like it," said Heather.

"Me either and don't be surprised if we become more involved. Let's see if there's a quick arrest. As for Charley's death, it wouldn't hurt for us to go to the ranch and look around. Marvin might have missed something."

It made little sense to Heather that they weren't doing more to find Charley's killer. Perhaps Steve knew things he'd not told her. If so, it was because she was so entangled in the acquisition.

She ambled toward the head of the table. "Do you remember Hector DeLeon from your hunting trips?"

Steve tapped his fingers on the table, a sign the two murders weighed heavy on his mind. "Hector was as much a part of the Voss family as the children. Perhaps more than Charley, who was a loner with a distant gaze in his eye. It was like he looked to the past for something he'd lost or missed along the way." Steve shook his head. "Maybe I'm reading more into him than I should. Don't let me color your opinion of Charley if we start a full-blown investigation. As for Hector, I remember him as having a sanguine personality, happy all the time and content with life."

Steve paused. "Why don't you ask Sue Ann about him? If I remember right, he carved wooden figures of cattle and horses for her to play with."

"Who should I talk to about Charley?"

Steve shrugged. "Take your pick of any of the children."

She knew the door had closed on further discussion about Charley and Hector, at least for the time being. Then another question rose to the surface. "What's wrong with Sheriff Blake? He looked odd wearing house shoes in the cafe."

"Gout. He can't get his boots on. They say gout can hurt as bad as childbirth."

"I wouldn't know about either," said Heather. "At the rate I'm going, I'm more likely to get gout."

The chuckle seemed to do Steve good, but he soon settled into himself, as if he were a turtle.

Roy's voice preceded him throwing open the door. Sue Ann entered two steps ahead of him saying, "Don't be so mean. Grant's doing the best he can."

"If that's his best, I'd hate to see what he's like when he isn't trying. He's mean to you and the kids and lousy with money. Somebody's going to come along and cheat him out of what could be a better life for you."

"If there's a cheater in the family, it's you. Now leave me alone. I don't want to talk about Grant anymore."

Roy looked to Heather and Steve and flipped a dismissive hand in the air. "Don't pay any attention to us. It's a Voss tradition to have arguments." He issued an inappropriate laugh. "Some families serve food around the table. We throw it at each other."

To his credit, Roy skipped a seat between him and Sue Ann and remained quiet until Mae walked in with chin lifted an inch too high.

"All rise for the queen," said Roy. "Where's the court jester? Didn't Pat come with you?"

"Zip it, Roy. I'm only here to tell Rance I'll accept his estimates on the livestock and to insist he sells every head and we divide the money evenly."

"Little Rance may have something to say about that. I hear he's quite attached to one or two of the heifers." Another obnoxious laugh came forth.

Mae settled in her chair and turned to Heather and Steve. "Where's Rance? It's five o'clock, let's start without him."

"He's on his way," said Steve. "We'll wait."

Five long minutes passed. Mae examined her manicured nails and huffed every sixty seconds, as if to remind everyone her valuable time was being wasted. Roy took a deck of cards from his shirt pocket and performed tricks displaying his dexterity. All the while he whistled the tune, *Oh What a Beautiful Morning,* from the musical *OKLAHOMA!* Heather realized he increased the volume at the place with the lyrics "I've got a beautiful feeling, everything's going my way." Yet another goad to annoy Mae.

Sue Ann's downcast eyes focused on the blank cover of a thin file with the edges of pages peeking from the top right corner. Every few seconds her lips would move. It reminded Heather of the way people memorized lines or prayed.

The door opened and Rance entered with shoulders rounded and his gaze downcast. Following him was Patrick, with Sheriff Blake bringing up the rear.

Roy stopped whistling while Mae narrowed her eyes. "What is this, a parade?"

"Leave the jokes to me," said Roy. "I know how to read people and this isn't the time."

"Before anyone asks," said Steve. "I changed my mind. I'm allowing Patrick to attend the meeting."

The attorney gave Mae a grim-faced nod and put a finger to his lips to clue her not to speak.

Rance took off his hat and ran fingers through his hair. The whites of his eyes were puffy and pinkish, where yesterday they'd been bright and clear. He sat three seats down from Roy, close to the floor-to-ceiling window, and turned so he wouldn't have to look at anyone in the room.

"I believe everyone knows me, but just in case, I'm Stoney

Blake, the sheriff of Llano County. Today, around noon, we found Hector DeLeon dead at the Voss Ranch."

Heather tried to look at everyone at once. Mae clenched her fist, but said nothing. Roy remained uncharacteristically quiet and gave nothing away in his expression. Sue Ann jerked her head up and mouthed the word. *No.* Rance didn't turn around.

Roy broke the silence after a few seconds. For once, his tone suited the moment. "Is this another murder?"

The sheriff gave his head a nod. "Somebody shot him. The investigation is ongoing."

"Good Lord," said Mae. "Somebody's trying to kill us all."

Patrick patted her hand. "We don't know that." He brought his gaze to the sheriff. "Can you give us any details?"

"Dispatch received the call at thirteen minutes after noon. Chief Deputy Marvin Goodnight arrived at the ranch house at twelve thirty-nine."

Mae gasped. Her grip left Patrick's hand pink when she released it.

Roy asked, "Could it have been an accident?"

"People don't shoot themselves twice."

The sound of abject grief has a tone all its own. Heather had heard it many times when she was a cop. Delivering news of untimely deaths was something she never got used to, nor did she want to. The moaning ache coming from some deep place within Rance brought back a flood of unpleasant memories. Still, was this level of grief normal? He was a young man who dealt with the cruelties of nature in animals every day. He was no stranger to blood and death, albeit with livestock, animals, and their prey.

Roy stared straight ahead and tapped the deck of cards. He seemed to be processing a bet. The corners of his mouth turned upward. "I know why you're here, Sheriff. You need to question each of us to see if we have an alibi."

"I already told you," said Mae. "I left the ranch as soon as I could after graduation. I haven't been on that property since."

"Did the guilty dog just bark?" asked Roy. "Got something to hide, Mae?"

"Of course not, and if you weren't so stupid, you'd see what's going on. One of you three is responsible for both killings." She cast her gaze to each of her siblings. "No. You three are working together on this and I'm next. That's why you bashed Dad's head in."

"Explain Hector," said Roy in a challenging tone.

Mae hesitated. She looked to her attorney but found nothing to guide her until he said, "It's possible that Mr. DeLeon might have overheard a plot to kill Charley Voss."

Roy came back with, "It's also possible that you have something to do with the murders. After all, you make up lies for a living." He laughed and said, "Don't look now, Mae, but your paranoia's showing."

Sue Ann's weak voice broke in. "I was at home all last night and today with the kids."

"Prove it," shouted Mae.

Something like a geyser erupted at the far end of the table. Rance sprang to his feet shouting, "Don't you people have any respect? Hector was more of a father to all of us than Dad ever was. Mae, he bought you makeup when Dad took yours and called you a tramp. Did you know he watched you when you'd sneak out at night? He made sure you were all right until you got in the truck with your boyfriend and he'd watch until you snuck back in. How old were you when that started? Thirteen? Fourteen?"

Rance's gaze shifted to Roy. "Hector may not have gone to school, but he was smart in different ways. How did you learn to read people so well? He taught you how to read cattle. You knew what to look for if they were restless, frightened, or hurt. You applied the skills he taught you to people at a poker table. Did you ever thank Hector for the education he gave you?"

"I'll put an arrangement on his grave."

Rance took a step toward Roy but stopped when he saw Sue Ann's tear-filled gaze. "Sister, do you remember all the animals Hector carved for you? Dad wouldn't let any of us have toys, so we had to make our own. Mae stuffed hay in Hector's empty bags of coffee so she could pretend they were dolls like the other girls had. Those got passed down to you. Hector could see that you needed something extra, so he spent hours whittling animals out of mesquite. He didn't have to do that."

Roy stood and clapped. "Thank you for that touching account of our wasted childhoods. If there's one thing I learned from that old Mexican it's that life is tough." He looked around the room. "The sheriff is here because he thinks one of us might be responsible. Mae's so loco she thinks we all are. I know I didn't do it. Sue Ann's afraid of her own shadow, so that leaves you, little brother. What's your alibi?"

Rance stormed from the room.

"Little brother seems touchy today. I had no idea he cared so much for Hector."

Sue Ann stood, closed to within arm's length of Roy, and unleashed a roundhouse right that caught him square on his left cheek. The sheriff didn't make a move to stop her as she bolted from the room.

Roy wasn't smiling when he picked himself up off the carpet. A trickle of blood oozed between his fingers.

"Get cleaned up," said Sheriff Blake. "Come back in or you'll be looking at a jail cell tonight."

The unexpected punch had a sobering effect on Roy. All he could utter was, "Yes, sir."

Patrick spoke as soon as the door closed behind Roy. "Sheriff, is there anything else you need from my client?"

"Did either of you kill Hector DeLeon?"

"Of course not," said Mae.

The attorney shook his head. "I did not."

"Do either of you have any knowledge of who might be responsible?"

Both Mae and Patrick said they didn't.

Sheriff Blake leaned back in his chair. "Are you going back to Austin?"

Patrick shook his head. "Instead of driving back and forth every day, Ms. Richards thought it best to stay at Horseshoe Bay."

"Here at the hotel?"

Mae spoke up. "I'm booked in one of the waterfront condos through Tuesday. You have my number if you need to ask me anything else."

"What about you, Mr. Shaw? Are you going back to Austin?"

"I need to converse with my client about today's developments and how they might impact the inheritance."

The sheriff sighed. "Why do lawyers use a dozen words to skate around a question when a simple yes or no would do? I'll send someone around to take statements from both of you about where you were last night and today."

Steve spoke after he heard the door click shut. "Mae's already spending her inheritance."

Heather noticed the sheriff grimace.

He pursed his lips together. "Don't get old and fat, and above all, don't get gout."

Heather jerked her head around. Marvin held the door open for a woman who looked to be in her mid-twenties. Her hair was a soft brown. The olive complexion made it hard to tell if her heritage was Hispanic, Italian or a mix. One thing was sure, her dark eyes had been crying. The long lashes glistened with fresh tears.

"This is Angelina Perez," said Marvin. "She's Hector's granddaughter, and she'd like to talk to Mr. Smiley and Ms. McBlythe."

"Do we need to stay?" asked Sheriff Blake.

"Please do," said Angelina.

The young woman worried a tissue that was fast becoming shreds of fiber. She eased herself on the edge of a chair nearest Steve. "Marvin, eh, Deputy Goodnight, tells me you're private investigators who specialize in solving murders. I want to hire you to find my grandfather's killer."

Steve leaned into Heather with a cupped hand. He whispered so low only she could make out the brief sentence. "We have a client."

"It's about time."

10

Adrenaline coursed through Heather's veins. Steve must have experienced the same thing. It wasn't his movements or words but the sudden stillness of amplified concentration that charged the air around him. It meant every word to follow would have the singular purpose of solving the murder of Hector DeLeon.

Cementing the agreement with the granddaughter would have to wait as Sheriff Blake expressed his condolences and turned to his chief deputy. "You left the crime scene?" His words sparked with accusation.

"The people from the State Forensic Lab are there, and I had Roger put up a perimeter. All we could do was stand around with our faces hanging out. The word must have got out back in Llano. Angelina showed up while I was on my phone talking with a state trooper."

"Don't blame Marvin, Sheriff," said Angelina. "As soon as I heard, I left home and drove to *Abuelo's* cabin. I had to know what happened." She ducked her head and waves of hair spilled on her face. She used both hands to push it back after she raised her chin. "I lost it when I saw my *abuelo* being placed in a black bag."

She looked at Heather as if asking if she understood. Heather nodded. "*Abuelo*. Your grandpa. I'm sorry."

A hard stare from the sheriff pinned Marvin. He didn't offer any additional defense.

"I'm sorry you had to see that," said Sheriff Blake.

"It was my fault," said Angelina. "I broke away from Roger at the roadblock and outran him to the cabin."

Instead of commenting further, the sheriff stood. "If you'll excuse us, Marvin needs to give me an update. We'll be in the hall."

Marvin swallowed hard. It probably wasn't his fault, but he was due a lecture all the same. In her mind's eye, Heather envisioned Deputy Roger as a plump young man manning a roadblock. He wore heavy cowboy boots and all manner of gear. She could almost hear his footfalls and protests as he tried to keep up with a trim young woman wearing running shorts, a figure-accentuating tank top and tennis shoes.

Heather made a mental note that she'd have to give Steve a physical description of Angelina later.

Steve used his most comforting voice to say, "Ms. Perez, let me express our sincere condolences. Words always ring hollow, but they're all we can offer, except our desire to help you. Are you serious about wanting us to investigate?"

Angelina's gaze dipped, but only for a second. This was the second time she'd displayed the same unconscious habit. Heather read it as something akin to shame, or perhaps uncertainty. She'd ask Steve's opinion on it later to see if he agreed.

Shame or not, she raised her chin and firmed her voice. "Yes, Mr. Smiley. I'd like your help, but I'm not sure I can pay you up front. I have a few thousand dollars saved, but I may have to work out terms for your services."

"You needn't worry about payment," said Heather.

Steve didn't belabor the point other than to say, "We do require you to sign a contract, but I remember Hector and it wouldn't be right taking from his granddaughter."

Her eyes went downward a third time. "That's very kind, but I won't accept charity. I've already written a check for a thousand dollars."

Steve ignored Angelina's last words. "To get started, tell us about yourself. I take it you live in Llano?"

"With my mother. Her name is Anna. Anna Perez. And before you ask, I'm single, twenty-four, five-feet-three-inches tall, and I weigh a hundred and fifteen pounds in the summer and a hundred and twenty-five after Christmas tamales."

Steve patted his belly. "My pants get tight around the holidays, too."

"I graduated second in my class from high school and went to college in San Marcos. My degree is in accounting and I failed my first CPA exam. Fingers crossed when I take it again in the fall."

"Are you working now?"

"For the county treasurer."

The longer the young woman talked, the more Heather liked her. Angelina knew her strengths and weaknesses.

Steve pressed on. "Any serious romantic relationships?"

The head dipped again. "Not anymore. I was engaged in college, but that didn't turn out the way I expected."

"Ah."

The pause gave time for Angelina to square her shoulders. "I'm a third generation Texan, Mr. Smiley, but I come from common stock. I passed muster with my fiancée's parents until they met my mother. She preferred to speak Spanish, even though she converses well in English."

Heather bristled as she remembered how her father would treat any young man she mentioned. The bloodline had to run true-blue, and the Standard and Poor's credit rating had to be above reproach.

"But don't get the wrong idea," said Angelina. "My mother's preference to speak Spanish was just the first drop in the bucket. It really had nothing to do with my heritage. The real reason was money. They didn't want their son's portfolio tarnished by my student loan debt. You might say I come from the wrong side of the financial tracks."

Steve's next question brought Angelina back from the unpleasant memory. "How did you hear about your grandfather's death?"

"Do you know how many people live in Llano County? Less than twenty-five thousand in a land area of nine-hundred and sixty-six square miles. In the city of Llano, if you can call it a city, you can't sneeze without somebody blessing you. News travels fast."

Steve had drawn Angelina into a conversation that got her mind off her grandfather and established himself as a safe person. It wouldn't be long before his questions hit closer to the heart.

"When was the last time you saw your grandfather?" asked Steve, right on cue.

"Yesterday. I took him a big bowl of menudo Mama made for him. Enough for several meals."

"How did he seem?"

"What do you mean?"

"Was he upbeat, nervous, calm, worried?"

Her eyebrows drew together. "Mr. Charley's death hit him hard. We talked about how he missed him and my grandmother Rose. He cried."

"Hector seemed to be a good man. I never saw him without a smile," said Steve. "Of course, it's been a while since I last saw him. I didn't come back to this area after I lost my father, except once with my wife."

Angelina took a moment before she continued. "Mr. Charley's death hurt my grandfather. Mama was super-worried about him. That's why she cooked for him."

"Do you think he might have worried about having to move from the ranch?"

She took her time answering the question. "He seemed worried about something, but it wasn't about finding another job. Over the years, he turned down a lot of offers from ranchers that paid more and offered him a better place to live. He always chose to stay at the Rocking V. Now that I think about it, *Abuelo* considered himself part of the Voss family. That's odd since the only Voss child that treated him with respect was Rance." She paused. "That may not be a fair thing for me to say. Rance told me Sue Ann had a good relationship with him. I don't know how the two oldest treated him. He wasn't one to discuss negative things with me."

"How well do you know Rance?"

A smile of familiarity parted her full lips. "He was three years ahead of me in school. I knew him when I was growing up because he spent so much time with *Abuelo*. He was always nice to me, but the age difference and my living in town meant we had little in common."

Heather broke in with a question. "Rance is handsome and well educated. You're a beautiful young woman with a promising future. Is there any chance you and Rance might—"

A peal of laughter came from Angelina, cutting Heather's question short. "Me and Rance? Hardly. His heart belongs to his cattle and my long-term plans are to move to a place where thick, green grass grows instead of things that stab or bite you. Besides, it'd be like kissing a brother. Yuk."

"Yeah. Yuk," said Steve. He tapped his index finger on the table. "Would it be possible for us to visit your mother in the next few days?"

"Let me talk to her first. She's devastated. I called several of her friends and I'm sure they've packed the house with food by now."

"And your grandmother, Rose? She died several years ago?"

"I was young when she passed."

"One more thing," said Heather. "Can you think of anyone who'd want to harm your grandfather?"

Her chin quivered. "He was such a good, cheerful man. How could anyone do this?"

The door opened, and Marvin entered with hat in hand. "I'll take you back to your car, Angelina, whenever you're ready."

Heather made eye contact with the grieving granddaughter. "I'll call you in the morning to check on you."

"Thank you. And thank you, Mr. Smiley." She brushed his cheek with a kiss and walked out the door with Marvin leading the way.

Sheriff Blake grimaced as he hobbled back in the room and all but fell in the nearest chair. "Did she have anything interesting to say?"

Steve shook his head. "We were establishing background and getting a feel for the case. She said Hector had been down in the dumps since Charley died. That's not the Hector I remember."

"Me either. Do you think the same person killed both of them?"

The air in the room took on weight, like a force was compressing it. Steve took off his sunglasses and rubbed his sightless eyes. "How many head of cattle are there in Llano County?"

The sheriff's face twisted into a question. "If memory serves me, there's about forty thousand head, give or take. Why?"

"Two murders on the same ranch, less than two weeks apart in a county with twice as many cattle as people. What are the odds?"

The sheriff fingered the brim of his hat. "Roy is the expert on giving odds, not me."

Steve put his sunglasses on. "I'll ask him tomorrow, along with the others."

The heaviness in the room lifted when Steve's stomach made a sound not unlike a washing machine.

"You need to feed that thing," said Sheriff Blake.

Steve pushed back from the table. "I've got a hankering for some good Mexican food. Is there a restaurant nearby?"

"Go out to the main road and turn left. There's one not more than a mile, on your left."

"Care to join us?"

"Do you want another funeral? If the food didn't kill me, Clara would. It's carrot soup and a salad without dressing for me tonight."

11

Heather nodded her approval as she led Steve to a booth in a newly remodeled restaurant that boasted spotless tables and a smiling hostess. Mariachi music came from speakers in the ceiling, loud enough to enjoy but not overpowering like in some dining rooms. As usual, she chose a booth and put herself where she'd have the best view of the room. A dark-haired beauty arrived promptly with a single menu. Most servers missed the fact that placing a menu before Steve was a waste of time. With two orders for iced tea committed to memory, the server scurried away.

"Do you know what you want, or do I need to read the menu to you?"

"Get me one of everything. The cinnamon roll is a distant memory."

"Tuck your napkin in your shirt. She's coming back with drinks and chips."

Steve did as instructed, and Heather pointed at a spot in front of him for the server to place the basket of chips and a small bowl of what looked like pureed tomatoes, cilantro, onions and minute chunks of jalapenos.

He found the chips on the first try, but reached too far to the left for the salsa. After easing his hand to the right, he located the bowl and dipped his first chip of what Heather knew would be most of the basket.

"You'd better bring us some extra napkins," said Heather. "I'm still training him to dip and not scoop."

The server giggled and padded off.

After stuffing three more chips in his mouth, Steve said, "Surprise me. Order whatever looks good."

Heather studied the menu. "How does a fried avocado, stuffed with shrimp and cheese sound? It comes with rice, refried beans, and a chalupa."

"Throw on an enchilada or two."

Heather noticed an order being delivered to a nearby table. The generous portions told her Steve would be more than full with one extra enchilada. She spotted a salad topped with sizzling fajita meat that came in a bowl the diameter of a medium pizza. The menu went to the edge of the table.

Steve continued to reduce the stack of chips but spoke between bites. "Tell me about your trip to Montana."

"Something's fishy up there, and it's not rainbow trout. I think the mine could be on its way out, but that's not what the results of the drill holes say."

"Keep talking."

Heather explained the reduced usage of electricity, increased housing availability, and how much diesel fuel is being delivered as compared to past months and years.

"That doesn't sound good," said Steve. "Have you told your father?"

A deep sigh escaped. "He dismissed the facts I uncovered. If it had been Webster bringing him the information, it would have been a different story."

"Who's Webster?"

"Father's personal assistant and the son he never had."

"Ah."

"Yeah, 'Ah.' I think Father was grooming him to take over the company until I came back in the picture." Heather sensed her face warming, and the salsa wasn't to blame. "Father said he and Webster had already discussed the issues I brought up and there were logical explanations for them." She took a drink of iced tea and smoothed the napkin on her lap. "I sort of lost my temper and told Father I was going out on my own. I'm wiring him the money for the full price of the airplane tomorrow morning."

"Ouch. That was a Christmas present, wasn't it?"

A pang of guilt hit her, but she needed to defend her decision. "It was, and it wasn't. A tax write-off to the company, but Father seemed pleased to give it to me."

Steve stopped eating.

"Did I make a mistake?" asked Heather.

Steve lifted the basket of chips. "Take these away from me or I won't have room for the main course."

Heather did as asked and waited.

"There are two issues, but they're intertwined. The first is your responsibility to make a sound business decision based on the best information you could gather. He put you in charge of that project, but you didn't see it through to the end."

"He didn't let me. Webster's been in his ear ever since he gave me the assignment."

Steve leaned back. "Do you want me to continue?"

Heather rewound a tape of the conversation with her father in her head. She'd snapped at her father, and now she was doing the same thing to Steve. It was time to muzzle her mouth and listen. "Sorry."

He leaned forward. "If you're right, McBlythe Enterprises stands to lose millions of dollars."

"Hundreds of millions in direct losses and future earnings." She knew that wasn't all. "There's also the loss of reputation.

Father doesn't often make mistakes when it comes to something this big."

"And if you're wrong, what happens?"

"The deal will go a competitor, and McBlythe Enterprises will lose out on what Father calls the deal of a lifetime."

"Isn't everything based on projections?" asked Steve.

"Yes, but there's solid science to support them."

"Perhaps. But that's not the point. Your father gave you an assignment and you quit before you completed it."

Her stomach clenched. "That's not fair. He told me he was going ahead with the deal without me."

"And you did what?"

"I quit."

Steve leaned forward more. "You didn't just quit, you lashed out against your father in a way you knew would hurt him."

The words stung, but she knew they were true.

He continued, "The second issue is a bit broader. You're wondering if you'll be happier if you're free from McBlythe Enterprises. That's something to answer on your own. How you handled the gold mine and your decision to cut the business strings from your father's company are two different issues."

"Steve."

"Yes?"

"Your hand is in salsa you spilled on the table."

"I know. I'm going to smear it on my avocado."

The tension broke, but this would be a conversation she'd remember the rest of her life.

The server warned Steve of a hot plate. They ate in silence, except for the multiple moans of delight and comments on the quality of the cuisine. Heather thought the meal would be enough for Steve, but he had other ideas. "Get on your phone. There has to be Dairy Queen in Marble Falls. My sweet tooth is acting up and a strawberry sundae will help put the fire out from the jalapenos I ate."

On the way to town she asked, "Which one of the Voss children do you want to interview first tomorrow?"

"Let's start with Roy. I think that smack in the face might have taken the starch out of him. Let's get him before his defenses rise again."

"Do you want me to do a background check on him?"

"Already done. I'll send you the files I made on each of the Voss clan while you were in Montana."

Heather glanced to her right in time to see him smile. "You've been busy."

"I had time after Bridget Callahan dumped me for a real golfer."

"Are you disappointed?"

"Let's say I'm getting over it fast."

"Who do we talk to after Roy?"

"I thought we'd go for Rance. I'm interested to see if his grief is still as deep after a night's sleep."

"Or lack of sleep," said Heather.

"Right. Then we'll talk to Sue Ann. It seemed a little odd that Grant wasn't with her today."

Heather thought back to the punch she landed. "That wasn't as odd as the way she reacted to Hector's murder. That was an awesome punch. Split the skin on Roy's cheek bone wide open. He may show up with stitches."

"I didn't have her pegged as being violent," said Steve. "That's a reminder that people do unexpected things under pressure."

"That leaves us with Mae," said Heather. "What do you expect from her tomorrow?"

"More of the same. She's not likely to agree to anything because she's the first in line for the inheritance. I wonder if Charley left her a bigger cut or if he divided everything equally?"

"I guess we'll find out tomorrow."

Steve shook his head. "He gave them five days to decide. Tomorrow starts day five, but it's not complete until 5 p.m. on Tuesday. That's when I'm to receive the second part of the will from a local attorney. Mae won't like it, but that's the least of her problems."

Heather put on the car's blinker. "What do you mean?"

Steve leaned away as she made a sharp turn and scooted into Dairy Queen's parking lot. He righted himself as he said, "She's swimming with sharks. Lawyers like Patrick Shaw and his bosses will take bites out of her inheritance until there's nothing left. She doesn't know it, but she might be better off if Charley didn't leave her anything."

"Would he do that? Cut one or more of the children out of the will entirely?"

Steve unbuckled his seat belt. "He was a sour man that kept himself to himself. I'm a little surprised he married."

"Speaking of," said Heather. "What was his wife like?"

"I met Pearl a few times. She was more than a decade younger than Charley and wore her blond hair in a ponytail. No makeup, and she liked long skirts and loose blouses. I once noticed a yellow tinge under an eye. I don't think Charley was kind to her."

"Did you do a background check on her?"

Steve reached for the door handle. "I thought I'd leave you something to do."

12

Heather looked at the notes she'd made on a yellow legal tablet, the ones concerning Pearl Voss. She still needed to type them into her computer so Steve could use his program to change the text to audio. She glanced at a file on the gold mine and stuffed it into a box. After examining her hair and makeup in the mirror, she checked the time, smoothed her blouse and headed to the conference room. Roy and Steve were probably already there.

She was only half right. Steve sat by himself. "Am I early, or is Roy late?"

"I'm not sure he owns a watch. Did you have a productive day?"

"I stayed busy. How about you?"

"Kate called. She's sending me the latest edit of my book tomorrow. We had a nice long talk about me writing something else."

Heather's mind went back to last December when she and Steve were guest lecturers at a womens' mystery writers' conference. While there they solved a murder and Steve caught the eye of the group's president, Kate Bridges. He denied anything more than a teacher-pupil relationship, but Heather believed otherwise. Either way, Steve had found something to keep him occupied between cases.

"Did Kate want you to take notes about this case for your next book?"

"She wants me to work on short stories. Says I need to learn to walk before I try running with another novel."

The door opened and in shuffled Roy Voss. Gone was the smile and pointed banter. On his left cheek he wore a quartet of Steri-Strips. The swelling seemed minimal, but his countenance bore the look of a man whose luck had changed for the worse.

Steve invited him to sit down and asked about his face.

"I've been in worse shape. It's an occupational hazard for gamblers to run into people who think you're cheating them when they're drunk and making silly bets. It's not that way on the professional circuit."

"Do you goad your opponents the way you do your brother and sisters?"

He flipped a dismissive hand and leaned back. "All part of the game. I do that to get a read on people. Pressure causes them to reveal what's going on beneath the surface. Mae is easy, and so is Rance. I thought Sue Ann was, but she surprised me."

"That's interesting," said Steve. "You never saw her lash out like that before?"

Roy spoke in a somber tone with eyebrows pinched. "This has me worried. I haven't missed a tell so bad in years. It's shaken my confidence, and that's the one thing I can't afford to lose."

"You didn't answer Steve's question," said Heather. "Was Sue Ann violent when you grew up?"

He jerked back in his chair. "Heck no! All she did was play with the wooden animals Hector brought her. I'm sure you noticed, but she doesn't dazzle people with her brilliance. She always tried hard, but life didn't deal her the best hand."

"Do you think she's capable of harming your father or Hector?"

Roy stood and paced. "If you'd asked me that before yesterday's meeting, I would have laughed in your face. Today? I don't know. Like I said, I didn't see the punch coming."

"Are you going to press charges against her?" asked Heather.

His head came forward. "It was my fault. I mentally replayed what happened all day, and I still can't find her tell. It's driving me nuts."

Steve moved on. "Did Marvin Goodnight talk to you today?"

Roy nodded.

"Respond verbally," said Heather.

He threw up his hands. "See what I mean? I'm so rattled I can't even tell there's a blind man asking me questions."

Heather bit her lip. The words she held back would have served as payback for some of Roy's antics, but they wouldn't aid in gaining information.

Steve plowed on. "Did the police talk to you?"

"Yeah. Once at dawn and again around noon. I wasn't very communicative the first time around."

"And what did you tell them?"

"I sat in on a game last night here in the hotel and lost a wad of cash. Against amateurs, no less. There were only two inches of scotch left in the bottle when Marvin came to my room this morning. I tell you, Mr. Smiley, this is serious. The Rocking V Ranch is jinxed."

"Do you plan on leaving soon?"

"I can't. Marvin said I'd need to stay until the sheriff said I could go."

Beads of perspiration formed on Roy's forehead. He mopped his face with the sleeve of his shirt.

Steve used his soothing voice. "I'm glad to hear you'll be here for the reading of the will tomorrow."

"Tomorrow? Isn't this Monday? The first meeting was Thursday. He clenched his fist and popped out a finger with each day he recited. With the last finger extended, he said, "Monday."

"I made the same mistake," said Heather. "From Thursday at five until Friday at five is one day."

Roy banged his head on the table. "I can't count to five using my fingers. How can I count cards?" He looked up from his misery. "Mae and her attorney are going to pick my pockets. You've got to help me, Mr. Smiley. Don't let me agree to anything stupid."

"No one's going to force you to do anything," said Steve. "You can sit out today's meeting if you want to."

He nodded with vigor and stood to leave.

The door opened and Rance entered, dressed like he'd climbed down from a horse in the hotel parking lot.

"Sorry I'm late."

"You're early," said Heather. "We didn't expect you until five-thirty."

"I couldn't reach him," said Steve. "No worries. Roy was leaving."

"I want him to stay," said Rance, with more determination in his voice than Heather had heard before.

"All right," said Steve. "Roy can stay if he wants to."

Rance remained standing and tossed his hat on the table. "I'm sick of all this fussing and fighting. I want to finish rounding up the cattle, take 'em to auction and sell every last one."

"Whoa, cowboy," said Roy. "What's got into you?"

Rance took a red bandanna from his back pocket and scrubbed a layer of grime from his neck. "I'm ready for a fresh start. I'll take my fourth of the money from the sale of the livestock and leave anything else I might get to you and Mae and Sue Ann."

He looked at Heather. "Ms. McBlythe, could you draw up the papers and make it legal for me to renounce any other part of an inheritance I might get?"

Heather needed to stall for time. He'd second guess a decision like this the rest of his life. "I can draw up an agreement like that, but I can't do it today." She went to a refrigerator and retrieved two bottles of water. "You look parched. Have a seat and cool off."

He nodded in agreement.

Roy addressed his brother without sarcasm, something that sounded out of character. "This is a big decision, Rance. If you don't mind me asking, why are you willing to settle for so little?"

Rance paced like a caged animal looking for a way out. "That ranch has been a source of pain and misery for all of us. You know better than me how Daddy treated people, especially Momma and you and Mae. He slacked off on Sue Ann because of the way she is. By the time I came along, there wasn't enough left of him to do much harm. I had it the easiest because he pretended I didn't exist. Hector filled in as best he could, and now he's gone. Give me one good reason for staying and fighting over land that ain't fit for anything but heartaches."

Roy walked to the windows, looked out and then turned. "You're right. I don't blame you for leaving, but don't do it like Mae and I did. Play your hand smarter. I bet you can get the whole herd if you don't fold. Then you can sell and start someplace else with more chips. Mae only wants the land, not the money from the cattle. I don't need it. If you want to be noble, split the money from the sale of the herd with Sue Ann."

Rance slowed his steps. "I'm afraid I'll do something stupid if Mae and her lawyer keep pushing."

Steve broke in, "What if you didn't have to listen to any

more fighting? You could come to the reading of the will and leave as soon as Heather finishes."

Rance ran his finger down the side of the bottle. "I could do that?"

"Who's going to stop you?"

Eyes shifted back and forth as Rance slowed long enough to give consideration to Roy and Steve's words. "I have my eye on a ranch fifty miles northwest of College Station. A two-way split from the sale of the cattle and what I have saved will be enough to get me a fresh start." His gaze shifted to a spot on the wall. "Why is life around family so complicated? Everything makes more sense when I'm on horseback."

Roy went to Rance and put his hand on the younger brother's shoulder. "Sleep on it one more night. You'll know what to do after you hear the second part of the will. I'll back you no matter what."

"Thanks, Roy." He straightened his shoulders. "I guess I was a might hasty in giving up too much. I'll take some of your advice, but not all of it." He cast his gaze to Heather. "I'd appreciate it if you'd pass this on to Mae. I want to give up my claim to any land in exchange for the cattle and horses. Sue Ann's getting the other half, but I don't want her to know it until Mae and Roy sign a release."

He turned to face Roy. "I'll leave it up to you to convince Mae to give up her portion of the herd."

Rance shifted his gaze back to Heather. "I'd like everything ready to sign at tomorrow's meeting. One less Voss for you to worry about might help speed things along."

Roy looked at his baby brother with what appeared to be admiration. His countenance shifted as his head tilted. "How did you figure out the reading of the will wouldn't take place until tomorrow?"

Rance shrugged. "Sundown to sundown is one day. Today is the fourth sundown."

The two brothers left together, talking about finding a cold beer and a hot meal.

Heather made sure Mae wasn't eavesdropping in the hall. She stretched and asked, "What did you make of that?"

"Rance is a man of integrity."

"I was thinking," said Heather. "It must be tough on him living at the ranch where his father and a man who took him under his wing were both murdered."

"He's not living at the ranch. He packed his truck this morning and is staying with a friend in Llano."

"How do you know that?"

"I spoke with Sheriff Blake today. Remind me to tell you what he said after we talk to Sue Ann and Mae."

"Why not tell me now?"

Steve dipped his head. "Sue Ann's going to knock in 3...2..."

Timid raps sounded.

"Missed it by one," said Steve.

13

The door tentatively swung open. Sue Ann entered the room, head down, and pulled out a chair to sit down. Heather immediately noticed a dark circle under one eye and a red welt under the other. She stuffed down her immediate reaction to ask what happened and said, "Thanks for coming, Sue Ann. Grant didn't come with you?"

"He told me to come by myself. He couldn't take no time off today."

Steve looked toward her and smiled. "That's fine, Sue Ann. I'm glad you could come. You have a lovely voice, but I'm having a bit of a hard time hearing you. If you could speak up a little that would help me out."

She agreed, but the words showed no appreciable increase in volume. If it weren't for the bandage on Roy's eye, Heather would never believe this shrinking violet would ever raise her voice, let alone a hand, in anger. Perhaps Sue Ann's still waters had turbulent undercurrents.

"How are the children?" asked Steve.

"They're fine, I guess."

Sue Ann's tepid response came only after she seemed to

choose her words with extra care. She also made a mental note that Sue Ann winced when she sat down. A swollen eye and unseen damage elsewhere had the hallmarks of an abusive husband's handiwork.

"Tell me about your day," said Steve.

A look of confusion crossed Sue Ann's face. Her eyes darted as if she was checking for a way out of the room. "It weren't nothin' special."

Steve took on a jovial tone. "That can't be right with four kids running around the house. I bet there was plenty of activity."

"Matthew cut his foot, but not bad. He hates to wear shoes."

"I did, too. But I grew up in Houston and my mom loved thick grass. With all the rain on the coast, Dad and I were kept busy cutting it."

"We have a four-legged lawn mower that gives milk."

Steve smiled. He was putting Sue Ann at ease with inconsequential conversation and questions. Heather had seen him use the same tactic numerous times when he detected someone's resistance to answering questions. It took time and laughter, but her answers stretched longer and contained more details.

"How's Grant's job at the granite quarry?"

"He don't like it much, but there ain't much else around here for him to do."

Steve rocked back in the executive chair. "I guess some inheritance money would come in handy."

She included a firm nod with her verbal reply. "We got a stack of doctor bills. That don't count all the normal things."

"What days does Grant work?"

"He's supposed to work Monday through Friday, but most weeks he takes a day off."

"Does he have any hobbies?"

"He knows every inch of the lake and he's good at fishin'. If nothin' else, we can always eat fish and hush puppies, and fresh vegetables in season. I do a lot of cannin' this time of year." She straightened her posture. "I grow a passable garden and we raise chickens. Between what Grant brings home huntin' and fishin', milk from the cow, eggs, the garden and what we get from the government and churches, we always have enough."

"You're a resourceful woman. Do you go fishing and hunting with Grant?"

"Used to. Before the kids came along."

"Did you hunt much before you married?"

A laugh pealed out from her. "You've seen where I grew up. Mama taught all us kids how to shoot. You never knew when a snake or coyote might come around the house. I got me a fox tryin' to get in the henhouse when I was eight."

"Did you hunt deer?"

"Sure. I don't anymore because Grant wants me to stay home with the kids while he goes."

Heather made notes on a legal pad. Steve was picking Sue Ann's brain for clues and she didn't realize it. So far, he'd verified they were behind on bills and needed help to survive. Grant and Sue Ann could both handle a boat and firearms. Grant worked Monday through Friday, but not every week. She'd need to verify if Grant missed work on the days the murders took place.

Heather gripped her pen when Steve asked his next question.

"How many times has Mae talked to you since Thursday?"

"Three."

Sue Ann's wide eyes telegraphed she hadn't meant to answer the question.

"You can't tell her I told you, Mr. Smiley."

"Did she want you to sign something?"

"I'm not supposed to say. That lawyer told me I couldn't."

Heather huffed. This wasn't good for Sue Ann. There's no telling what trick or pressure they used to get her to sign some-

88

thing she couldn't understand. That also might explain the red eye and why Sue Ann kept her left elbow pressed against her ribs.

"Grant found out, didn't he?" asked Steve.

Sue Ann looked like a balloon leaking air. Her shoulders rounded over and her head dipped.

Steve reached his hand toward Sue Ann. "Take it, and look at me."

She inched fingers with gnawed nails toward him as she blinked back tears.

"Have you signed anything yet?"

"I told them I might today after the meeting."

Heather put her pen on the legal pad. "Don't worry, Sue Ann. We won't let anyone cheat you."

Steve released her hand. "Let's not borrow trouble until we see what the second part of the will has to say."

Sue Ann took a breath and leaned over. She brought a purse half the size of a bed pillow to the top of the table. "I was going through all of Daddy's papers when I did the inventory of the ranch house. I'm not sure, but I think this is a copy of the will."

"Both parts?" asked Heather.

"What's in the first envelope reads the same as the one you gave us."

Steve's voice held a hint of excitement. "Has anyone else seen this?"

"No. I didn't remember it until after Mae and Mr. Shaw left this morning."

Heather wasn't prone to get excited about wills, but this one had her heart racing. "Have you read the second part?"

"No. I didn't think it right for me to know before the others."

"Do you want us to keep it?" asked Steve.

"I think it's better that you have it. If Grant finds out I forgot to tell him, I don't know what he'll do." She pushed the envelope toward Steve.

"Did you find any other interesting documents?"

"Daddy wasn't much for keeping records, but I found some titles to land and all our birth certificates."

"Those are important," said Heather. "Let me have everything you brought and I'll give the birth certificates to your brothers and sister tomorrow."

"One more thing," said Steve. "What did you think of Hector DeLeon?"

Her face brightened, then fell. "He was the nicest man I ever met. When Daddy beat Mama, Hector would nurse her back to health. Daddy was a mean man. He beat all of us, but not like he did Mama."

"What about Rance?" asked Steve. "We heard he wasn't as hard on him."

Sue Ann looked beyond Steve, as if she could see into the past. "When Roy left home, the whippings stopped. Daddy would get mad, but he wouldn't hit me or Rance. Don't know why."

Heather made a note on her pad. Steve had no further questions, so he expressed his thanks and asked if she had anything else to add. Sue Ann slung her purse over her shoulder and promised not to tell that she'd given them the second part of the will.

Heather had the envelope open before Sue Ann made it three steps down the hall. She read it aloud and waited for Steve to respond.

"Leave it to Charley to make us work for answers."

"Why didn't he just write out who gets what?"

"He did. Sort of."

She made a sound like air coming out of a bicycle pump.

"What time is it?" asked Steve.

"We're ahead of schedule, by twenty minutes."

"Call Mae and tell her we'll come to her condo. The walls of this room are closing in on me."

Steve was right. A change of scenery after Sue Ann's tales of woe would be welcome. Even if it involved obnoxious Mae and her slimy lawyer.

PATRICK ANSWERED THE DOOR WEARING PLEATED SHORTS, A KNIT shirt, and deck shoes. "I hope you don't mind the informal attire. It's a relief to put the suit back in the closet. Mae will be out in a minute."

Two men and a woman entered through a sliding glass door that led to a covered patio overlooking the lake. Patrick took care of introductions. The men were identified as an architect and a civil engineer. The woman was a paralegal in the law firm Patrick worked for.

Of the three, it was the woman who caught Heather's attention. Her violet eyes were as startling as they were disarming. They reminded Heather of a color she'd seen at sunset when God took special pleasure in painting the sky.

Paralegal Cindy King stood nearest to Patrick during the introductions. Perhaps it was nothing, but Heather made a mental note that he touched the small of her back when he introduced her.

The three excused themselves with the unlikely excuse they wanted to find a Starbucks. A flip chart and white board on an easel gave evidence the trio were there to plot out the future of a lakefront development.

While Patrick saw them out, Heather looked around the condominium with its upscale touches. The open floor plan included hardwood floors in the living room, dining room, and breakfast nook. Rich, brown leather covered the couch, a love seat, and a recliner. The kitchen boasted stainless appliances and the obligatory granite counter tops. Thick area rugs spread over the living room's center and under the dining room table with seating for six. Abstract paintings of muted colors and soft designs looked down from the walls.

As impressive as the inside area was, the covered deck caught Heather's eye and held her gaze. A hardwood table and chairs sat at one end of the deck, while a more intimate conversation circle of a glass-topped table and padded outdoor furniture anchored the other end. Heather's gaze swept over the shimmering water and an arc of homes and condominiums. She noticed most of the homes came with drive-in boat garages, complete with boat lifts. It was the type of real estate where if you had to ask the price, you probably couldn't afford it.

Mae breezed in with a long-stemmed wineglass held in a hand weighted down with rings. She wore a one-piece jumper with one too many top buttons undone. Heather took one look at the exposure and knew a surgeon had enhanced Mae's assets.

"Have my siblings come to their senses? Please tell me they have," said Mae as gold bracelets jangled.

Steve spoke first. "We might have made a little progress today. Can we sit down and talk about it?"

"The view is so much nicer outside," said Mae.

"Nothing like a magnificent view," said Steve.

Heather knew he threw that line in to see how deep Mae's self-absorption went. Her absence of response answered the question.

"I think the deck is divine," said Mae. "Especially this time of day when the traffic on the water settles down. It's so rude the way some of these boats fly about. The racket is unbearable."

Patrick cleared his throat. "I take it you have no objection to my sitting in."

"The more the merrier," said Steve in a jovial voice.

"Could I get either of you something to drink? Wine, beer, something stronger?"

Heather held up a palm to give her answer. Steve said, "Water for me. I'm driving." He cut loose with a boisterous laugh.

For once Mae laughed, but it sounded like the bray of a donkey. She must have realized her faux pas and said, "Let's take our drinks outside. I'm interested in what scheme *les cher infants* are plotting."

Steve chirped on about boats and a near-death experience trying to water ski after he lost his sight. Heather took in the scene of lakeside properties hugging the water. The panorama held a certain mystique that drew you in. It also came at a premium. Her thoughts shifted to the Voss ranch. Even if it wasn't the first development on the lake, it could rival this one.

Patrick delivered Steve's water and settled into a cushioned chair with a short glass of ice and amber liquor.

Steve asked, "How did it go with the sheriff this morning?"

"What do you mean?" asked Patrick.

Steve kept the lighthearted tone to his voice. "Sorry. Old habit. I used to be a homicide detective in Houston. I knew Sheriff Blake would ask you where you were at the time of Hector's death. Those are the kinds of questions I used to start a murder investigation with. It's no big deal, forget I asked."

Mae wasn't one to stay quiet. "He was rude. He all but accused me of killing Hector. I had nothing to do with that man when I was young and I didn't kill him."

"Of course not. What could you gain from that? It's not as if your father would leave anything in the will to him." Steve paused. "Would he?"

"How should I know what that crazy old man did?" She tapped a heavy ring on her wineglass. "But if he did, Pat says we have good cause to challenge the will. Isn't that right, dear?"

He squirmed in his chair. "I seriously doubt it will come to that."

Heather bit her lip when she heard the non-answer. Typical lawyer response.

"I can't imagine it coming to that, either," said Steve. "But, we did hear some things today that led us to believe Hector was much loved by most of the family. Is that true?"

"Not by me," said Mae. "He pretended to care, but I knew better than to trust him. Anyone who put up with Dad must have had a screw loose."

"That's not surprising," said Steve. "I saw your dad in action against Roy once. I'm glad I wasn't on the receiving end of his anger."

If fire could really come from someone's eyes, Mae could melt steel. "You have no idea, Mr. Smiley. I'm entitled to every bit of the inheritance for what that animal did to me." She drained her glass. "And speaking of the inheritance, I know my brothers are trying to cheat me. What I don't know is how?"

Heather noticed that Mae didn't mention Sue Ann. She obviously believed her sister would soon sign away her inheritance.

"It's nothing definite yet," said Steve. "Rance mentioned his desire to sell the herd and move to a place with literal greener pastures. It's possible he might be amenable to some sort of land-for-cattle trade."

"No!"

"I come in peace," said Steve with his hands raised. "Don't shoot the messenger. I wanted you to know that Roy told Rance he'd support him whatever he decided. They both seemed willing to talk again before tomorrow's meeting. Is that something you'd like to take part in?"

"Can't you see? They're ganging up against me. I'm telling you, Mr. Smiley, they're plotting something. It won't work. I'm the oldest and first in line for the inheritance. They may get an equal part, but I'll get the lakefront."

Patrick said, "Perhaps we shouldn't be so hasty, Mae. We could at least hear the offer."

Mae's highlighted hair swung from side to side. "I know Roy. He has more up his sleeve than his arm. The best way to deal with him is to ignore him. I'll win this hand. I know I will."

Steve and Heather stood at the same time. "Thanks for the water and the talk. Heather will read the second part of the will tomorrow at five, provided we receive it by then."

"You don't have it?" asked Patrick.

"I heard from the attorney that has the original," said Steve. "He'll hand deliver it tomorrow."

Heather waited until the door closed before she pushed out a full breath. "You skated around the truth on that one."

Steve had already moved on with his thoughts.

"Let's go to Llano in the morning. I'd like us to talk to Sheriff Blake and meet up with Angelina Perez and her mother. What was the grandmother's name?"

"Rose DeLeon."

"I don't remember ever meeting her." Steve tapped his cane in front of him. "Is tomorrow too soon after Hector's death to pay a visit to Anna and Angelina?"

Heather pulled her phone out of her purse. "One way to find out."

14

Steve surprised Heather by not wanting to go out for breakfast. His silence in the SUV on their drive to Llano meant he'd retreated into that secret place within himself where he did his deepest thinking. She pulled into a parking space in front of a newer building north of Llano with light-colored stone walls and a shiny metal roof. "I expected to see something that looked like a fort with bars on the windows. This is nice. The sheriff must have done some fancy talking to get a new building like this."

"Are we early?" asked Steve.

"Ten o'clock. Right on time."

"Let's see how much information we can swap with the sheriff."

Once settled, Steve inquired about the lawman's gout.

"Better." Sheriff Blake sat behind an aged wooden desk in an office bristling with plaques and photos. "One or two more days in house shoes and I should be back in boots. That's provided I keep eating right and drinking water like a five-pound bass."

Steve brought an ankle over a knee, looking like he was at

home settling in to listen to a movie. "Yesterday, we changed our methods by speaking with the four Voss children individually."

The sheriff's head turned a single notch. "Did that help?"

"A little more productive and a lot less noisy."

The sheriff shifted his gaze to Heather. "I heard Sue Ann put Roy on the mat the day before yesterday."

Heather nodded while Steve said, "She rocked his world in more ways than one. He thinks he's lost his mo-jo. I knew gamblers were superstitious, but he's scared he'll lose his shirt in a game of wits with Mae."

"I guess you'll find out this afternoon when you read the second part of the will."

"That's something we need to talk about, Sheriff."

Heather pulled an envelope from her purse and slipped it in front of the sheriff. "This is a copy of the second part of the will. Sue Ann found it when she took inventory of the contents of Charley's ranch house. It came to us sealed."

Sheriff Blake's eyebrows lifted as he slipped out the single page and took his time reading it. He read it again and put it back in the envelope. "You say she found this in the house?"

"That's what she told us," said Steve.

After placing his reading glasses on his desk, the sheriff rubbed his temples. "I told Marvin to have the house searched from top to bottom. Those knuckleheads he assigned were to bag any documents that looked important or suspicious. I guess they didn't think a copy of a will mattered. Did Sue Ann take any more documents that you know of?"

Heather retrieved an envelope containing the Voss children's birth certificates and handed them across the desk. "If you don't object, I'll pass these out to each of the Voss children this afternoon."

The sheriff seemed to talk to himself with his next comments. "Don't see why not. I can get certified copies from the hospital if I need to." He tapped the envelope containing the birth certificates. "I need to send Marvin to Sue Ann's and see if she took anything else."

Steve played peacemaker. "Don't be too hard on him. He tried to delegate and homicides in this county are infrequent as eight-inch rains."

"Point taken. But crime scene training seems in order, don't you think?"

Steve nodded.

The sheriff winked at Heather and pointed to Steve. "You have more experience in homicide than anyone I know. You interested in training my deputies? I've got enough money to pay you for a couple of days."

The offer met a quick response. "I'm busy now, but we could talk about it after we solve these murders."

"It appears we're horse trading. So far, you've anted up information, a couple of documents, and a possible training session with my deputies. Is it my turn to put some chips on the table?"

Heather concluded the sheriff had played this game of trading information before. Steve got right to the point. "How was Charley killed?"

"Blunt force trauma to the back of the head. One blow with something flat and heavy. It dropped him where he stood, just outside the barn at his ranch."

"Did you recover the murder weapon?"

"Nope."

"Did the coroner give any clue what the weapon might be?"

"Flat and heavy was all he said in his report." He handed Heather a folder. "I figured you'd be asking for a copy of the report."

Not only had the sheriff played the game before, he knew Steve wouldn't have come without information to trade. "No transfer of trace materials?" asked Heather as she skimmed over the document.

The sheriff narrowed his gaze. "I know what you two are thinking, and it's a real head scratcher. How can something hit hard enough to fracture a skull and not leave microscopic traces?"

Steve asked, "Any tire tracks or footprints?"

The sheriff smiled like a patient grandfather. "It's been a hot, dry spring. Must be one of those weather patterns caused by the Pacific Ocean temperatures. Never can remember which one it is." He brought his thoughts back to the tracks. "Charley spent two full days lying there before Rance found him. It doesn't take much wind to wipe out tracks made on hard-scrabble ground."

The sheriff shifted in his chair. "What else do you have for me, Ms. McBlythe?"

It was her turn in the game of give and take. "In yesterday's meeting, Rance was eager to get out of the county and start fresh. Roy had to talk him out of a quick decision to give up any claim he had to the ranch. All Rance wanted was to sell his portion of the herd and leave. Roy convinced him to hold out for a better deal."

"You say Roy talked him out of it? That's not the Roy I know."

Steve added, "I told you he lost his lucky rabbit's foot when Sue Ann put him on the carpet. He wasn't mad that she hit him, but because he didn't read her and know the punch was coming."

The sheriff interlaced his fingers and placed his hands on his desk. "How do you think he's going to react when he hears the second part of the will?"

Steve brought his foot down from his knee. "I'm not sure how any of them will react." He chuckled. "I don't know how I'm going to react."

Heather asked, "Can you make sure Marvin is there?"

"Marvin and I will both be there. This'll be something I'd pay money to see."

Steve lifted the tone of his voice. "What about Hector DeLeon? How was he killed?"

"Completely different. We don't have the autopsy results back, but I can tell you what it'll say. Two gunshots from a high caliber rifle. One in the leg and one in the chest. We found a blood trail from his cabin that ran all the way to the porch of the ranch house."

Steve scratched his chin. "If I remember correctly, Hector's cabin is about forty yards north of the barn and nearest the lake. The house is fifty yards south of the barn."

"You have an excellent memory," said the sheriff. "The blood trail started outside Hector's front door. It went from there to the barn and on to the ranch house. We believe the first shot hit Hector in the leg. He limped his way to the front porch and turned. The second shot put him down."

Steve nodded as he spoke. "You can see Hector's cabin from the water. It's possible that the killer came by boat. It's even possible the first shot came from a boat."

"We think Hector might have been trying to get to one of Charley or Rance's rifles. We found the casing of a 30-30 by the barn. That's where we believe the second shot came from."

Heather noted that the conversation was like watching a tennis match. Each man took his turn and volleyed a piece of information or a theory. It was Steve's turn.

"If the killer was waiting for Hector, he might have broken into the ranch house, stolen the rifle and then used it to commit the crime. Of course, he could have brought his own rifle. You said a 30-30 casing? I'm guessing it was a saddle rifle. There's no shortage of those around."

"Where was Rance at the time of the murder?" asked Heather.

The sheriff went to a map of the county and pointed. "Says

he was rounding up cattle on a small piece of property out toward Enchanted Rock. I think he's telling the truth. There were six head in the trailer hooked up to his truck when we found him at the ranch waiting for us. No witnesses yet to back up his story."

"What about the rest of the Voss children?"

"Roy says he sleeps until noon or later every day. Sue Ann was at home with the kids. Mae and Mr. Fancy Pants claim they were on their way from Austin to Horseshoe Bay and don't remember when they left or when they arrived."

It was the sheriff's turn to ask questions. "The will's not cut and dry. Do you know how you're going to handle it?"

"I'll award what I can today, but I'm going to hold off on the land."

"Mae won't like it."

"Neither will her lawyer," said Steve. "That's why I have Heather as a partner. She can come up with some legal excuse for me."

All three rose from their chairs. The sheriff gave Heather a nod. "Good luck this afternoon. I'll make sure there's no more bloodshed." He spoke to whoever wanted to answer. "What's your next step?"

Steve unfurled his cane. "We're going to pay our respects to Anna and Angelina."

"Speaking of," said the sheriff. "Marvin said he saw Rance's truck at their house last night. You know anything about Rance and Angelina getting friendly?"

"I doubt it," said Steve. "I think it's more a case of both of them caring for Hector."

Heather said nothing, but the sheriff's remark made her wonder. The more she thought about it, the more she thought there might be something between them.

"One thing about a town the size of Llano," said Heather. "It doesn't take long to get from one side of it to the other."

"They may crack five thousand residents in another twenty years, if they keep growing," said Steve. "Tell me about Anna's home."

Heather shifted the transmission into park and cast her gaze to the dwelling. "The front has brick halfway up, but everything else is wood that's painted white. Plain tan roof shingles. It's a rectangle. I'm guessing they built it in the sixties or seventies. There's a one-car attached garage, and the driveway is gravel. No curb or gutter on the street. The grass in the yard is sparse, but looks better than the neighbors. I noticed a chain-link fence in the back."

Steve responded with a grunt and mumbled, "It's what I expected. How many cars are here?"

"The garage door is down, but there's one clunker in the driveway."

"Details, please."

"Fifteen-year-old light blue Ford Tempo with a creased left rear quarter panel and student parking decals on the back window."

"Angelina's car," said Steve. "Let's go."

Angelina opened the door and pushed back a storm door before Heather could speak. Hector's granddaughter had traded in her running shorts and tank top for a business casual look of white blouse and black slacks. Pulled back hair opened up her oval face, made even more attractive with judiciously applied makeup. Red lipstick showed off perfect Cupid's bow lips.

"I hope we're not intruding," said Heather. She led Steve inside and looked for a place to deposit him.

Angelina must have read her searching eyes. "Let's put Mr. Smiley in the green chair by my mother."

"Thanks for allowing us to come," said Steve. "I expected a sizeable crowd."

A voice with an accent answered, "We're between shifts, Mr. Smiley. If you'd been here thirty minutes ago, you'd still be waiting in the yard. I'm Anna Perez."

He gave the customary condolences for both himself and Heather.

"Thank you. I must still be in shock. It all seems so unreal."

Steve swallowed. "I know what it's like to lose someone you love."

It only took a handful of words, but something bonded between Steve and Anna. You couldn't see it, but the emotion of grief looked for someone who understood and latched on to the kindred spirit.

"You lost your wife, didn't you, Mr. Smiley?"

He gave his head a single nod. "Another senseless killing."

"I'm sorry. She must have been very special."

When Steve didn't answer, Angelina came to the rescue. "We have more food than the refrigerator can hold. Have you eaten?"

Steve spoke for both of them. "I'm saving myself for a place I heard about that serves giant barbecue pork chops."

Angelina's laugh came without effort. "You mean Cooper's. I worked there when I was in high school. How about a cup of coffee and a slice of pecan pie to tide you over?"

"You have a customer," said Steve.

"Just coffee for me, and I'll help you," said Heather.

It was the size home where, if you were in the kitchen, you were also in the dining room and the living room. Privacy wasn't a problem, because there wasn't any until you reached the hallway leading to the bedrooms.

From the kitchen, Heather heard Steve speak. "Heather and I are trying to find out who killed your father. Are you up to answering some questions from strangers?"

"My Angelina has a good head on her shoulders. If she trusts you, I do too."

"Good. Tell me your fondest memory of your father," said Steve.

"Ah, that's easy. It was at the ranch. After a long day in the hottest part of the summer, Papa came home, and we walked to the lake and went swimming late in the afternoon. He looked so funny wearing his blue boxer underwear and cowboy boots. There's a sandy beach and a sandbar in front of that part of the property, and it's not far up a path to his cabin. I walked out what seemed like a long way in the lake, but it was still safe. Of course, he was always with me. Mama brought watermelon. It was simple, but I thought it was heaven."

"I can taste the melon," said Steve. "How old were you?"

"I must have been four or five at that time, but I remember we went a few times every summer."

After several seconds, Steve said, "You don't have to tell me what happened between your parents, but it might help to talk about it," said Steve.

"There's not much to talk about. Papa lived at the ranch and Mama and I lived in town. Papa came to see me every weekend, and he never stopped giving Mama money. They seemed to get along, but it was never the same without Mama. She lived until I was out of high school. I married that same year."

"This is a tough question, but did your mother and father ever live together as man and wife?"

"I know what you mean, and the answer is no."

"Did Hector still come see you after your mother died?"

"Almost every Sunday, unless there was a heavy rain that washed out the water gaps or the cattle broke down a fence."

"Did your father ever hit you?"

"I can only remember once. I was playing with a knife and he swatted my hand. I felt awful for upsetting him."

Steve rubbed a palm against his face. "I don't understand.

Everyone we've talked to loved Hector. Can you think of anyone that had anything against him?"

"No, Mr. Smiley, I can't. Even Mr. Charley liked him, and he didn't like anything or anybody." She paused. "Perhaps he didn't like Papa as much as he respected him." She smiled, "Who am I to think such deep thoughts? I'm just a simple woman, not a psychologist."

Angelina delivered pie to Steve while Heather placed his cup of coffee on a table beside him. She took a seat on a dining room chair next to Steve. "Anna, did Hector leave a will?"

"Yes. I understand you're an attorney. I think I understand it, but could you read it and tell me if there's anything unusual about it?"

Angelina hustled down the hallway and soon returned with a hand-carved wooden box and a confession. "I hope I didn't get Rance in trouble. I called him yesterday and asked him to look around the cabin for any of *Abuelo's* papers. He brought this to me last night."

"Was the police tape still up?" asked Steve.

"Rance said it was. That's why I hope he won't get in trouble."

Heather asked, "Did you look inside the box?"

"It was locked, so I gave it to Mama."

Anna issued a mischievous smile. "It wasn't much of a lock."

Heather wondered how Steve wanted to play this. By all rights they should take the box to the sheriff, or at least call him and let him know what Rance had done.

"Is there anything else in the box the police need to know about?" asked Steve.

Anna didn't hesitate. "Nothing that concerns them. Ms. McBlythe is welcome to take the box and read everything."

Steve asked Angelina a leading question about her quest to become a CPA. Heather knew that would give him time to finish his pie and to weigh the pros and cons of not divulging Rance's misdemeanor to the police.

As they rose to leave, Steve said, "Anna, there's been enough heartache and grief. Hector would want you to have that box. Angelina's our client and we hold what she says in confidence. As long as there's nothing in the box that pertains to the murders, we won't tell the police about it."

"Thank you both," said Angelina. "Rance is a fine young man. I'd hate to see him get in trouble for doing a good deed."

Heather put Steve's hand on her shoulder. They thanked Rose and Angelina and walked into a hot midday sun.

"You're getting soft," whispered Heather.

"We need Rance at the meeting this afternoon, not being detained by some overzealous deputy. We can always tell the sheriff later if we have to."

"Were you serious about wanting barbecue for lunch?"

Steve didn't reply.

"Silly of me to ask. Where is this place?"

"Go to the intersection of highways 16 and 29. It's six blocks to the west down 29. If that's too complicated, I'll hang my head out the window and guide you by smell. I think I'm getting a whiff from here."

"You're going to outgrow everything you own."

"Speaking of, be sure to wear something you can move fast in to the meeting. I might need protection."

She didn't know if he was kidding, or not. "Is there anything else we need to do before the meeting?"

"One stop on the way home. I have a job for you if the police have cleared out."

"This sounds like something that might get me arrested."

"When's the last time you heard of a lawyer going to jail?"

15

Heather took one look at Steve, gripped his shoulders, and turned him around. "I told you to change shirts. You ruined the one you wore to lunch."

"Sorry. I forgot to tuck a napkin under my chin. Admit it, the pork chop and sauce were worth the cost of that shirt. If memory serves me, I picked it up at a thrift store for three dollars."

Once again Heather marveled at how thrifty Steve could be while still caring about his appearance. Trends for men were definitely not his main concern, as evidenced by his reaction to wearing a pink shirt on the day they arrived. From now on she'd stick to the basics when she bought his shirts.

Steve unbuttoned his stained shirt and changed the subject. "I've been propped up in bed, thinking about the will and how the Voss children will react. By the way, did you get the samples sent off?"

"Next day delivery. We should have the results in less than a week."

She stepped to the closet and examined the choices. "Do you want long or short sleeves?"

"Long, and my blazer. No tie." Changing the subject, he asked, "Heard from Jack?"

Heather handed him a clean shirt, tossed the blazer on the bed and moved to the window overlooking the pool. "I'll call him tonight."

"What about your father? Talk to him?"

"The same. As far as I know, he and Webster went forward with the deal." Steve's question caused split-screen images of her father and her boyfriend to appear in her mind's eye. Had she ruined both relationships?

While she stared into space, the door to Steve's room opened. He stood holding it for her with cane in hand. She crossed the room and gave him a pat on the arm. "You look rather dapper, Mr. Smiley."

"Thanks. This should be a meeting to remember. Remind me to call Kate tonight and tell her how things went."

Steve jabbered until the elevator deposited them on ground level. The first voice to reach them as they traveled down a long, carpeted hallway belonged to Mae. "You're late and some group from a tech company is having a meeting in our room."

Heather took over. "We're to meet across the hall. You must have missed the sign on the easel that reads VOSS FAMILY."

Mae harrumphed her displeasure and took short, quick steps into the room, with Patrick Shaw a half-step behind her. The heads of all the other attendees turned to meet the latecomers.

Roy greeted his older sister the way Heather expected. "Forget your glasses, Mae? You and Pat walked right past the sign."

"You could have said something."

She received one of Roy's trademark laughs in reply.

Heather took stock of the venue and spoke in a low voice to Steve. "This room is smaller and there's three round tables, each with eight chairs."

He whispered back. "You and I will sit at one table by ourselves. Let's give them a choice where they sit. It might be interesting."

Heather addressed the crowd. "Steve, Sheriff Blake and I will sit at the table in front of the whiteboard. You may sit at either of the remaining tables, wherever you feel most comfortable."

Rance, Roy, Sue Ann and Grant chose the table on the left while Mae and Patrick took the table on the right. Marvin Goodnight stated that he'd prefer to stand.

"I can tell by your voices that everyone is here, except Grant," said Steve.

"I'm here," came the voice to Sue Ann's left."

"Excellent. Let's get started."

Sue Ann opened a spiral notebook and dug a pen from her purse.

"Before Heather begins," said Steve, "I need to tell you, there will be no dispersal of funds today. We should make excellent progress, but the settling of the estate and the distribution of checks will take additional time."

"Why?" snapped Mae. The others had a variety of reactions, ranging from looks of acceptance to disappointment.

"You'll soon find out," said Steve in an even tone. "Heather will now read the second part of the will. You'll not receive copies of this part until she's finished and we take care of something stated in the document."

Heather stood. "Like the first part of the will, Mr. Voss wrote this in his own hand and it bears his signature and the signatures of the same two witnesses." She slowed the cadence of her speech.

"I'll start with the youngest two, since they turned out better than Mae and Roy."

Glancing up, Heather saw Mae's eyes squint in anger. Roy showed no emotion. She continued reading before Mae interrupted.

"To Rance I leave the herd and the horses. I also leave him the house and barn."

Rance nodded. The entire herd was his. He could sell them and give half the proceeds to Sue Ann without having Roy negotiate for him.

Roy responded to Rance's glance with a thumb up and a nod.

"I want Hector to have the cabin and any money that's in my checking account. He can stay as long as he wants, and so can Rance, but I doubt either will."

Patrick scratched furiously on a legal pad. His face remained placid, but Mae couldn't contain herself. "That ruins everything. Did that old fool have any idea that Hector's cabin is in the center of the most valuable property?"

Patrick put a hand on Mae's arm and said with force, "Mae. Be quiet."

Mae shot him a dagger stare, but it shifted to Steve as soon as he spoke. "That's sound advice for everyone. Emotions are running high, but I assure you, everyone will get something. In fact, I have a feeling everyone will get what they deserve."

Heather continued:

"Since you're all listening to this, that means I'm dead. I had a feeling this was coming, so I took out some insurance policies. Rance, you get $1 million. Sue Ann, you get $1 million.

Roy and Mae, I don't want you to say I played favorites

between you two. There's a third policy for $1 million, and then there's the land that needs to go to someone.

Roy and Mae, you deserve nothing, but I'm feeling charitable. I'll let lady luck decide. Whoever wins a hand of poker will have their choice: You can take the money or get what's in the last part of the will. That won't be read 'til after the hand of poker is played."

Blank stares and silence filled the room as those assembled realized that a multi-million-dollar hand of poker would settle the bulk of the estate. To everyone gathered, it appeared Charley left the biggest prize to one of the two eldest.

Steve broke the spell of silence that the unorthodox will had cast. "I'll deal the hand at this table. The only Voss children allowed at the table are Roy and Mae. I asked Chief Deputy Goodnight to stop by a store and pick up a new deck of cards. Mae and Roy can examine, but not touch the sealed pack. I'll fan the cards on the table face up and Ms. McBlythe will remove the jokers. Again, Roy and Mae can look, but not touch. I'll then shuffle the cards ten times and cut them after each shuffle. The game will be five-card stud, played face up."

"Why face up?" asked Mae.

Roy answered for Steve. "All the chips will be on the table. You only deal the first ones face down if you plan on raising the stakes or bluffing. This way we don't have to touch our cards. No way to cheat."

"That's right," said Steve. "Mae and Roy are to play without touching their cards. Questions?"

"I'll need a few minutes with my client," said Patrick.

Steve nodded, and the couple retired to the hallway.

Roy moseyed to Steve's side. "That old buzzard is still after me. I don't have a chance. Mae's going to get all the property and snare a new husband while she's at it."

Heather cast an inquisitive gaze to Roy and tilted her head to further ask him to explain.

"Don't be so naive, Ms. McBlythe. Patrick is just as much a gold digger as Mae is. He'll put a ring on her finger, get control of the property and drop her like a hot horseshoe."

While Heather pondered the possibility of a change in Mae's marital status, Steve focused on Roy and the gambler's perception of his chances to win the hand of poker. "Still haven't found your lucky rabbit's foot?"

"I couldn't win a stuffed doll at the fair with a hundred darts and balloons the size of a basketball. I might as well tell her she can have the land and not play."

"That's not possible. I can't read the last part of the will until someone wins this hand of poker."

Roy stuffed his hands in his pockets and took his seat at the table. Mae and Patrick reentered, and she sat rigid in a chair on the opposite side of the table from Roy.

Steve raised his voice. "I'll ask everyone else but Heather, Sheriff Blake, and Deputy Goodnight to stand in a line behind me. The sheriff will sit facing me and Heather will monitor each player. Once everyone is in place, we'll begin." He paused. "I almost forgot. Heather, would you take my coat and roll up my sleeves?"

Once Steve settled with hands and forearms exposed, she said, "Everyone's in place."

Deputy Goodnight stepped toward the table and handed the deck of cards to the sheriff. He said, "I'm showing the deck to Roy first. As you can see, the seal is intact. Do you agree?"

"Looks good to me. A standard deck of cards."

"Mr. Smiley, I'm now showing the deck to Mae."

Mae lowered her head to within inches of the deck and examined the plastic cover with more care than a diamond cutter. After looking at it from every imaginable angle, she said, "I guess it's all right."

The sheriff asked, "Do you want me to break the seal?"

Steve shook his head. "I'll do it. Slide the deck my way." The deck came across like a slow-moving hockey puck and bumped against Steve's hands. He tugged off the wrapper, pulled the deck from its case, and fanned the cards on the table. "Count the cards after Heather removes the jokers."

Grant said, "Stop counting, Sue Ann. He was talking to Roy and Mae."

It took Roy only a second to say, "They're all there. Ace of spades down to the deuce of clubs."

Mae, of course, took her time. She looked at Patrick and he nodded. "Let's get this over with."

Steve slid the cards together into a single stack. He split the deck evenly and the first of ten flutters filled the air. Between each shuffle he divided the cards left over right.

Once finished, Steve placed his palms on the table. "Are both of you satisfied that I shuffled the cards to ensure a fair deal?"

Both responded in the affirmative.

"I'll now cut the cards a last time and take the top card and place it in front of Roy, face up."

"The four of hearts," said Heather.

"And now for Mae's first card," said Steve.

A king of diamonds appeared. Mae nodded her approval.

Roy's next card proved to be the seven of hearts, while Mae drew a five of spades.

Heather announced, "No help for Roy. Mae still has the high card."

The third cards were a ten of hearts for Roy while Mae paired her five.

"Possible flush for Roy. One pair for Mae," said Heather as the tension in the room increased.

"What does that mean?" asked Mae.

"It means you're ahead so far," said Steve.

The fourth cards slid beside the others. Roy drew the ace of hearts. Mae frowned as a two of diamonds joined her pair.

After Heather announced the cards for Steve's sake, he said, "Still a possible flush for Roy and a high pair if he draws another ace. Mae still has the high hand with a pair of fives."

Heather noted the rapt expressions on everyone's face but Roy's. Despite him having two potential winning hands, his head shook, and his down-turned mouth showed no confidence. If he won, he'd likely be the most surprised person in the room.

Steve's hand reached for the deciding card. If it were a heart or an ace, Roy would have his choice of a million dollars or what the last section of the will revealed. Eyes widened around the table as the top card flipped to reveal a red face card. A heart? No. The face of the jack of diamonds stared at Roy as if to mock him. No matter what card Steve turned over next, Mae won the hand with a lowly pair of fives while Roy sat with a busted flush in front of him.

Patrick Shaw threw a fist skyward and shouted, "Yes. We have it."

Mae asked, "Did I win?"

Heather announced, "Yes, Mae. You get to choose. What will it be: A million-dollar insurance settlement or whatever is in the unread portion of the will?"

"Are you kidding? I choose the land."

Steve asked, "Are you saying you're choosing to take whatever is in the remaining portion of the will and not the million dollars?"

"Of course. I'd be a fool not to."

"Very well. Heather has drawn up documents for you to sign that state you made this decision of your own free will and that your choice is irrevocable. Furthermore, you promise not to make any claim to the monies or property distributed to any of the rightful heirs. She's drawn up similar no-contest documents for the other heirs to sign that state they will not make claims on the awards assigned to others."

Heather handed the original and a copy to Patrick Shaw. "It's a standard release. Add your signature as a witness. I made a copy for you to take with you, and I'll notarize all the signed releases. Then, we can get on with the meeting."

She took care of the legal formalities while Roy, Rance and Sue Ann took on the appearance of siblings at a normal family reunion.

With chin out, Roy said, "First hand I ever lost and came away with a million dollars. Looks like my luck is changing."

Mae, of course, had questions about the necessity of the document, but Patrick assured her it was all legitimate and would give them a leg up in case Roy challenged the outcome of the game.

Steve rolled his sleeves down and buttoned the cuffs. "We're almost finished. They're all yours, Heather."

She raised her voice above the chatter. "If you'll take your original seats, I'll finish reading the will." By the time she'd taken a drink of water, everyone had returned to their chairs. She passed out copies of the will and instructed everyone to follow along where the reading stopped. Once again, she put enough inflection in her voice to tone down her Boston accent.

"I'm an old fashioned man forced to live in a lousy, modern world. A part of me wanted my oldest boy to get the land. The other part of me said it should go to my firstborn girl. I'll let the cards decide. I hope they did their job. That's about it. Adios."

Mae couldn't contain herself. She thrust herself up from her chair and sent it rolling. Shouts of "Yes! Yes!" accompanied the upraised arms. Patrick made a less dramatic rise from his chair, but soon the two were locked in a spinning embrace.

"I told you, Pat. I told you the land would be mine."

"Ours," said Pat.

"Of course, darling. We'll take care of that as soon as we can get a license."

Heather cast her gaze to Roy, who mouthed, *I told you so.*

Three of the Voss children and Grant cleared out after Steve explained he would get with the insurance company and tell them who to make out the checks to. He left it up to Heather to tell Mae and Patrick that the land would require a survey and easements to Rance's property and Hector's heirs.

For once Mae let Patrick do the talking. "That won't be necessary. We plan on buying both properties."

Heather didn't dispute their intentions and knew they'd pressure Rance and Anna to make a quick sale.

Steve returned to his chair after wishing each of the family members a good night. Heather retrieved a bottle of cold water for him and placed it on the table. "Water's at your six."

"Thanks. How do you think it went?"

"Better than I expected."

"Now our work really begins. We still have a murder to solve."

Steve took a drink and screwed the cap back on the bottle. "Tomorrow I want to go back to the ranch. Something doesn't feel right. I missed something important."

16

Steve struggled to come out of the fog of a dream before he realized his phone's command to be answered. Unlike his waking hours, the time spent in dreams came painted in colors and images, making it harder to come back to reality. After groping the top of the nightstand, he retrieved the unwelcome mechanical intruder and placed it to his ear.

"Yeah, Smiley here."

"Sorry to wake you, Steve." The gruff voice of Sheriff Blake sounded void of remorse. "I'm at the Voss Ranch. The ranch house and Hector's cabin are smoldering piles of ash. Nothing but rock chimneys left standing. The barn fared a little better, but not much."

Steve threw back the covers and swung his legs over the side of the bed. "What time is it?"

"Seven in the morning. The first call came in a little after midnight. You probably remember the houses and barn are about three miles off the nearest paved road. By the time the first pumper-truck arrived, the house had already collapsed, and the cabin looked like an Aggie bonfire, back when they had 'em."

After rubbing his sightless eyes, Steve said, "Two homes and a barn don't set themselves on fire at the same time."

"A state arson investigator is on his way."

Steve rubbed his palm across whisker-stubbles. "Mae and her future husband come to mind first, but they don't strike me as being dumb enough to do it themselves."

"I thought the same thing. Marvin and I are on our way to see them. Do you want to come along?"

Steve pondered the invitation, but not for long. "I think it best if I stay out of an arson investigation and concentrate on the homicides. I'd look along the shoreline to see if there're any traces of a boat pulling to shore last night. It would be a lot easier to come in from the water."

"I have deputies there now. I'll let you know if we find anything."

"Good luck. Arsons are hard to unravel and even harder to prove. At least you have a good idea of motive. Mae and that lawyer needed those buildings gone so they could develop the land. They told us yesterday they were going to buy Anna out. This may speed the process."

"What about Rance? Do you think he might have done it?" asked the Sheriff.

"He'll have a million dollars and whatever he gets from the sale of the livestock. Heather didn't find any documents of insurance on the dwellings or barn. Even if there's an insurance settlement on everything that burned, it wouldn't be worth the risk to him."

"I talked to Rance at daybreak. He confirmed what you said about Charley not having insurance on the house or cabin."

"How did Rance sound when he heard about the fires?"

"Surprised at first, but then relieved. Said he was going to give the house to Mae anyway. He also said he'll talk to Anna about taking whatever Mae offers her for the cabin and he'll pay her an equal amount so she and Angelina don't have any ongoing dealings with Mae or Patrick."

"That's generous."

The sheriff's voice changed. "I'm pulling up to the condo Mae rented. It won't hurt my feelings one bit to wake her."

After the phone went silent, Steve rose to his feet and stretched. Mae was a nasty piece of work, but that didn't mean she killed her father or Hector. But what about Patrick? He had ample motive. He also had the money to hire people to do the dirty work. How long had he known Mae and when did he start their relationship?

While brushing his teeth, Steve's thoughts continued to focus on the attorney. Patrick didn't hesitate to correct Mae about the property soon belonging to both of them. If he killed to gain half ownership of the property, what would keep him from killing again to get all of it?

"Too many questions and not enough answers," said Steve out loud.

He reached for his phone and told it to call Heather.

Her panting words and a whining noise told him she was on one of the resort's treadmills. "What are you doing awake?"

"The sheriff called. Someone torched the ranch house, barn, and cabin last night."

Heather remained silent until the whirl of the treadmill ceased. "It didn't take Mae and her lover long to pressure Anna to sell, did it? What do you want to do first?"

"Take a shower and eat breakfast. Let's go back to the Bluebonnet in Marble Falls. We'll make a plan for today while we eat. Let's concentrate on Patrick. This evening I want us to go to the ranch and have a look."

"It will be a crime scene. Don't we need the sheriff's permission?"

"They'll have the gate to the property locked and maybe post a deputy, but we won't drive in."

"We won't?"

"Can you drive a boat?"

"I'm a blue blood from Boston. I can row, paddle, sail, and dock a yacht without chipping the paint. If it floats, I can operate it. Give me forty minutes and I'll be at your door."

HEATHER THROTTLED UP THE ONE HUNDRED-FIFTY HORSEPOWER engine of the rented pontoon boat. It took only seconds before she and Steve were skimming into the sun of Lake LBJ, her auburn hair whipping behind her. The ease at which the boat reached speed surprised her. The bulky appearance of the craft hid its versatility. It could seat eleven and clip along fast enough to pull a skier, even with a full complement of sun worshipers.

She shouted to Steve, who sat three feet to her left. "I'll keep it in the channel until we get to the ranch."

"How deep is the water here?"

Heather checked the depth finder on the boat's dashboard. "Forty-eight, but the girl at the rental said it's ninety feet in some spots."

Steve turned his baseball cap around so he wouldn't have to hold the bill. The cap was a purchase they made after Steve ate himself into a state of contentment at his newest favorite cafe. They stopped at Walmart to purchase inexpensive shorts, t-shirts, and tennis shoes for what Steve had in mind.

Heather's thoughts turned to the progress they'd made. She'd spent her time doing research on Patrick Shaw. He'd been a middle of the pack law student who started out in a reputable firm, but didn't last long. The reasons for his moving on were still obscure, but it had something to do with promising more than he could deliver. He played leap-frog with his career over the next ten years until he settled in with his present firm, where rumor had him in line to be a junior partner. A check of

Yelp reviews revealed a three-star average with some entertaining and original comments about customer dissatisfaction. By reading between the lines, Heather gathered Patrick might try to collect more than the agreed upon fee, especially if the case involved the divorce of an attractive client. She'd been able to distill the least complimentary comments on Patrick Shaw down to three words: slippery, slimy and scum.

Steve shouted above the noise. "Are we in the middle of the channel?"

"Yes," hollered Heather.

"The old riverbed is the dividing line between Llano and Burnet Counties. It's the Colorado River and the primary source of water for a big part of Central Texas, including Austin. It empties into the Gulf of Mexico between Galveston and Corpus Christi."

The trip continued without words until Heather eased off the throttle. She checked a map of the lake and looked for landmarks along the shore while keeping a sharp eye on the depth gauge.

"We must be close," said Steve. "The wind is out of the southwest and I can smell burnt wood." He pointed. "Try that way and look for a sandy beach."

Sure enough, Steve's sensitive nose led them to the sandbar Angelina remembered wading on as a child. Heather cut the engine and allowed the boat to drift until the depth gauge read four feet. "I'm going to drop anchor here. I'll swing the boat around so the stern faces the bank. You should be in three feet of water when you climb down the ladder by the motor."

"Can you see what's left of the cabin from here?"

Heather had already moved to the stern to manipulate the ladder to its full extension. She raised up, shielded her eyes from the late afternoon sun and said, "There's a path and I see a chimney. There's still puffs of smoke now and then. Too much brush to see anything beyond the cabin."

She descended the ladder into clear water that reached halfway up her chest. By pushing the starboard side, she maneuvered the rear of the boat over the sandbar and into shallower water. By now, Steve had his foot on the top step and his hands gripped the ladder's sides.

"Come on down," said Heather. "The water's deep enough that we won't have any trouble getting out of here."

They trudged their way the first few steps, but soon walked through coarse dry sand.

"Say Hector's name," said Steve.

She did and waited.

"Nothing." said Steve. "Let's go to the cabin."

Steve's hand stayed on Heather's shoulder as she walked a narrow path, avoiding cactus and warning him of rock outcroppings. The smell of smoke increased the closer they came to what once was Hector's lakeside cabin.

"Say his name again," said Steve.

"Hector DeLeon."

Steve shuddered like he had a chill. "Red, but not bright red."

Heather knew what this meant. An impression of the color red came over his mind. His "gift," as she called it, was associative chromesthesia, a phenomenon more common with artists and composers. Certain colors manifest when some artists are deep into their creativity. If a person was murdered, Steve saw red. Accidents and misadventures that result in death didn't rate color. A suicide might register pink. Negligent homicides and various categories of manslaughter moved up the color wheel. Murder topped the chart at bright red.

"That's not a surprise, is it?" asked Heather.

"No. But they only found one casing from a rifle shell. I wonder if the first shot came from a boat anchored where we did. That would explain why they didn't find the first brass. It also might explain why the shot caught Hector in the leg. A wave from a boat that passed might have reached the shooter and caused the boat to dip."

"That's possible," said Heather. "Where to next?"

"The barn. Or what's left of it."

"Didn't you say the sheriff told you they found a spent cartridge by the barn?"

He grunted a positive response. "I want to confirm that's where the shot that killed Hector came from. I should see red."

The path to the barn was clear of most obstacles. Other than it being uphill, the fear of becoming a pincushion to cactus thorns came into play, so Heather tread with particular care.

Unlike Hector's cabin and the main house, the remnants of the barn didn't look so apocalyptic. "It's still standing," said Heather before she qualified her statement. "The major support of the walls is metal poles. They look like drill stem pipes, but spaced far apart and covered with corrugated metal. The roof has partially fallen in. It must have been mainly wood framing. The loft is gone."

Steve said, "Somebody had to work hard to do this. Do you see scorching running up the sides of the metal?"

The telltale sign of arson started at eye level and ran down to the ground, where someone doused an accelerant and then set it ablaze. "Most likely they used gasoline," said Heather.

"Where would you steady a rifle to take a shot?" asked Steve.

Heather scanned the immediate area. "There's a corral about thirty yards to the west, but my guess would be the corner of the barn."

"Take me there."

She did and said the name Hector DeLeon without being told to.

"Bright red. This is where they fired the kill shot."

Steve's gift of associative chromesthesia didn't come free. The price he paid was absolute certainty that he was standing in the spot a killer had stood. More than likely he'd get to relive the vision of what happened in tonight's dreams.

"Do you want to go to the house? There's not much left."

"Might as well since we're here."

Heather explained to him what she was seeing, but there's only so many words to describe mounds of charred wood and memories.

Steve's head jerked up. "Somebody's coming."

Heather strained to hear, and in a few seconds, she heard tires on gravel. "Do you want to make a run for it?"

"Is there crime scene tape?"

"No."

"Then we should be all right. Besides, my days of running down trails bordered by cactus are long gone. Let's see who it is."

"It's a pickup truck," said Heather. "It looks like Rance, and there's someone with him."

"Ah," said Steve. "That should be Angelina. Good. This will save us a trip."

17

Heather took a lengthy look at Rance's one-ton Dodge Ram pickup. Although less than five years old, the diesel four-wheel-drive modern version of a work horse appeared battered and bruised. The green paint along the sides bore deep scratches. It looked as though the student body of an entire high school used keys in an act of vandalism. The windshield boasted a crack streaking like lightning from the inspection decal to where it ran out of real estate on the passenger's side.

Both front doors slammed shut at the same time. Rance and Angelina wore boots, jeans, and clean t-shirts. It wasn't unusual to observe two young people dressed in similar attire, but they both carried themselves like adults, with chins slightly lowered and shoulders squared.

In an uncharacteristic move, Rance spoke first. "I didn't expect to see you two here. Did you swim?"

"Not quite," said Steve. "We rented a boat that's anchored on the sandbar."

"Perfect place to swim," said Angelina.

Heather cast her gaze to the gravel road that Rance and Angelina came from. "Aren't the gates locked and posted?"

Rance nodded. He'd traded his cowboy hat for a baseball cap branded with the name of a feed store in Llano. The t-shirt and cap gave him a more adolescent, carefree appearance. "I called the sheriff and got permission for Angelina and me to see if we could salvage anything. He said there might be some tack in the barn that isn't beyond repair."

"I need to search and make sure for Mama's sake," said Angelina. Her voice held a sharp edge.

"Take a stick to prod around with," said Heather. "There's still some hot spots."

Angelina's brown eyes squinted. Heather waited for what she suspected was coming.

"We all know who's responsible for this. That shady lawyer came by the house this morning. He said the will was vague about who owned the land the cabin was built on and insinuated it already belonged to Mae. Then he said he wanted to help with some funeral expenses and avoid any legal complications Mama might have." She used air quotes to emphasize the words 'legal complications.' "He made no secret of telling us what a prestigious law firm he worked for and how they knew ways to get what they want."

She faced where her grandfather's cabin had stood, mere hours earlier. "First, they kill Mr. Charley. Then they kill my grandfather and now that snake has the gall to pressure Mama into selling with a ridiculous offer of a thousand dollars."

"That's all?" asked Heather. "What did your mother say?"

Angelina described the encounter as much with her hands as with words. "Mama never had a chance to say anything. I told him and Mae to get out and that he had some nerve talking business before we buried Grandfather."

"Good for you," said Steve. "Don't be in a rush. The land Hector's cabin sits on is the key to their plan."

126

"What about you, Rance?" asked Heather. "Did Mr. Shaw contact you with an offer?"

"He tried. I was working cattle most of the day and ignored his calls after I listened to the first two voice messages."

"Will you sell to them?" asked Steve.

He shrugged. "I was thinking about giving it to Mae as a wedding present, but I'm having second thoughts." He glanced at wisps of smoke rising from the remains of the only home he'd ever known. "I'll stay mad for a day or two and then make a decision."

Angelina threw up her hands in frustration. She stomped off toward the cabin, mumbling in Spanish about how she hoped to send them a Hallmark card when they moved to their jail cells.

Rance watched her pick up a rock and throw it against the side of the barn. "She's got a bit of a temper," he said. Admiration, not condemnation, laced his words.

The trio allowed Angelina to get well out of sight. The smell of charred wood and the faint odor of gasoline gave the air a pungent smell. Steve asked, "Can you take us to the exact spot you found your father?"

"Sure. It's right in front of the barn."

Heather allowed Steve to walk unaided as they strode three abreast across open ground. Rance stopped and said, "I know this is the right spot because there's a divot in the ground."

Steve bent his knees, shifted his cane to his left hand, and felt. "Was this always here?"

"Could have been, but I don't remember it," said Rance.

Steve turned toward the barn. "Describe it to me, Rance."

"Simple pole barn with a loft on the front. The loft's gone now."

Heather asked, "Did the firefighters cut that opening over the doors?"

"That where a loading door used to be. We'd bring bales of

hay to the barn on a trailer. We call 'em square bales, but they're rectangular. It was easy to load the top rows right into the loft. When we unloaded enough of them, we'd back the trailer into the barn and stack the bales from the back of the barn forward. It's hot, nasty work."

Heather noticed the setting sun. "Steve, if we don't want to be on the water in the dark, we need to leave."

"In a minute. Rance, this is going to be hard, but I need an answer. Did your father ever abuse Mae, other than beat her?"

Rance stuck his thumbs in the front pockets of his jeans. "Wasn't like that. Pa would get drunk and use a belt on the oldest two. The whippings always took place in front of us other kids, and we couldn't turn our heads or make a sound. Then he'd leave and wouldn't come back for a day or two." Rance cast his gaze toward the cabin. "If that's all, I need to see if Angelina needs help."

Steve grabbed Heather' hand, a signal to not follow the young man.

With Angelina and Rance's voices in the distance, Steve said, "Say Charley's name."

"Charley Voss."

Steve squatted down with his hand in the indention. "Say it again. I want to be sure."

She complied. "What did you see?"

"Pink."

"Pink? What does that mean?"

"It means things just got more complicated."

18

The extra-long shower not only washed away lake water and the smell of smoke, but gave Heather an opportunity to organize her thoughts. After blow drying her hair, she replaced the fluffy white robe she'd purchased in the hotel's gift shop with a football jersey and sleep shorts. The first thing she reconsidered was Steve's silence on the boat ride back to the marina. He rode in a seat near the bow with the full force of the wind pinning back his hair. He must have been so deep in thought he forgot to turn his hat around. It flew into the darkening waters and he hollered to not go back for it.

What did his seeing pink at the spot Charley Voss died mean? Perhaps Steve wasn't standing close enough to the site. Maybe it wasn't murder, but manslaughter. After all, Charley had an explosive temper. If so, who could be the suspect? Rance? Try as she might, she couldn't see him killing his father.

She kept pondering, allowing her imagination to run free. The only other person who should have been at the ranch when Charley died was Hector. She whispered the name aloud. Why not? All the Voss children said Charley had a mean streak in him, wider than the lake was long. Did Hector receive his wrath too? Heather stood looking at clothes hanging in the closet but not seeing them. Her theory of Hector being the killer didn't match the descriptions they'd received of a gentle soul with a happy-go-lucky disposition. She'd spent enough time as a cop and detective in Boston to see plenty of cruel husbands, and the occasional violent wife, who didn't live up to their peaceful reputations. After all, everyone has their breaking point. Did Charley find Hector's and then pay the price?

Her training as an attorney kicked in and she argued the case from the standpoint of the defense. She remembered Steve saying he called Sheriff Blake and asked about the alibis of all the suspects. According to Rance, he and Hector were making their bi-weekly rounds of working cattle on some more remote tracts of land in the county. For three days and two nights they'd slept under the stars on bedrolls, much like cowboys of old. Each gave the other an alibi. Unless they'd agreed to a conspiracy, or someone came forward that had seen them on or near the main property, no proof of opportunity existed.

One other thing bothered her. Why hadn't the forensic report shown traces of the murder weapon in the wound? Heather had to admit her imagination couldn't stretch far enough to come up with a single answer, so she reached for her phone.

"Where do you want to eat supper?" she asked.

Steve's answer came after a yawn. "I'm beat. I'll call room service tonight."

"Are you sure? I thought we might talk about the possibility of Hector killing Charley."

"He didn't kill Charley."

Heather plopped on the bed. "Are you positive? I know there's no evidence, but—"

"Listen to me. Hector did not kill Charley. Focus on who killed Hector."

It wasn't like Steve to border on being combative, and it didn't sit well with her. "I can see you'd not be fit company tonight."

"You're right. I need to think, eat and sleep, but not in that order."

"Fine. Eat, think and sleep all you want, you grumpy old man."

The phone had already clicked off before she finished saying fine, which was just as well. Her temper had a nasty habit of keeping her apologies coming at a steady pace.

With one theory dashed against the rocks, Heather focused on other aspects of the case. She corrected herself and said, "Cases. Two deaths. Two cases. I don't care what Steve says."

She found the menu to J's Restaurant and Bar on the hotel's website and called down her order to room service. She chose the grilled Scottish salmon, which came with braised crispy potatoes, grilled asparagus and a selection of breads she had every intention of eating to the last crumb. With that chore out of the way, she fluffed her pillows and sat with legs crossed in quasi yoga style and put her mind to work again. If Steve was so sure about Hector's innocence in Charley's death, she'd focus on two people who were anything but innocent. Patrick and the future Mrs. Mae Shaw.

She spoke the name again, followed by a giggle. "Does that poor man have any idea what grief awaits him?" She concluded they deserved each other.

Uncrossing her legs, she wiggled her toes and realized Mae and Patrick's alibi was like Rance and Hector's as it related to Charley's murder. Two people giving each other an alibi. Mae and Patrick told police they were in their rented condo at the time of Hector's murder and when the fires consumed the dwellings at the ranch. That didn't mean they didn't lie or pay someone to commit either crime, or both. In fact, they had the most to gain. No, that wasn't right. Mae didn't know who would get the land. Charley had seen to that by making her and Roy play a high stakes game of poker.

Heather separated Patrick from Mae in her mind and once again let her imagination take off with possibilities. Patrick knew about the land and that the only things standing between him having excellent chances of getting his hands on it was a wedding ring and an old rancher. He'd put off the wedding part of the plan until after Steve announced Mae the big winner. Patrick played fast and loose with truth. Hector DeLeon's murder and the burning of the homes at the ranch made sense if you twisted your mind enough to think like a man who wanted to score big and didn't mind how he achieved his goal.

Mae popped up next. She spent her life hating her father. Her looks were fading, and she had little to show for her life. Behind her lay shipwrecked marriages. Ahead was an uncertain future, trending toward wrinkles and sags that surgery couldn't solve, and loneliness that her personality all but ensured. It was easy to see how the land could be a way to a brighter future, and payment for years of physical and mental abuse. She'd said as much. She'd also counted Hector as something less than warranting full status as a fellow human being. Who would miss an old Mexican cowboy?

Heather shook her head. Being inside Mae's thoughts wasn't a pleasant experience. She needed to get back to the three basics of any investigation: motive, means and opportunity. She'd concentrate on those after she finished her meal. In the meantime, she switched on the television and spent an indeterminate amount of time searching in vain for something that interested her.

The knock on the door came as a welcome interruption. Room service wheeled in a cart, bringing with it a bouquet of pleasant aromas.

Eating at a table wasn't an option. Boxes of files related to the gold mine, notes pertaining to the murder cases, electronic devices, and personal items covered all surfaces. Despite being a stickler for order, after the better part of a week in a hotel room, it didn't seem as large as when she arrived. Options were to clear the small desk or balance a plate on her lap in bed. Hunger won out. She took the cover off the plate and settled against several pillows.

The quality of the meal lived up to expectations, but the atmosphere brought the dining experience down to a lament over what could have been. She'd expected to be sitting with Steve at a table with muted lights and soft jazz playing in the background. She also wanted to get Steve's thoughts on him seeing pink. Instead of the new dress she'd picked up in the hotel gift shop, she dined wearing what she would sleep in. A disappointing evening all the way around.

Halfway through the meal, she reached for her glass of white wine. She hadn't consulted the wine list, but expected the hotel to provide a quality house wine. Instead, it must have been something that came in a box. The Lambrusco wasn't that bad, but she'd set her palate on something not so bright and sweet. A shiver coursed through her body, causing her to lose her grip on the glass. The potatoes softened the stemware's landing, but chilled wine filled her plate and cascaded onto her shorts, legs and bedding. The surprise of cold vino on her bare thighs caused her knees to jerk upward, tossing her plate upside down on her chest. Invectives followed.

After scraping the remnants of soggy fish, potatoes and asparagus off her t-shirt, she put the serving cart back in the hall and padded her way to her second shower of the night. Steaming water helped calm her jangled nerves, but she didn't look forward to a night of vapors rising from the food-stained side of the king bed.

Back in the bedroom, she took stock of the condition of her room and decided she was overdue in bringing order back into her life. First, she gathered all her clothes that needed washing and filled a plastic laundry bag. Next, she emptied her suitcase and placed all the remaining clean clothes into a dresser. Items related to the gold mine came next. On her way to fill the remaining drawers, the yellow legal pad she'd made notes on in Montana caught her eye. She noticed something she hadn't told her father. Perhaps one more item might be enough to persuade him to delay the purchase.

She found her phone under a pillow and placed the call. It rang five times before the clipped voice of her father answered.

"Father, I was going through my notes and remembered something else about the mine."

His voice still had that condescending ring to it. "I'll listen, but it doesn't matter now."

"Did you sign the contract despite my warning?"

"I told you time was of the essence." He paused. "What is it you wanted to tell me?"

"If you've already signed the contract, it doesn't matter now."

"Tell me, child."

Why was it that after thirty seconds with him she was a little girl, seeking her Father's approval and never quite measuring up?

"All right, I'll tell you." She gathered the top of the robe tight in her fist. "My copilot went to a bar and met a woman who works in the company payroll office. She told him the company president wanted payroll projections for a fifty percent cut in personnel for all workers at the mine."

After a long sigh, her father's condescending tone and words returned. "Am I to understand you base business decisions on rumors picked up in a bar?"

The haughty attitude that drove her away from her father after she graduated from Princeton reignited a desire to flee. "I use every source available, and I've been quite successful because I look beyond traditional sources and don't take for granted what I hear from people who live in ivory towers."

"Business doesn't run on rumors, especially those picked up by untrustworthy sources in a bar somewhere in Montana."

Heather's frustration matched her anger. "Of course you're right, Father. You always are."

Heather took in a full breath and continued. "I'm sorry to have bothered you. I'll wire the funds for the airplane to you tomorrow and I'll inform my staff they're to send everything pertaining to McBlythe Enterprises back to your office in Boston."

His voice held its own edge. "I thought you had sown your wild oats after wasting ten years as a police officer. I should have known you haven't changed your bohemian ways."

The words stung.

"Father, I see no use in carrying on this conversation. Give my love to Mother." She paused. "I hope you and Webster enjoy a long and prosperous relationship. After all, he's the son you wanted instead of a daughter."

She pushed the disconnect icon on her phone before he could respond and tossed her phone on the bed. Then, she dressed in her workout clothes and went to the hotel's recreation facility, only to find it closed. Off she went into the night, hoping to sweat more than she cried. Running mile after mile brought a measure of release. She returned thoroughly winded and glowing from more exertion than she'd expended since running a half-marathon.

After the third shower of the night, she needed to talk to a friendly voice, someone she trusted. Grabbing her phone, she placed the call.

"Hello," came back the enthusiastic sound of a woman's voice.

"Uh... is Jack there?"

She giggled. "He's in the shower. Can I take a message?"

It was the straw that broke the proverbial back. Instead of a camel's, it was the oak rod of emotions that held Heather erect.

She fell face first on the clean side of the bed and dampened the pillow with tears. The man she'd been dating longer than anyone else, the only man she'd ever seriously considered spending her life with, was back in Conroe, taking a shower while a woman with a perky voice answered the phone like she belonged there.

The flood of tears gave way to anger, an emotion which allowed self-pity and irresponsibility to join the party. She grabbed the house phone. "Send two bottles of champagne to my room... It doesn't matter what vintage. I'm after quantity, not quality."

19

Steve's phone announced the time to be 7:15 a.m. One week had passed since he and Heather arrived at the resort, and they'd begun the arduous task of reading and interpreting a strange hand-written will. In that week, sibling rivalries and long-held grievances surfaced like festering sores, not to mention blood shed on the carpet of a conference room and at the Rocking V ranch. A killer needed to be apprehended, and the final settling of the estate would take place in a matter of days. He needed Heather's help and hoped to catch her before she began her day with a morning workout.

His call to her cell phone went to voice mail. Perhaps she was in the shower. He dressed and put an ear to the adjoining door to see if he could hear running water. Tapping on her door produced no sounds. He exited into the hallway and used his cane to sweep the area before his steps. It warned him of an obstacle blocking his path. The smell of wine hit him hard. He ran his hand over the top of what he deduced to be a food cart and felt an array of items including damp material of various textures, an uncovered plate with soggy food, and an empty bottle laying on its side.

Did she have company last night? Heather never drank more than one glass of wine, unless she was with Jack.

Steve backtracked to his room and used the hotel phone to call her. All he received for his effort was a busy signal.

Back in the hallway, he heard wheels squeak as they passed by, accompanied by the smell of wine. "Excuse me. Are you from room service?"

"Yes, Sir."

The voice answering had a distinct Hispanic accent, but it didn't sound like it came from along the border. Perhaps from one of the Central or South American countries.

Steve continued, "My friend was celebrating last night. I hope she didn't make too big of a mess?"

"Not too big, *Señor*. Only two bottles of champagne."

"That's good." He reached in the pocket where he carried five-dollar bills and extended one to the worker.

"Gracias, *Señor*."

Steve gave Heather's door a triplet of knocks after he heard the cart rattle into the elevator and the doors swish to a close. He waited fifteen seconds and knocked again, this time with more force. After repeating the cycle two more times, he heard a raspy voice say, "Go away."

Now he knew. A party of sorts had taken place, but it didn't make enough noise to rouse him, which led him to believe his business partner had partied alone. Heather had downed two bottles of sparkling wine and now she paid the price. He continued to knock, but with more vigor.

Mumbled words preceded the sound of the door flying open. "What?"

"Get dressed. We have work to do."

Her footsteps drug across the carpet, and the bed seemed to groan when she fell on it. "Go away. I'm sick."

"No, you're hung over."

"Leave me alone," she complained in muffled tones. She must have covered her face with a pillow.

"Did you drink the wine or take a bath in it?"

The sound of a pillow being launched across the room came to him.

"If you must know, I spilled a glass of lousy wine on my plate last night. Things went south after that."

"Ah."

"There you go again with your nonsensical 'Ah.'"

"That one meant you can't drown your troubles in two bottles of fancy champagne."

"It wasn't fancy."

He laughed out loud. "No wonder you're in such terrible shape. A champagne hangover is bad. One with cheap champagne makes you wonder if you'll live through the day. I can tell you from experience that you will."

She countered with, "No lectures. I'm not in the mood for advice, suggestions, home remedies, or questions from anyone of the male species."

"Ah."

She must have found another pillow because her scream was even more muffled than the instruction to leave her alone.

Steve considered his options. He could coddle her and say he'd done the same thing after druggies killed Maggie. Only he'd stayed in a variety of bottles for a full month. That wouldn't do any good now. Perhaps later he'd tell her that sorry chapter out of the story of his life.

Instead, he went for what must have sounded like a merciless approach and used a no-nonsense tone. "I'll be by for you at noon sharp. We're going to see Sue Ann. Think about questions to ask her."

She groaned something into the pillow that might have been an affirmative response, but he didn't think so.

He left the room and went in search of answers to what had

driven Heather to such uncharacteristic behavior. She said she didn't want advice from a man. Something must have happened last night. He considered the possibilities and came up with three men who could press her buttons hard enough to bring on a two-bottle bender. It wasn't him. He wasn't sociable last night, but that wasn't enough to set her off. The next person was her father. It would be ticklish trying to extract information from the Boston aristocrat. That left Jack Blackstock, the only man Heather had ever been serious about. He and Jack were on a first name basis, and he would know what sent Heather into such a tailspin. Steve spoke Jack's name into his phone and Jack answered on the third ring.

ASPIRIN, A GALLON OF WATER, AND A LATE BREAKFAST OF TOAST and orange juice helped, but only marginally. Nothing but time would undo the damage Heather had inflicted on herself by downing two bottles of sub-par champagne. She put on enough makeup so as not to scare anyone and threw open the door to her room. Steve stood in the hall, waiting for her.

"How's the head?" he asked.

"I'm never drinking champagne again."

He said nothing else until the valet brought her rental around and they were on their way to Marble Falls.

Steve disturbed the silence by saying, "I talked to Jack this morning."

Her blood pressure must have spiked because the headache throbbed. "I don't care. He's nothing but a terrible memory."

"Don't you want to know who the woman was?"

Heather jerked her head to the right, making it hurt all the more. "I don't care who she is, and I don't appreciate you butting into my personal life."

Steve continued to face forward. "Don't blame me if you

jump to conclusions and make yourself useless in investigating a murder."

Heather applied heavy brakes and pulled into a parking lot occupied by a food truck. After the car slid to a stop, she turned to her right. "It's obvious you're going to keep picking at me until you tell me the juicy details. All right, Mr. Super-Sleuth. Who is this mysterious woman and what was she doing in Jack's home while he was taking a shower?"

Steve let out a sigh. "Rule number three in investigating: don't make assumptions based on incomplete information."

Heather huffed. "Would you quit drawing this out? I know what I heard. She had a voice that sounded like..." She took in a breath. "Like her chest measurements were more than her I.Q."

"If this detective gig doesn't work out, you might have a career doing stand up."

Heather's patience stretched to its limit. "Tell me so I can get on with my life."

"Her name is Lanni Blackstock."

"Lanni?" shouted Heather. "That fits. One of those cutesy names that ends in a y sound, like Roxy, or Barbie."

"She's his niece, oldest brother's daughter, and a junior in high school. Jack and his brother were working on her car. She tried to add a quart of oil, but the funnel slipped. Jack's hair got the worst of it."

Heather's hand went over her eyes as her head dipped.

Steve kept on with the explanation. "Jack said everyone got a big laugh out of it. One of those stories that will be told around the table at Thanksgiving for years to come. I told him how you reacted. It will serve you right if he mentions you in the tale's retelling."

Heather gripped the steering wheel with both hands and banged her head against it twice.

"I wouldn't recommend that with a hangover."

He was right. The second self-inflicted wound added

another layer of pain and stupidity to her actions. She glanced to her right. "Thanks."

It came out of the blue when Steve said, "You must have spoken to your father last night, too."

She sat upright. "Did you call him?"

"He's out of my league. Besides, that's a family matter, and where I draw the line on butting in."

Heather thought about telling Steve about the conversation with her father, but something stopped her. "Do you mind if we don't discuss what's going on between me and my father?"

Steve pointed toward the windshield. "Put this thing in gear. Sue Ann's expecting us."

The land east of Marble Falls wasn't as unforgiving as the Voss Ranch. Heather gave a running commentary as they drove east from town. "We're running parallel to the Colorado River. It's more like a river valley, but still rugged. You can probably tell it's very hilly. There's some nice meadows close to the river."

A voice from the car's GPS told her to turn right in two hundred yards. Heather followed the instructions and drove until the land made a gentle slope toward the river. A final instruction told her they'd reached their destination. Sue Ann and Grant's home exceeded her expectations, but not by much. She'd expected a small frame house in disrepair, with a couch on the porch and a couple of cars on blocks in the front yard. The home matched the image in her imagination for size but not condition.

"Is there a boat?" asked Steve.

"Not that I can see. The house could use a coat of paint, but the yard has nice grass and there's a lovely bed of roses in front and a quarter acre garden running along the east side. There's chickens in a pen, and I see a barn in the back."

"Give me a better description of the house."

"Toys are corralled in a baby's playpen. The porch has a

swing and I can see curtains on all the windows. Everything looks orderly."

Heather waved. "There's Sue Ann. Let's go in."

It wasn't stretching the truth to compliment Sue Ann on her home. Although modest and well used, order prevailed. It reminded her of a farmhouse out of a bygone black and white television show. It took a few minutes before she realized the windows were open and the hum of an air conditioner wasn't drowning out the clucking of chickens and the occasional moo of a cow. Somehow the room wasn't stuffy or warm.

Steve must have noticed it right away. "This reminds me of where you grew up, Sue Ann. You didn't have air conditioning on the ranch, did you?"

"Never did. You don't miss what you've never had."

The slamming of a screen door brought Steve's chin up. "The kids must have come in the back door."

"I'll get them to introduce themselves," said Sue Ann.

She left the living room and returned with four children whose blondish-brown hair looked identical in color. Their heights staggered upward from left to right, ranging from three to five-feet tall. Cut-off jeans and white t-shirts were the uniform of the day. From eldest to youngest, they stood erect and gave their names and ages.

"We already had lunch," said the youngest, a girl with her nose dotted by freckles. "Mama said we could have pie and milk when you got here."

Sue Ann hung her head. "It ain't much. If you're needing lunch, I can make you a peanut butter and jelly sandwich."

"We ate before we came, but pie and milk would be perfect," said Steve. "What kind of pie?"

"Rhubarb," said the middle girl. "I picked it from the garden yesterday."

Steve rubbed his stomach. "I can't remember the last time I had rhubarb pie. This is a real treat."

"Wash hands before you sit down," said Sue Ann. She looked at Steve and dipped her head. "I was talking to the kids, Mr. Smiley, not to you and Miss McBlythe."

Steve followed the children's footfalls. "I have to use my left hand sometimes to find my food. Washing my hands before and after a meal is something I try to do every time I eat."

Sue Ann fetched the pie from a pie safe that looked to have been built during the great depression. Wood, grayed with time, matched the perforated tin sheets that kept insects from enjoying what lay inside the cabinet.

Sue Ann said, "Lizzy, get the milk and pour everyone a glass." The tallest girl slid from her chair and retrieved a glass pitcher from a relatively new refrigerator, manufactured at least within the last fifteen years.

While the milk was being evenly doled out, Sue Ann cut pieces of pie, and they passed clockwise around the table until everyone had a slice of equal size. The children's gaze didn't stray from their mother until she nodded. Forks made quick work of something that took a considerable amount of time to prepare.

Steve savored his, giving moans and comments on the tangy-sweet taste of rhubarb and the quality of the crust. Heather had to admit, the pie could have won a blue ribbon in any county fair. The latticed crust gave it a special touch that took it over the top.

Steve tasted his milk, smacked his lips and said, "This is better than any milk I've ever tasted. What brand is it?"

The oldest boy said, "We call it udder delight." The other children broke out in squeals of laughter.

Sue Ann's face turned pink. "I'm so sorry, I should have told you. We don't buy milk from the store."

The oldest boy spoke up. "That milk is as fresh as it comes. I squeezed it out of Buttercup at five this morning. It went straight into the refrigerator. How does it taste?"

Heather had already enjoyed half a glass when the conversation about milk started. "Is it pasteurized?"

"Heck, no," said the youngest boy. "That would ruin it."

"Most people don't realize that laws about pasteurizing milk didn't start until the 1920s," said the lad who'd taken on the role of teacher. "The reason people get sick is because of poor hygiene with the livestock, the milking machines, and what the milk's stored in. Buttercup is pasture fed and only comes to the barn twice a day to be milked. We wash her udders and hand milk into a stainless-steel pail that's scrubbed after each use. We also hose down the concrete she stands on twice a day."

Steve nodded his approval. "It sounds like you've done a lot of research."

"I have. You can get sick from unpasteurized milk, but it isn't the milk that's the culprit. It's how it's processed. Of course, there are a lot of articles about how dangerous unpasteurized milk is, but those come from big dairies. They're usually written by people getting paid by the government or the dairy industry."

The small voice of the youngest daughter interrupted the lecture. "Momma, can Lizzy and I split the last piece of pie?"

Sue Ann shook her head. "What would your daddy do if he found out you and Lizzy ate his piece?"

Something just shy of terror shone in the young girl's eyes. "Can I go play?"

Sue Ann glanced at each of the four children. "Put your plates in the sink and don't let the door slam again."

Chairs scraped against the wooden floor and soon the sound of voices faded. Heather took Steve's plate and followed Sue Ann to the sink. She looked out the screen door. "You have two porches? One out front and one in the back?"

"That's our sleeping porch. It's open on three sides to catch a breeze and the oak trees shade it. There's cots and a couple of old roll-away beds for whoever can't sleep. Come late July and August most everyone will be out there."

"Did the house you grew up in have a sleeping porch?"

"Just the front porch. Daddy said if we couldn't sleep it was because we hadn't worked hard enough."

Steve spoke from where he sat, "Can I help do the dishes? I'm not much on washing, but I can dry with the best of them."

"The two middle ones will get it done after you leave," said Sue Ann. "Let's go on the front porch and swing a while. The kids will be down by the river and we can talk about whatever you want."

Heather placed Steve in a rocking chair while she and Sue Ann sat on the swing and began the motion that mimicked the slow ticking of time in this peaceful setting. But was it always peaceful? The discoloration under Sue Ann's eye told another story of this bucolic country life.

No one spoke for a couple of minutes, content to allow the taste of rich milk and rhubarb pie to fade. Steve finally broke the spell. "We need your help. Tell us about growing up at the ranch."

"I don't understand. What do you want to know?"

"Start with your first memory," said Steve.

Sue Ann closed her eyes tight. "It was at the funeral home when Grandpa Voss died. I remember the casket. It was made of wood and had gold handles." She opened her eyes. "They looked like gold."

"What kind of man was your grandfather?"

"I don't remember him, but then, there's some big gaps in my memory. From what Mae and Roy said, he was meaner than Daddy. They said he didn't like anyone in general and a lot of people in particular."

"Who in particular?"

"Mexicans and Blacks; called them all sorts of names, according to Mae." She shook her head. "Wait. That would be people he hated in general, not in particular." She gazed toward the garden. "I'm not good with words."

"Any people you can remember him saying he hated?"

"Roy said he didn't like Hector, but that's because he was different than us."

"What did you think of Hector?"

"I loved him because he loved me and Mama and Rance."

Heather took her turn. "What about your father? Did he hate Hector?"

Sue Ann's head shook with certainty. "He and Hector were close, kind of like they were brothers, but not really."

"This is a hard question," said Heather. "Did your father ever beat you or your brothers or sister?"

"All but me and Rance. I try not to remember those days and most of the time it works. Like I said, my memory has some big gaps."

"What about your mother? Did he ever beat her?"

A shiver caused the swing to lose its rhythm. "That was before Rance was born. It must have been shortly after Grandpa died. He only hit her once that I can recall, but it was hard."

The swing found its pace again, slow and steady. Steve lifted the tone of his voice and the mood changed. "This is such a nice place and your children are special. You and Grant must be very proud of them."

She stopped swinging. "Mr. Smiley, can I tell you something?"

"That's why we're here. Say anything you want."

"I married a man just like my pa. The kids are good because none of us have a choice. Do you understand?"

The rhubarb pie did a flip in Heather's stomach.

"I understand," said Steve. "What do you want us to do?"

She stood and leaned against a post supporting the roof of the porch. "Is there any way you can delay giving me the million dollars for a long time? As soon as I get it, Grant will take it all and blow it. The kids will be left with nothing and he'll be twice as mean as he is now."

Heather answered for Steve. "We might be able to delay the payment for a few days, but not long. To do what you want won't be easy. You'd have to go in front of a judge and get a restraining order against Grant. It would be best if you had proof of him assaulting or threatening you. You'll need to file for divorce, too. This is a community property state. Things would get complicated if he took the money and invested it."

Sue Ann continued looking out into a pasture. "I tried that once. He stayed locked up a few days and then made life worse than before."

"Let us work on it," said Steve. "I have a seed of an idea."

"Seeds are good," said Sue Ann. "Look at what the kids did with the garden."

Steve moved on. "When we drove up, Heather said she didn't see a boat. Isn't Grant a big fisherman?"

"He took it almost a week ago. I asked him about it and wished I hadn't."

"What kind is it?"

She shrugged. "It's a red and black fishin' boat is all I know. He's probably on the lake now. He quit his job."

"I figured he would," said Steve. "One more thing. You said you brought home some personal items from when you made the list of things in the ranch house. Do you still have those?"

"Uh-huh. They're mostly receipts and stuff that should have been thrown away."

"Do you mind if we take them and Heather checks to make sure you don't get rid of something important?"

"Sure. Take whatever you need."

They left Sue Ann standing on the porch. Heather turned to Steve after she put the car in gear. "Where to?"

"Llano. Let's talk to the sheriff about finding a boat."

20

Heather took Highway 71 out of Marble Falls and headed west.

"Sheriff Blake wants us to meet him at a coffee shop on the south side of town," said Steve.

"We should be there in about twenty minutes." A wall of silence met Heather's estimation of travel time. Steve cocooned himself inside an imaginary soundproof room, which was fine with her. She needed to process the information gleaned from their meeting with Sue Ann.

Most of the miles were behind them when Steve came out of his shell. "Sue Ann's a good mother, and a lot smarter than everyone gives her credit for. I think she trained herself to act in ways that make her appear dim-witted."

"Explain yourself."

"She grew up in an abusive home, but somehow avoided the beatings her older brother and sister received. Her house runs on a shoestring, but she finds ways to not only get by, but to teach her kids how to prosper. She's also smart enough to know she needs to get away from Grant."

Heather agreed, but that didn't answer something that had

been niggling at her mind. "What about Rance? How do you think he got by without incurring the wrath of his father?"

"I can't explain that." Steve pulled his seat belt away from his chest. "I don't like odd things or coincidences. Can you picture Charley as a man who'd go soft on his son?"

"Everything we've heard about him tells me he remained a misanthrope to the end."

Another mile passed in silence before Heather asked. "Do you have a plan for delaying the insurance settlement to Sue Ann and the others?"

"Yeah, but it has a few holes in it." He tapped his foot in a sign of impatience and asked, "How much longer?"

"We passed the city limit sign. Another minute or two and we'll be there."

"Good. I can tell my plan to you and the sheriff at the same time."

It didn't come as a surprise, that at mid-afternoon in a small coffee shop in Llano, Texas, the trio had the place to themselves. The lone exception was a pimply faced worker with wires running from a cell phone upward until they disappeared under a mop of curly hair. No wonder the sheriff chose this place; it held no customers and the lone worker appeared both distracted by music and disinterested.

Heather helped Steve to his chair and said, "Nice boots, Sheriff. Glad to see you're doing better."

"Almost good as new. What mischief have ya'll been up to?"

Steve took over. "We visited Sue Ann. She's worried, and so are we."

The sheriff took off his straw cowboy hat and placed it on the table. "I lost track of her after she married. What's the matter?"

"It's her husband," said Heather. "There are interesting colors under her left eye and she's convinced Grant is going to make off with the life insurance money."

150

Steve added, "All of it, and leave her and the kids high and dry."

Sheriff Blake directed his gaze out a window, even though there was nothing to see but heat radiating up from black asphalt. "Don't know what I can do about it. They don't live in Llano County."

"I know," said Steve, "but he fishes in Llano County."

"Sometimes. But the county line runs right down the middle of the lake. I imagine he puts in at some ramp in Burnet County."

As he was prone to do, Steve changed subjects. "Have you given thought to where the first round that hit Hector came from?"

"Either on the bank near the lake or, more likely, from a boat anchored on the sandbar."

Steve nodded. "That's the same conclusion we came to. We also wondered what happened to the first shell casing."

The sheriff chuckled. "I can guarantee it's not on land. We searched every inch from the shoreline to the house and used a metal detector. That only leaves the lake."

"True," said Steve. "But there might be one other place you could check."

"Oh?"

"We gave each of the heirs a copy of Sue Ann's inventory of the ranch house before it burned. Rance says a lever-action 30-30 is missing. Picture the shooter standing on the bow of a boat. A wave lifts the stern as he's taking the shot. The barrel dips enough to throw the shot low, and it hits Hector in the leg. What does the shooter do?"

Leaning forward, the sheriff said, "We know what he did. He followed Hector until he had a clear shot and finished the job."

"Agreed, but before that he missed a kill shot. What's the first thing an experienced hunter does?"

The sheriff's eyes darted back and forth until the answer came to him. "He ejects the spent shell and chambers another round."

Steve nodded. "And where did the brass go?"

"In the lake."

"Or?"

The sheriff squinted. "Are you saying the spent shell might be somewhere in Grant Blankenship's boat?"

"It could be worth a look," said Steve.

Heather spoke up. "I see where my partner's mind is going with this. We found out today from Sue Ann that Grant quit his job at the granite quarry. She thought he'd be on the lake all day celebrating his good fortune."

Steve broke in. "I don't picture Grant as a man who likes to fish and not have a cooler of beer with him. I could smell it on him at the meetings he attended. I suspect he's celebrating double now that he thinks he's in line for a big payday."

The sheriff took over from there. "Marvin needs something to do this afternoon. I think I'll send him around the lake and see if he can't find Grant's truck and trailer parked at a boat ramp. If it's on the Burnet County side, I'll have him contact their sheriff's office and tip them off to a possible drunk driver. They might need to look in the boat for a shell casing while they're at it."

"Who knows," said Steve. "He might have put in at Horse-shoe Bay. After all, he thinks he's a millionaire."

"Anything else?" asked the sheriff.

They both shook their heads.

The sheriff was in his car with a phone to his ear before Steve spoke again. "The chance of them finding that spent shell is so small I can't even imagine it, but that wasn't the point of this meeting with the sheriff. We needed to buy Sue Ann some time."

Heather looked up as two women entered and had to tug on

the employee's sleeve to gain his attention. The boy nodded and set to making something that didn't require him to speak. Regular customers, no doubt.

She refocused and asked, "Why do we need time?"

"If Grant's in jail through the weekend for DWI, you can set up an investment plan for her. She can sign over the million to you before Grant can get his hands on it."

The door to the coffee shop eased shut behind them, away from the women taking an afternoon break. It was times like this that Heather lived for. They'd beat Grant to the punch and Sue Ann would provide for her children. "I'll call Sue Ann from the car."

"Those kids shouldn't grow up in fear," said Steve. "I just hope it wasn't Sue Ann that killed Hector. Keep that in mind when you're setting up the investments for her."

"I can't see her doing it," said Heather as a rebuttal.

"It won't hurt to be careful."

"What next?" asked Heather as Steve found her shoulder with his hand.

"We don't have any proof of who shot Hector. Grant seems a likely candidate, but we need to eliminate suspects. I made a list on my phone of companies around the lake that rent boats. Let's see if any of the other siblings rented one on the day of the shooting."

Heather waited until they were both in the car. "You were busy this morning."

"One of us needed to be. How's the headache?"

She considered making a comeback to his jab, but decided a lighthearted answer would be best. "Buttercup's milk has strange restorative powers."

"That's what this case needs, a magic cow. Should you ask Buttercup who killed Hector DeLeon?"

"Good idea." Heather couldn't help herself. "I'll milk her for information."

"Ha-ha. You've recovered from your night of folly." He slipped his phone out of his pocket and gave it instructions to find the name and location of the nearest boat rental.

THE SEARCH BEGAN IN KINGSLAND, A TOWN UPRIVER FROM THE main body of the lake. It had a less aristocratic vibe, but was still a haven for water sports. Steve stayed in the car and let Heather do the legwork. It would save time since they had several businesses to visit.

Pontoon boats and more traditional ski boats bobbed in the water under the tin roof of a wood dock, ready for the next customer to enjoy. An almost empty rack of jet skis also caught Heather's attention. Those didn't seem likely candidates for someone carrying a rifle, so she needn't inquire about them. She entered the lakeside business as a customer left with two preteen boys in tow. All three wore sunburns and walked with shuffling steps.

"What can I get for you, today?" The man asking wore a collared knit shirt with the rental's business name embroidered on the right side of his chest.

"All I need today is information."

He tried to look serious but failed. "That's the most expensive thing we offer here." He added, "Just kidding. I've got the rates right here in this brochure." He handed her a folded piece of advertisement.

She took the glossy pamphlet but didn't look at it. "I'm a private detective investigating the murder of Hector DeLeon on the Voss ranch."

He took a step back. "I heard about that. It happened several miles from here, on the other side of the lake." His gaze narrowed. "What's that got to do with me?"

"Probably nothing, but one theory we're working on is the shooting came from a boat and not on land."

"And you think it involves one of my boats?"

Heather kept a serious tone to her words and didn't give a straight answer to his question. "There's two things I want to check. First, I need the names of anyone who had a boat out this past Saturday night."

The man scratched the whiskers on his right cheek. "I'm not sure I can do that."

"Sir," said Heather in a firm voice. "I'm an attorney and a private investigator. Is there anything in your rental contract that states you promise anonymity?"

"Well, no, but—"

Heather interrupted his balking speech. "Do you see that man sitting in the car in the parking lot?" Heather pointed to the rental.

"Yeah. I see him."

"He's a homicide investigator with over twenty years' experience, and he's my partner. A little while ago we were having coffee with the sheriff of Llano County. You can talk to me now and get this over with, or one phone call and you'll be receiving a visit that could cause loss of your valuable time and business. Sheriff Blake trusts my partner to conduct interviews and he's very thorough, not to mention a little scary."

Two twenty-dollar bills slid across the counter. "Forty bucks for telling me if you found a spent rifle shell in any boat that a customer turned in since Sunday morning."

The man folded the bills and stuffed them in the pocket of his shorts. "We go over the boats from bow to stern after each use. I have a collection of cell phones, e-readers, hats and half empty bottles of booze that people left behind, but I can't say we've ever seen rifle brass."

"Who cleans the boats?"

"My wife and daughters. They would have mentioned it."

Heather pulled out a business card. "Double check the boats that were out overnight on Saturday. That rifle shell would mean a lot to me and I can be very generous." She paused. "You look like an honest man and I'm in a hurry. If you find the brass, email the names of the overnight renters and their addresses. I'll call you with my credit card. How much is a deposit on a boat?"

"A ski boat rental starts at two-hundred and ninety dollars for four hours. There's a fourteen-day cancellation notice."

"Send me the list of names and I'll put a boat on deposit. Rent it to someone else if you can. I won't need it."

The man had nice teeth and didn't mind showing them. "Look for the email tonight if I find anything."

Heather returned to the car. "One down and four to go."

"Any problems?"

She responded with a scoff.

"You cheated and did it the easy way. How much did that set us back?"

"Time is ticking. We have four other stops to make before dark."

Steve shifted in his seat. "I'll take the next one. Give me ten minutes and it won't cost a penny."

Heather knew better than to bet against him, so she changed the subject. "We'll be starving by the time we finish four more boat rental places. Any suggestions for supper?"

He counted items on his fingers. "So far today you've had a piece a toast, orange juice, a slice of rhubarb pie, a glass of fresh milk and a cup of coffee. I think you've earned the right to pick."

She glanced over at him and gave her head a nod. "I want a chicken-fried steak in an out of the way cafe."

"There's hope for you yet, partner."

A mile passed before Steve said, "Tomorrow's Hector's funeral. How many of the Voss children do you think will show up?"

"Two," said Heather. "Rance and Sue Ann."

"I'll say three," said Steve. "Roy should be there if he doesn't get sucked into a poker game."

Heather thought for a moment. "Of course, Angelina and her mother will be there."

Steve nodded. "We need to make an appointment to see them again on Saturday."

The miles passed as Heather's thoughts about the day came back in flashes. That wasn't the only thing flashing as they approached Horseshoe Bay. County patrol cars and a local cop had a truck with a boat and trailer pulled over. She slowed. "Traffic stop. Marvin's putting Grant in handcuffs. A second deputy is searching the boat."

Steve rubbed his hands together like he was washing them. "I was right. Grant put in at Horseshoe Bay Marina. He's already spending Sue Ann's inheritance."

Heather tilted her head and asked, "Didn't Sue Ann say Grant's boat was red?"

"Red and black," said Steve.

"This one's gray and white. Do you think Sue Ann made a mistake?"

Steve wagged his head from left to right. "I need to call Sheriff Blake."

The sheriff answered after the first ring. "You do good work for a city boy. Marvin's happy as a puppy with two tails to wag."

"We just passed them," said Steve. "DWI?"

"Better. DWI and he's hauling a stolen boat. It's registered to a guy in Austin and the boat disappeared from Lake Travis a day after Hector was killed."

Steve congratulated the sheriff and told him Marvin should get a raise. That earned him a boisterous laugh.

After signing off, Steve said, "That's good news, bad news. Grant will be out of circulation and we can move unhindered to protect Sue Ann."

"What's the bad news?"

"Our search for the missing shell casing just got harder. I was hoping Marvin would find it and we'd know for sure that Grant shot Hector. The sheriff would've mentioned it if they found it. Now we have to keep searching the boat rental places. We knew it was a long shot to look for the last casing. More than likely it's in the lake." Steve turned her way. "Did you bring a bathing suit?"

21

Steve huffed his way from the boat rental office at Horseshoe Bay. "I never had that much trouble when I carried a badge."

"Relax," said Heather. "Three out of four wasn't bad."

Steve stopped before they reached the car. "What is it about places that cater to the rich and entitled? The people that bow and scrape to them think their privacy is something they're duty bound to protect. Don't they know many of these people spend their lives becoming famous? They want people to know about them."

Heather countered with, "All it took was a phone call to Sheriff Blake to get their attention." She felt a nudge on her shoulder and continued walking.

"I'm losing my touch. I couldn't talk that woman into giving me the time, let alone the names of who rented boats."

"The car's ahead of you ten feet."

He found it with his cane. "I didn't think it possible, but she's put me off my hankering for chicken-fried steak. Let's eat someplace else."

Heather considered the options. "I'll stop at the first place I see." She didn't have far to go before she spotted the Yacht Club Restaurant, the place Steve and his golfing date, Bridget, had dined.

"We're here. I hope we don't have to wait."

Since it didn't matter to Steve if they had a table with a view, Heather asked for first available seating. The only thing open was outside bar seating by the pool. That suited both of them. She read the menu to him and, as usual, didn't get to the end before he said, "Hamburger and fries."

"They have Joe's Hamburger or a Brontosaurus Burger."

"Brontosaurus meat sounds old. I'll stick with Joe. I never met a cook named Joe that couldn't make a decent burger."

Heather ordered the Hill Country chicken wrap and iced tea. An orange sky in the southwest contrasted against the ever-darkening blue to the northeast. Night never hurried in mid-June. She closed her eyes and formed mental pictures of those coming to dinner via watercraft instead of cars. She parted her eyelids and saw her vision come to life. Gleaming boats delivered customers to waiting dock workers decked out in the resort's shorts and shirts. The arriving men wore Rolex watches and the women flashed gold and diamonds. Some did so to impress. Others, because that's the way they lived. Displays of wealth didn't bother Heather as long as people treated others with respect. It was the pretentious, the pretenders and the wanna-be's that stood out. She made a vow years ago not to be one of those.

Opening her eyes, she inspected Steve. There he sat in his dark world, yet cognizant of sounds, smells, tastes and touches that others couldn't understand. His thoughts went far deeper than most, and he even had a special gift of seeing red.

That reminded her. "Steve, have you figured out why you saw pink at the Voss ranch?"

He reached for his glass of iced tea. "Still thinking about it." He immediately raised his glass to his lips and took several sips.

She'd been around him long enough to know that meant he knew more than he was telling, or wanted to tell.

Steve set his glass down and turned into the wind. "Unless I'm mistaken, Mae and Patrick are somewhere near."

Heather looked in the direction he was facing. Sure enough, the couple walked arm in arm. She wore a dress with deep slits traveling north to south on the top and south to north on the lower half. Her gold bracelets jangled when she walked.

Heather leaned into Steve and whispered, "Did you hear her or smell her first?"

"Smelled, but it didn't take long before I heard her bracelets."

As they came behind, Steve spun on the swivel seat of his chair and said, "There's the happy couple. When's the big day?"

Mae held her head high and issued a full grin. Patrick looked at Steve with a suspicious gaze, as if he'd had a cop's flashlight shine in his eyes. Heather gave him high marks for making a good recovery, but Patrick's initial reaction puzzled her.

"Saturday," said Mae while broadening her smile. "We got the license yesterday morning and have to wait seventy-two hours. It'll be a simple ceremony. The resort is handling everything."

"It's good you decided on keeping it simple," said Steve. "I'm not sure if Sue Ann could get away from the kids."

Patrick perked up. "Why? What's happened?"

Heather answered. "On our way back to the resort this afternoon, Grant was being pulled over and handcuffed."

Steve added. "I was curious, so I called Sheriff Blake. Grant will be in jail all weekend, sitting out a DWI."

"Serves him right," said Mae with venom lacing her words.

"The interesting thing," said Steve. "He was pulling a stolen boat and trailer."

Mae's chin lifted in an obvious show of superiority. Patrick broke eye contact and looked toward the lake.

Steve asked, "Did Sue Ann tell you Grant was getting rid of his boat?"

"Of course not," said Mae. "You know I don't stay in touch with any of my siblings."

"It doesn't matter, but I asked myself why Grant would steal a boat when he already had one. And days away from a million dollars, why didn't he wait? It's almost like somebody set him up."

Patrick had a firm hand on Mae's arm. "Come, darling. We don't want to be late for our reservation."

"Before you go," said Steve. "Did you come here by boat?"

Mae couldn't get it out fast enough. "We had such fun this weekend, we rented another boat today to come to dinner. It's not as nice as what Patrick said we'll buy, but it gave us a taste of what will come."

Patrick gave her arm a squeeze. "We really must be off. They're real sticklers about reservations in the peak season."

Steve waited until he was sure they were out of earshot. "We spent hours going from one boat rental place to the next when all we had to do was come here, drink iced tea and wait for Mae to come by with her unfiltered mouth."

"That's at least two with the opportunity to kill Hector," said Heather. "Three if you add Grant to Mae and Patrick."

"We should divide Mae and Patrick now," said Steve. "I give that marriage the time it takes to melt an ice cube on the parking lot."

The meal arrived. Steve's hamburger rose a full six inches off the plate. After one attempt to bite into it, everything slid between the two over-sized buns onto his plate. Heather went to work with a knife and made bite-sized pieces, separating the vegetables, meat and bread.

After pulling his napkin from the top of his shirt, Steve said,

"Best hamburger steak, salad and a roll I've had in a long time." He felt for his plate and put the napkin beside it. "What's your evening look like?"

Heather pushed an empty plate away from her. "The first thing I'm going to do is grovel. I should have trusted Jack."

"Humility is a much maligned and unappreciated character trait."

While waiting for the server to run her credit card, Steve asked, "Will you have time tonight to look at the things in the box Sue Ann gave us?"

"I should. It all depends on how much humble pie I have to eat. What will you be doing while I'm slaving away?"

"Probably sleeping. That and getting addresses and phone numbers to boat storage places away from the lake. It's possible Grant stored his boat somewhere nearby."

"Do you think Grant was dumb enough to hang on to that boat?"

Steve shrugged. "Grant doesn't impress me as an intellectual giant."

Heather waited until they were in the parking lot before she spoke again. "Do you think Patrick and Mae set Grant up?"

"Someone set him up. Tell me more about the boat you saw today."

"It was a fishing boat. It had a fancy paint job and looked new."

"Was it fiberglass or metal?"

"Fiberglass. Long and sleek."

"A big motor?"

"A lot bigger than the one on the boat we rented. It also had a trolling motor on the front."

Steve nodded. "A flat deck on the front and back?"

"Uh-huh. And two mechanical poles on the back of the boat that looked like spider legs."

"They're called power poles. They allow to anchor the

boat in shallow water with the push of a button. Professional bass anglers have them on their boats and don't mess with anchors when they're fishing in fairly shallow water."

Heather operated her key fob, and the vehicle chirped to announce the doors were unlocked. "It looked expensive."

"Expensive and easy to spot."

She spoke over the hood of the car. "What makes you think Grant's old boat is still nearby?"

Steve opened the door and slid in the car before he answered. "I'm trying to think like Grant and the person setting him up at the same time. Grant has the mentality of a pauper. He'd like to keep his old boat as a spare."

"Mae or Patrick?" asked Heather.

"Or Sue Ann. Or Roy, or Rance, or someone we don't know."

In mere minutes they were back at the hotel. She saw Steve to his door and told him they'd meet for breakfast. An arrangement of flowers awaited her when she opened her door. The card read, *Missing you. Jack.*

Her cell phone needed a charge, but she placed the call anyway.

"Hey, beautiful."

"Hey, handsome. Thanks for the flowers. Have you ever been to Horseshoe Bay?"

"Can't say that I have."

"Then it's time you came. I have some serious apologizing to do and it needs to be done in person. When can you get away?"

"If I work all weekend, I should be able to drive there Sunday evening and stay two or three days."

"Three. And you're flying. Expect a phone call from my pilot tonight."

"How's the investigation?"

"Steve's getting to where he's thinking more than talking. That usually means we're getting close. I'd say another three or four days."

"That means you'll be free on Monday, but you've been out of the office for a long time. Are you sure you don't need to get back to work?"

"You and I are going to play golf. Bring your clubs."

"You don't play golf."

"You can teach me. I've been told I need to relax and take up a hobby."

"I'm liking the sound of this. Are you sure I'm talking to Heather McBlythe?"

"The new and improved version."

Heather wanted to stay talking with Jack until the sun came up, but she'd already cost them a half day's work. "I hate to say it, but I have a big box of documents to go through and come up with an investment plan for a mother and her four children, and—"

Jack interrupted her with a laugh. "I'll be up late protecting the rights of the innocent."

"And I'll be catching the bad guys. What a pair we are."

"Yeah. What a pair."

22

The digital display on the treadmill read eleven laps. One more and she'd finish her three-mile run. Heather panted as sweat dripped from her nose. The past week had been full of trials, but last night's phone call with Jack turned her emotional ship around. She made a flurry of commitments to changes. No more seventy and eighty-hour weeks to impress her father. Corporate profits would take a back seat to time spent with Jack. Taking up golf had been a spur-of-the-moment decision, but it would be a good start for the new Heather. Besides, what better place to learn to play than at this resort? He could help her pick out the right clubs and she'd need shoes and clothes. Her mind raced with mental snapshots. Looking down, she realized she'd passed the three-mile mark.

She left the hotel's gym after picking up another brochure for the spa on her way out. Back at the hotel, the Starbucks near the front desk drew her in with the smell of freshly ground beans and the sputter of frothy milk. A tall coffee and a copy of the Wall Street Journal was how she loved to start her day. She'd go out on her room's small patio, sip her coffee, and allow the sun to rise enough so she could scan the headlines. The only thing that could make the morning better would be if Jack was with her.

First light had already made its debut when she reached the patio. She sipped her way through half of the dark stimulant and reached for the paper. The headline was a repeat of yet another dire warning about rising interest rates. She flipped the paper over and scanned the articles. Her heart skipped a beat. Below the fold, on the right side, near the bottom, a tag line read: McBlythe Falls For Fool's Gold

What followed was an uncomplimentary account of her father's purchase of the gold mine in Montana. She wondered how the reporter had gleaned so much information so fast. The more she read, the more she realized someone with firsthand knowledge must have fed the reporter details that only a few within McBlythe Enterprises would know. Her anger rose with every detail until the article ended with the obligatory statement that although the reporter reached out to Allister McBlythe, neither he nor a company spokesperson had returned their call.

Heather paced her room, fury growing with every step. She hated the reporter, hated the company that sold the mine, and, most of all, hated herself for not doing more to protect her father. She considered calling him, but what would she say? He wasn't a man to receive pity. She practiced a few lines, but they came out sounding either trite or accusatory. Perhaps Steve would have a suggestion.

A shower and clean clothes helped to dull the sting of the newspaper report, but not much. She looked in the closet and found nothing suitable for attending a funeral that afternoon. The hotel gift shop might have a dress that didn't splash with color. If not, she'd have to make do with slacks and a blazer.

She expected to find Steve alone in the restaurant. Instead, he sat with Marvin. The chief deputy took notes as Steve spoke.

The only sentence she caught as she approached was Steve saying, "That should keep you busy this morning."

Marvin closed a notepad and shoved it in the right pocket of his shirt. "The sheriff wants me to be at the funeral by one o'clock."

"We'll see you there," said Steve.

"What was that about?" asked Heather after Marvin left the room.

"Change of plans. Marvin's going to do our leg work today. We need to go to Llano this morning and get Rance out of jail."

Heather plopped on an empty chair. "What did he do?"

"An anonymous call came to the sheriff's office. They told the dispatcher that Rance killed Hector and the rifle he used was behind the seat of Rance's pickup. Sheriff Blake woke Marvin before dawn. He rousted Rance out of bed and Rance gave permission to search. Sure enough, the rifle was there."

Heather shook her head. "That's too easy."

"Of course it is. But the sheriff has to go through all the formalities. He'll dust the rifle for fingerprints and there won't be any. Rance will say he has no idea how it got there and he's sure it wasn't there the last time he checked behind the seat."

Steve took another sip of coffee. "This is a positive development. Someone's scared and they're not too smart."

When Steve didn't make a move to stand, Heather asked, "Don't we need to go?"

He waved a dismissive hand. "Plenty of time. Marvin and another deputy are checking out the boat storage places for us. It will look better for him if he finds Grant's boat."

Heather picked up the menu. "Do I have time to eat and stop in the gift shop and look for a dress?"

"Rance isn't going anywhere except to Hector's funeral, and that isn't until this afternoon."

The server appeared to take her order. She chose yogurt, fresh fruit, and a slice of whole wheat toast.

As soon as the server tucked her order book in the pocket of her apron, Steve asked, "How's Jack?"

Heather tried not to sound like a giddy schoolgirl. "He's wonderful and he'll be here Sunday night. I told him he deserved a face-to-face apology, so I'm flying him in with the pilot and co-pilot and the pilot's wife. They deserve a mini-vacation, too."

Steve leaned forward and spoke in a low voice. "The only paying customer we have is Angelina Perez, and she's still paying off student loans."

"You worry about solving a murder, I'll worry about paying for it. Besides, you told me I needed to do something besides work. I'm taking up golf, and Jack's going to teach me." The very thought of it caused her lips to part in a smile.

"Good for you. I'll show you the ropes on the resort's rich man's putt putt course. It will be an even match if we can talk them into turning off the lights."

Their laughter gave way to silence. She sensed Steve was several steps ahead of her on the investigation into Hector's death, so she brought up something he didn't know, the newspaper article she'd read. "I want you to listen to something that came out today."

Her emotions flared as she read the article. She folded the paper and looked at Steve. He'd interlaced his fingers and dipped his head. His silence became uncomfortable until he said, "What made your father think this was a worthwhile investment to begin with?"

"Samples from drill holes. They showed solid veins of high-quality ore."

"Do you think they were fake?"

"Not at first, but it made little sense that the mine was slowing production if they knew there was more gold. I wanted Father to slow down."

Steve took in a deep breath and let it out. "The details in the newspaper article bother me. Let me think on this. In the meantime, we have a client that expects results in solving the murder of her grandfather, and there's the little chore of making sure we faithfully observe Charley's wishes."

Heather's meal arrived. She'd hoped for Steve to rattle off a simple solution to how she was to interact with her father. Why didn't he ask more questions? No need to ask. He'd gone once again to that secret place.

RANCE SAT IN SHERIFF BLAKE'S OFFICE WITH HIS RIGHT BOOT resting on his left knee. He looked up at Heather with smiling eyes and nodded a greeting. His hair lay flat against his head, and a tan line creased his forehead where his cowboy hat shielded part of his face from long days in the sun and wind. "Glad to see you. I thought I was going to miss the funeral."

Heather cast a questioning gaze at the sheriff. He answered her unasked questions. "No bail. No paperwork to sign. Rance and I have been talking cattle. I'm keeping the rifle for now, but whoever put it there wiped it clean, too clean. With a truck like Rance drives, it should have at least had dust on it. And speaking of dust, we're not finished dusting his truck for prints. He can pick it up after the funeral."

The sheriff shifted his gaze to Steve. "Thanks for the tip. How did you know they'd try to frame Rance?"

"I had a similar case in Houston. Did Marvin find Grant's boat and a casing?"

"Yep. Right where you said it would be. Brass from a 30-30."

Steve rested his hands on top of his cane. "The markings on the brass will match the rifle, but I don't believe the casing found in the boat is from the first shot fired. The brass from the first shot at Hector is in the lake."

"Another example of trying too hard to point the finger at Rance."

Heather realized her mouth hung open. She let Steve and the sheriff talk without interruption. Steve added, "Someone's trying too hard to direct suspicion away from themselves. They overplayed their hand by putting the rifle in Rance's truck and calling in the tip. They should have ditched the rifle in the lake."

Sheriff Blake stood. "Let me know when you find out who it is."

Steve scratched his chin the way he did before he stretched the truth. "My money's on Marvin coming up with the name."

Rance and the sheriff both grinned but said nothing as handshakes and farewells followed.

After trading the claustrophobic jail for bright sunshine, Heather looked at her phone. They were in and out of the county jail in minutes. Even Jack, as good of a defense lawyer as he was, couldn't get a murder suspect out of jail that fast.

Steve interrupted her pleasant thought. "A little air conditioning would be nice. It works best if you start the engine."

She pushed a button, and the car came to life. Looking at the handsome young man in the back seat, she said, "Tell me where to go."

"Back into town. Turn west on 29. It's not far past the city limits sign."

He directed them to a home overlooking the Llano river and explained that the river was still flowing steady, but that would diminish as the summer wore on. They traveled a hundred yards down a gravel road. Rance pointed at a travel trailer parked under a tin shed. "My buddy's letting me live in the trailer. Are you sure you don't mind waiting while I shower?"

"No problem," said Steve. "I'm sorry we didn't get here

earlier. I planned on taking you to lunch, but someone had to go shopping."

"My fault," said Heather. "I found a dress with no trouble but started looking at a few other things. Time got away from me."

Rance slid out of the SUV and jogged to the trailer's door before she could add to her apology.

He returned wearing starched jeans, dress boots, a clean white shirt and a straw cowboy hat without the stains from sweat like the one he wore into the trailer.

Once Heather pointed the car toward town, Steve began a conversation with Rance. "Tell me your fondest memory of Hector."

"Heck," said Rance. "Most every memory I have of him is fond. He taught me all I know about being a cowboy." He paused. "More than that, he taught me how to treat people. He said a man needs tough hands and a soft heart."

Heather swallowed a lump.

Like a water valve opened, Rance carried on with a steady flow of words. "I don't know why Mae hated him so much. I asked her once, and she said she had good reason and told me never to ask her again."

"When was that?" asked Steve.

"She was about to graduate high school, so I dropped it. After that, she left."

Steve turned his head so Rance would be sure to hear him. "How close was Hector to Roy and Sue Ann?"

"Roy didn't have any use for the ranch, so he and Hector never found common ground. There wasn't any bad blood between them. In fact, Hector stood up to Dad once when he got too rough with Roy. Dad hit Hector with a hay-maker but Hector just spit out the blood and told him to take another shot if he wanted to but not to hurt Roy or else."

"Or else, what?" asked Heather.

"No idea." Rance paused for a moment. "I always thought

Hector knew something about Dad, had something on him. He's the only ranch hand that ever lasted more than a month or two. In a way, they reminded me of brothers."

"And Sue Ann?" asked Steve.

Steve couldn't see it, but Rance smiled. "Sue Ann's smarter than she puts on. Hector and Mom knew it, but Dad never did. Mom encouraged her to stay out of Dad's way, especially when he'd been drinking."

Heather had been quiet long enough. "What did you do when he started drinking and getting mean?"

"I'd walk down to Hector's cabin. Dad never came looking for me or bothered me if I went past the barn. I stayed there many a night."

"Tell me about your mother. I understand her name was Pearl," said Steve. "Nobody's given me a good physical description of her."

"Have they described Mae and Sue Ann to you?"

Steve said that he could picture them both with blondish-brown hair and fair skin, medium build and eyes of a blue tint.

"That's about right," said Rance. "Mae's smaller than Mom was and Sue Ann's taller."

Steve shifted a little, trying to face more toward the back seat. "Was your mother happy living at the ranch?"

"It's funny you asked. Mae and Roy remember her as being miserable until I came along."

Rance pointed. "Take the next right. The funeral home is down two blocks on your left."

As they pulled into the parking lot, Rance said, "I'll be darned. Mae and that lawyer she's supposed to marry are here."

23

Heather glanced at the funeral home's parking lot that was filling fast. She guessed the ratio of cars to pickup trucks to be one to four. Steve's hand rested on her shoulder and she told him the approximate distance to the front door. Rance walked alongside, matching her pace. Mae and Patrick were almost to the door when they moved away from those entering and stood off to the side. Mae nodded at something he said and followed the direction his head nudged. She led the way toward them, and it didn't take her long to cover the distance.

"I thought you were in jail," said Mae in an accusatory voice.

Steve stopped and faced Mae. "Why would Rance be in jail?"

"I wasn't talking to you, but since you asked, it's all over town they found the rifle that killed Hector in Rance's truck."

"They did," said Steve. "But whoever put it there made some big mistakes. I can't go into detail on what they are, other than to say someone tried to set Rance up and failed. The rifle and Rance's truck are being examined now by top forensic experts. I pity the person who put it there and thought they were too smart to get caught."

Heather knew Steve stretched the truth on the last statement. She also knew he counted on her to look for reactions from Mae and Patrick. Mae put on a cheerful face and said, "I knew it couldn't be you, Rance. You and that old Mexican were like this." She held up the index and middle fingers of her right hand held tight together.

Patrick dabbed sweat from his brow with a monogrammed handkerchief. Heather didn't know what to think of his reaction since the temperature was in the mid-nineties and climbing.

"I'm glad you're not in jail," said Mae. "That will save me the trouble of hiring local riffraff to round up the cattle and send you a bill. I want those cattle off my property."

Rance straightened his spine. "I've been working dawn till dark to do just that. I'm not dragging my feet, Mae. It takes time. We can't push the horses all day in this heat."

Mae took a step toward him. "I didn't ask for excuses. Every stinking cow is to be off my land by Wednesday."

Rance tilted his hat back on his head. "What about the other parcels?"

"Who cares?"

Heather hoped Rance would tell Mae to take a long walk off a short pier, but it took more than his eldest sister's selfish rant to provoke him. He resettled his hat and shrugged in a way that communicated he didn't have a care in the world. "If I can find another hand or two, and if we work all weekend, I might have them penned by Wednesday. Of course, there's no guarantee I can find good cowboys on short notice. There's also a chance we miss a few strays."

Patrick spoke up. "That's no problem. In fact, several cattle on the land will allow us to claim an agricultural exemption until we develop it. The surveyors are out there now. I've given them instructions not to get in your way."

Heather expected Steve to say something about starting work before he'd formally awarded the land to Mae, but he remained silent.

"Steve," said Patrick. "The two senior partners in our law firm have offered to help with title transfers."

It took all the self-control Heather possessed to keep from releasing a tactless refusal to Patrick's offer.

Steve spoke while she was forming her rejection. "That's very generous. I plan on getting the family together one last time Monday afternoon. I'll reread the entire will, make my last awards of the land and Heather will distribute the settlement checks for the life insurance policies."

From over Heather's shoulder, she heard a man's voice. The jovial words could only belong to Roy. "Did someone say we're having a family reunion? I'll bring the old-style lawn darts. The way Mae's luck is running, she'll eliminate all three of us and rake in the whole enchilada."

It occurred to Heather that Roy had a way of expressing gallows humor that made it hard not to smile. She turned to face him. "One final meeting on Monday. The insurance company said the checks will arrive that morning."

"Meeting at the hotel at five," added Steve. "I've arranged for us to be in the Live Oak room."

Roy looked at Mae. "Tie the knot yet?"

"Tomorrow morning." A smile that didn't reach Mae's eyes accompanied the curt reply that didn't include an invitation.

"Try getting someone who doesn't tie a slip-knot this time."

"Run along, Roy. The grownups are talking."

Roy responded with a boisterous laugh and walked away.

Everyone turned to leave when Heather spotted Sue Ann and motioned for her to join them. Instead of waiting for her, Mae took Patrick by the arm and pulled him away. Heather concluded that what Mae lacked in manners she made up for with a nasty personality.

The smile on Sue Ann's face told Heather that her sister's snub didn't bother her in the least.

Steve must have caught Sue Ann's scent. "How are you holding up with Grant in jail?"

"The hens laid two more eggs than usual, there's fresh tomatoes and the kids slept through the night. I think everyone is enjoying the peace now that Grant's not around."

Rance spoke up. "Why don't you and the kids come live with me once I get a new place?"

Sue Ann's eyebrows arched. "Where?"

He shrugged. "Somewhere between I-35 and I-45 and not too far from A&M. I'm looking for several hundred acres with good land and water. I think a million dollars and the money from the sale of the cattle will get us started."

Sue Ann looked at Heather. "Is there enough money for me and the kids to build a house? I don't want Rance to feel crowded."

Heather had to clear her throat before she answered. "You have plenty to build a house, and a barn for Buttercup, and a chicken coop."

Rance nudged his head toward the door. "Come on, Sue Ann. Let's get inside. I'll show you some places I found online later. One already has a four-bedroom house and a mother-in-law house in the back. That bungalow is all I'll need."

"Before you go," said Heather, "I have something for Sue Ann." She pulled a stack of Visa gift cards from her purse. "There's ten of these and they have a thousand dollars credit on each one. Buy whatever you need for yourself and the kids until we work out how much you'll be getting from the investments I'll make for you."

Rance looked skeptical, so Heather included him. "I expect

you to help us this coming week in deciding how to allocate her funds."

He agreed, and the two youngest siblings walked ahead. Heather noted their differences. He was dark and lean. Sue Ann tended toward a fuller figure, light hair and fair skin.

"Are we going to stand in the heat all day?" asked Steve.

"I was giving them some space," said Heather.

"You can't fool me. I heard you digging in your purse for a tissue."

"Guilty as charged, and glad of it. It's not every murder case I get to cry for the right reason."

Steve reached out his hand and Heather placed it on her shoulder as he said, "Let's hope we both aren't crying before this is over. We're heading into the home stretch and things may get rocky."

As they reached the door, cool air met them, and so did Angelina. "Thank you for coming, Mr. Smiley. And you too, Ms. McBlythe."

Steve leaned toward Angelina's voice and whispered, "Take us away from all these people."

Angelina led the way down a hallway opposite the crowd's direction. Halfway down, they slipped into a room filled with rows of empty caskets, their lids open and price tags displayed.

"No one can hear us in here," said Angelina. "I wanted to tell you I've been looking everywhere for what you wanted and I can't find it."

"Did you ask your mother?"

"She says it might be in her safe deposit box at the bank. We can't get to it until Monday."

Steve rubbed his chin. "That will cut it close. If worse comes to worst, I'll postpone the final meeting until we're sure." He pointed to the door. "You need to be with your mother. Are we still on for tomorrow morning?"

"Ten o'clock." Angelica stopped at the door. "We'll have coffee and Mama's special pumpkin cream cheese empanadas."

Heather tented her hand on her hips after the door closed, leaving them in a room of caskets. "When were you going to tell me about all the things you did while I was in Montana?"

"Don't blame me. Flying off in the middle of a case wasn't the deal we had. You agreed to drop everything whenever we have a case to work. If that wasn't bad enough, you got tanked and had to nurse a hangover. That lost another half a day. You can't blame me for making unilateral decisions if you're off doing your own thing."

Heather looked around the room. A strange place for a business meeting, but Steve was right. Regardless, he wouldn't like it if she didn't put up a defense. "You're not fooling me. You always keep something back so you can amaze everyone when you unravel the crimes."

He chuckled. "That's better. Let's pay our respects to Hector and I'll bring you up to speed on most everything on our way back to the hotel."

"Most everything? That means you'll be holding out on me."

"Sure. I'm not the only one who hasn't laid all my cards on the table. You haven't told me all you know."

"I certainly have."

He shook his head. "What did you find in the box of documents that Sue Ann gave you?"

"Nothing of value. Ranch receipts. Bank statements. Some family photos and the marriage license for Charley and the kids' mother, Pearl."

"See," said Steve. "You have your little secrets, too. I'm not complaining. Just stating a fact."

"Nothing was important," said Heather. She knew she'd made a mistake, so she cut him off. "I know what you're going to say: 'Everything is important in a murder case.'"

He nodded. "How many years passed between the time Charley married and Mae was born?"

Heather had to think for a minute to get the timeline straight. "Nine years."

Steve smiled. "That's important. I'll tell you why after the graveside service. I need you to tell me if Mae and Patrick go to it." He stopped. "Come to think of it, look for them in the service we're almost late for. I bet they've already left."

She was glad she didn't take the bet. Mae and Patrick must have accomplished what they desired by speaking to Rance and had no intention of attending the funeral. The service passed without drama until Rance stood to speak. His heartfelt eulogy left tissues shredded and handkerchiefs damp.

24

Saturday morning began without a cloud daring to mar the clean canvas of a summer sky. It would be another hot Texas day, with the resort's swimming pool frothing with children, parents and more seasoned guests. Heather dismissed the thought as she drove northwest to Llano, the diminutive county seat and home of Anna and her daughter, Angelina. She nuzzled the rental close to the back bumper of Angelina's car and asked, "How sure are you of this theory?"

Steve released his seatbelt. "About seventy-five percent. I'm hoping to get it up to ninety-five percent this morning."

Angelina had the front door open before they climbed onto the porch. "Come in. Coffee and empanadas are waiting for you. Would you rather eat at the table or in the living room?"

"A table works best for me," said Steve. "I have a habit of wearing as much food as I eat."

The kitchen and dining room were one and the same. A retro table with chrome legs and padded chrome chairs fit snug in an alcove, providing a cozy place for mother and daughter to partake of their meals. Steve moaned in delight at the first bite of his baked treat that looked like a fried pie.

Heather had to admit, the spicy pumpkin with cream cheese filling and light crust had her taste buds dancing. She wished she'd not eaten breakfast so she could have a second one, like Steve did.

Once Angelina cleared the dishes, Steve cracked open the lid to his proverbial box of questions.

"Mrs. Perez—"

She cut him off. "I insist you call me Anna."

"Only if you call me Steve."

With the pact formed, Steve continued. "Angelina told us you haven't been able to find the document we're looking for."

"It's not here. The longer I think about it, the more convinced I am that Mother's marriage license is in the safe deposit box along with mine."

"How old was she when she married Hector?"

"Almost nineteen. I followed Mama's footsteps and married Angelina's father right after high school."

Steve always nodded at the right times to communicate he understood and to encourage complete answers. "Tell me about your mother. Describe her to me."

"She was a beautiful woman with classic black hair and eyes the color of dark chocolate. She loved to dance. I can still see her spin in a circle and her skirt flare. She danced with such grace, almost like she floated. There was an excitement about her that didn't fit the monotony of ranch life. But then, I was nine when she died, so schoolgirl fantasies may taint my image of her."

"How long did you live on the ranch?"

Anna shook her head. "Mama and I never did. Hector, my papa, would come into town once a week and give Mama money. We didn't go to the ranch when I was little."

"Why not?"

Her shoulders rose and fell. "I'm not sure. They never had a cross word that I heard, but they never talked long, either."

Heather entered the conversation and hoped the question didn't sound too harsh. "How did your mother die?"

Angelina squirmed in her seat. The question obviously hit a nerve.

Anna pursed her lips, but then sighed and spoke in halting phrases that grew stronger the longer she spoke. "It was a long time ago. I still miss her. She died in childbirth, as did the baby." She paused and gave Heather a look that told her there was much more to the story. "At least, that's the official story. I find it hard to believe."

"Why?"

"Mama wasn't showing when she went to Austin by herself. That was over forty years ago. Medical care back then wasn't what it is today, but it was good. Babies and mothers didn't both die in the first trimester because of a miscarriage. She came home sick and depressed. She refused to go to the local doctor until it was too late."

Steve changed the subject, but only slightly. "Anna, tell me about your relationship with Hector. Did he want you to come live on the ranch with him after your mother died?"

"He was a good provider and my aunt needed the money. It made more sense that I live with her in town."

Heather clarified. "Was your aunt you mother's sister or Hector's?"

"Mama's. If Hector had any brothers or sisters, he never mentioned them."

"He sounds like a man of mystery," said Steve in a joking way.

Angelina jumped in. "He never talked about himself, and if he did, it wasn't necessarily the truth. Not that he was devious, he made a game of it. Every time I asked him where he was born, he'd give me a different town or country and then he'd laugh."

Steve reached for his cane, a sure sign he'd heard all he

needed, but then he stopped short of rising. "One more thing for each of you. Have you ever had a run in with any of Charley Voss's children?"

"Not me," said Angelina. "Unless you count Rance telling me to be more careful when I came to visit Grandpa. I thought he was bossy, but we played together and we'd go swimming. He's not so bad now that I'm out of college and working."

"Papa never wanted me to come to the ranch," said Anna. "He didn't let Angelina come out until she was older. She went every week or two."

"How old was she?"

"Ten," said Anna. "I remember because it was after Charley's father died. Mr. Charley was real nice to me and Angelina after that."

Steve thanked them again for the coffee and didn't turn down two empanadas to take with them. Heather expressed her appreciation. She planned to eat one of the pastries on the trip back to the resort. After all, Steve didn't need two.

Angelina followed them to the front porch.

"Be sure your mother gets that marriage certificate out of the safe deposit box on Monday. Also, get birth certificates for both of you," said Heather.

Angelina nodded but said, "You haven't told me why those are so important."

Steve faced her. "I can't tell you yet, and the less I say today, the better. Heather and I both have your phone number. Is there any way you can get your mother out of the house today?"

"We have an appointment to pick out a gravestone this afternoon. Why do we need to be out of the house?"

"Do you have to be with her this afternoon?"

"I don't want her going alone."

"After we leave, I want you to pack enough clothes for you and your mom to stay somewhere else for at least two nights.

Also, if there's any important papers or documents in the house, put them in the trunk of your car."

Angelina's eyes opened wide. "You sound serious, Mr. Smiley. Are we safe?"

"You should be if we prepare properly. I'll call you later today."

He turned to face the street. "Let's go." Halfway to the car he asked, "Have you ever crashed a wedding?"

HEATHER EXITED HER ROOM AFTER REWORKING HER MAKEUP AND putting on something more appropriate for a wedding reception than the walking shorts and polo shirt she'd worn to see Anna and Angelina. She smoothed the aqua-marine skirt and slipped the matching jacket over a white silk blouse. Her image rose three full inches in the mirror when she put on black heels.

Steve was waiting for her knock on his door. He spoke as soon as he verified no one could hear him. "The sheriff called me back and agreed to my plan. He's not comfortable with Anna and Angelina staying in Llano tonight, either. As soon as we're finished here, we need to pick them up. I've arranged for them to share a room down the hall from us."

"Are they all right with staying in their room for two days?"

"This will be the last place anyone will expect them to be, especially if you take them shopping."

"What about the stakeout tonight and tomorrow night?"

"Marvin's in charge of it. The sheriff will be around in case he can't handle it."

The elevator arrived and whisked them to the lobby. Heather led him down a hallway to an open door and peeked in. "The ceremony's over. About twenty-five people are milling around on the patio, drinking champagne and eating wedding cake."

Steve stopped and spoke in his deadpan voice. "Stay out of the bubbly. Remember what happened last time."

"You'll look funny walking around with your cane broken in half and a lump on your head."

"Tell me what you see," said Steve as they approached a sliding door leading to an outdoor shaded patio.

Heather took in the view. "There's a table with jumbo shrimp, various finger foods, and what's left of a small wedding cake. A server is doing a brisk business keeping champagne glasses full. It looks like the architect designing the new resort brought his wife. The civil engineer and his wife are with them. Another huddle is a group of eight men and women, maybe from the law office. They're pretty chummy. Mae's standing with a third group of women. I bet they're her real estate buddies. Now Mae's making the rounds, flashing her newest diamond. The legal group is dividing into two groups. One looks like support staff. The other is Sid and Sydney Walsh, Patrick and that woman named Cindy with the eyes I'd kill for."

"I get the picture."

A wave of hot air hit Heather when she pulled open the sliding door. It occurred to her that the reception wouldn't last long. They were going through the allotted bottles of chilled champagne and the men were shedding their jackets. It was fast becoming a day to stay in chilled air unless you were wearing a bathing suit.

Mae spotted them and approached with a scowl. "What are you two doing here?"

Steve played off the challenge with a laugh. "Congratulations, Mae. I smelled free food and couldn't help myself." Steve's first laugh was nothing compared to the second.

"Just kidding," Steve said as a follow up. "We already ate, I don't drink champagne and Heather's on the wagon until the judge tells her she can take off her ankle bracelet."

Mae looked down to see nothing but tanned legs and black shoes.

Whatever it was, Mae found something funny. People looked their way when Mae's donkey bray laugh cut across the patio. She drained her glass. "You know, Mr. Smiley. You're not too bad when you stop being such a stuffed-shirt."

"Seriously, Mae," said Heather. "We came to wish you all the best."

What Heather didn't say was that Mae might need the best divorce lawyer she could afford in the not-too-distant future.

Mae grabbed another glass from a passing tray. She switched hands to make sure her new ring sparked whenever she took a sip. "Well, I must mingle. Have something to eat."

Patrick Shaw filled the void Mae left. "I didn't expect to see either of you two here. There isn't anything wrong, is there?"

Heather noticed beads of sweat on his brow and lip but refrained from answering him with a question of her own. Instead, she waved a dismissive hand. "Nothing wrong. We came to wish the happy couple a long and prosperous life."

"Anything new on the murder case?"

"Which one?" asked Steve.

"Huh? Oh, yeah. I forgot about Charley Voss."

"How could you forget him?" asked Steve. "If it weren't for Charley dying, you wouldn't be here."

Patrick's smile retreated. "Is that a veiled accusation?"

"Should it be?"

Patrick took a step back. "Find your way out. I don't remember Mae putting you on the guest list."

"Don't worry," said Heather. "We're not eating or drinking. It's a good thing you're bringing home this deal for your senior partners. Mae has expensive tastes, and I understand she only sold six houses last year, even in a hot market."

Patrick stuttered something unintelligible and went to Mae's side.

"Let's get out of the heat," said Steve. "We can catch Sid and Sydney as they leave."

Before they could turn, Mae shouted, "We're going to the condo to continue the party. Everyone's invited. Give us a few minutes to freshen up." She pointed to the table. "Someone bring the champagne."

Heather led Steve out of the way as Mae and Patrick sped past on their way to their new life together. Heather whispered, "Patrick wasn't smiling."

Steve said, "I'd slash my wrists, drink poison, and hang myself if I were him."

Heather was thankful the crowd had consumed enough champagne that their decibel level rose to the point they didn't hear her laugh. She cleared her throat when a woman stared at her. "Here comes Sid and Sydney."

"Good," said Steve in a soft tone. "We won't have to chase them down."

"Ah, Mr. Smiley and Ms. McBlythe," said Sid. "I'm glad you're here. Do you mind if we step out of the sauna and find a cool spot to talk?"

"Music to my ears," said Steve. "Let's find another room that's more private."

Sydney spoke next. "Good idea. I have a feeling everyone will grab two glasses of wine and come in here for relief before they go to the condo."

Heather led the way to the smaller of the two rooms she and Steve used to discuss the will with the Voss children.

Sid led things off. "I was wondering what time you wanted to meet tomorrow to go over the property deeds. I understand not all are in Llano County?"

"Before we get into that," said Steve, "I need to tell you

there's been a development. It's come to our attention that a subsequent claim on the property may be made."

The muscles in Sid's jaw flexed. His attorney wife and business partner kept a stone face and issued a demand. "Explain."

Heather responded. "Charley Voss may have been married prior to his marriage to the mother of the Voss children. If that's true, then we'll do more investigating to see if they conceived a child."

Sydney took in a deep breath. "That's a big if. Who is this mystery wife?"

"It wouldn't be prudent to say until we know for sure," said Steve.

Heather added. "We haven't even established that Charley married prior to his marriage to Pearl. I don't think Mae and Patrick have anything to worry about."

Steve took his turn. "Please don't mention it to Mae and Patrick since they're on their honeymoon. We should have it straightened out by Monday afternoon, if the rumor turns out to be false."

Sid unclenched his teeth. "This is absurd. Do you have any idea how much our firm has already invested?"

Sydney cut him off. "A two-day delay won't be a problem. After that, we'll do what's necessary to protect Mae and Patrick."

Steve nodded with vigor. "I don't blame you one bit. Believe me, this would be a lot easier on us if this so-called heir hadn't popped up. We were both police detectives and we can tell a bogus lead when we see one." He paused, "Or, in my case, when I hear one."

Steve stuck out his hand to Sid. "Come to the meeting Monday."

Heather added, "I'll turn over all the property records to you as soon as Steve tells me his decision is final. The meeting will be at five o'clock sharp in the same room Mae and Patrick exchanged vows."

Sid grabbed Steve's hand and squeezed it harder than necessary. "At five-thirty Monday, I'd better be walking out of here with a box of deeds."

Sydney pulled her husband away and nodded a salutation.

Steve rubbed his hand after the door closed. "Let's give them enough time for the valet to bring their car around. Watch to see which way they turn out of the hotel entrance."

Heather didn't need to wait long. Sid and Sydney were in the driveway pacing when Heather placed Steve at a table in front of the coffee shop. She peeked often enough to track them, but not so often they'd notice her. She hadn't practiced tailing someone in quite a while, but this was simple. Simple, until a black SUV from the airport pulled in front of the hotel. She recognized the occupant of the back seat as soon as she stepped out. The equally familiar figure of a tall man in his early sixties joined the woman and stepped toward the sliding doors.

"Holy smoke," said Heather.

"What is it?"

"My parents are here."

"Did you know they were coming?"

"Of course not."

"Do you still have eyes on Sid and Sydney?"

"Sorry, I lost concentration. I'll ask the valet."

"Don't worry. It's being taken care of."

Heather looked down to make sure she still looked presentable. Why did her father always make her nervous?

Steve was on his feet before she realized he'd risen. "Quit fussing. You look fine. Stand up straight and walk like you own the place."

"Not this one," said Heather. "Father might if he likes it and can get it at a good price. I should do some research on it tonight."

Steve grabbed her by the arm. "Have you already forgotten? You're working with me until this case is over. Understand?"

She shook herself back into detective mode. "Understand, partner. Are you ready to face them?"

"I'll picture them as two cuddly Teddy bears. It's one advantage of being blind. I can make people look like anything I want them to be. What time is it?"

"Three-thirty."

"Make introductions and leave them to me. You need to pick up Anna and Angelina."

"But—"

"But nothing. I'll have Papa and Mama Bear eating out of my hand by the time you get back. What time do they like to eat supper?"

"Seven sharp."

"I'll have a table for four reserved. Wear your pearls. Jack says they make you look fabulous."

"Holy, holy smoke. I forgot Jack's coming tomorrow. How am I going to juggle a murder investigation, my parents and my boyfriend all at the same time?"

Steve didn't answer.

25

Looking like scared mice, Anna and Angelina Perez opened the door to their room. Despite the quality clothes Heather bought them in the gift shop, they fidgeted with their hair and couldn't look her in the eye. Heather marched them back into the room for a pep talk. "What's wrong?"

Anna spoke first. "I'm nervous and it's not just because someone may want to harm us. We don't belong here."

Angelina took her turn. "I went to a sorority rush party my second semester in college. Those snobby girls took one look at me and gave me the cold shoulder. I made the fashion mistake of not wearing designer jeans. That's all it took for me to decide that world wasn't for me." She paused. "Not that we're not grateful for everything you've done for us."

Heather nodded she understood their concerns. "That's why we want you here. You'll hide in plain sight."

Anna continued to wring her hands. "I don't know how to act when we go to that fancy restaurant downstairs."

"It's easy," said Heather. "Pretend everyone is a Teddy bear. When you order, say, you'll have the chicken or fish or steak.

The server will compliment you on your choice. Remember that everything is charged to the room. Don't worry about a tip, they'll add it on."

Heather looked them over. "You'll do great if you stand up straight with shoulders back and walk with your chin up. Put your sunglasses on and don't take them off until you get to the restaurant. They keep the lights low in there and we don't want you to trip. Questions?"

Both women wagged their heads.

Heather nodded and opened the door. "We'll stop at Steve's room." She continued the instructions as they walked down the hall. "He and I will get in the elevator first. Pretend you don't know us if anyone else gets on. We'll follow you to the restaurant and I'll be watching to see you leave. I'll be behind you all the way back to your room."

On the elevator ride down, Steve said, "If you two look half as good as you smell, we may have made a mistake in letting you out of your room. Men will want to take you dancing tonight."

"Can we?" asked Angelina.

Anna added, "Not me. Angelina dances like her grandmother. I'm a hazard to men's feet."

Heather looked at them and frowned. "There'll be time for fun later. Right now, everyone's job is to keep you two safe."

Angelina looked down. "You're right."

The elevator dinged, and the door opened. Heather gave last second instructions. "Shoulder's back and imagine everyone's a Teddy bear."

Steve whispered as they lagged in the hallway. "How do they look?"

"Like they flew in on a private jet."

"Good. I knew they'd be nervous, but I didn't want them caged up all weekend."

They arrived at J's Restaurant and Bar at fifteen minutes

before seven. Steve planned it that way so Anna and Angelina would be seated before the Bostonians arrived. Heather settled in a chair that gave her a view of her two charges while also allowing her to see any threat approach.

"Take your own advice," said Steve. "Everyone here is a stuffed animal. That includes your father."

Heather sensed the tension ease from her shoulders as soon as she let them drop.

Anna and Angelina were eating their salads when Allister McBlythe IV and Rebecca McBlythe entered the restaurant. As always, her father wore a dark suit with a burgundy tie. Her mother surprised her by wearing dress slacks and a linen jacket. Also, she'd cut her hair since Heather last saw her at Christmas.

They approached the table. "Mother. Father. I'm glad you were able to join us."

Steve continued to break the ice by asking, "Were you able to get in a nap, Rebecca?"

"A short one. It was a little hard to sleep with Al's incessant jabbering on the phone."

"I was in the next room," he said in his defense. "Ever since that article came out about the gold mine, I've been doing damage control. I should have listened to Heather."

"Yes dear, you should have."

It was the first time Heather had ever heard her father come close to an apology. Something was different about her mother, too. The haircut made her look younger and more alive. And slacks instead of a dress at dinner? Unusual, to say the least.

Heather's mother reached out and took her hand. "Al told me you're working on a case here at the hotel. How exciting!"

Heather knew her father's gaze would bore into her, so she looked only at her mother. "Part of it has been taking place here at the hotel, but the deaths occurred at a ranch in the area. I'm also helping Steve with the inheritance that's tied to the deaths." She purposefully said *deaths* instead of *murders.*

"Are you making progress?" asked her father.

Steve answered for her. "We should have everything wrapped up in a couple of days. Of course, we act in coordination with law enforcement. That keeps us out of harm's way."

"Don't be so modest," said Heather's father. "I can tell a man who makes things happen when I meet one. As for Heather, she's always been prone to run headlong into danger."

"She takes after you," said Steve.

Heather noticed the look on her father's face that mixed puzzlement with incredulity.

"Me? I don't chase after killers."

Steve nodded in agreement. "True, but you swim with the biggest sharks in the financial world every day. I'd say Heather's jobs in law enforcement, and now working with me, are tame compared to what you do."

"He's right, Father," said Heather. "I've been trying to copy you and it's much harder than I ever imagined. Knowing that a decision I make could put a thousand people out of work, or possibly create as many jobs, keeps me awake at night."

Her father's business face seemed to crack. "You have an interesting perspective on business. Do you really think about gains and losses in terms of people and their jobs?"

Heather dipped her head. "Not as much as I should, but yes, I do."

The server arrived to take orders, putting conversation on hold. Heather played it safe and ordered a salad. She wasn't sure how her father would steer the conversation and things might get testy. They had a long history of disagreements, many times at the dinner table.

Silence fell over the table until Heather's mother lifted her chin and said, "Al. It's time for your *mia culpa.*"

"I suppose it is." Her father cleared his throat and looked

Heather straight on. "I came to apologize to you. You were right about the gold mine. I should have listened to you and taken my time in purchasing it. I thought I was too old to get gold fever, but apparently there's no fool like an old one."

Heather didn't know how to respond, so she didn't.

"Go on," said her mother in a firm tone. "Tell her everything."

"Webster turned in his resignation after I signed the contract."

Heather sighed. "Steve told me he would."

Her father sat with mouth hinged open. He cast his gaze to Heather and then to Steve. "How did you know?"

Steve placed his palms on the table. "The only thing I know about gold is there's two crowns on the bottom molars of my teeth, but I like to think I know something about how people act. Heather told me how close you were to Webster. How you trusted him. It must have been a shock when you took the responsibility for the gold mine from him and gave the project to your daughter. Not only that, you gave her carte blanch to decide how much to pay for the acquisition and how to structure the deal. Webster realized then the future didn't include him at the helm of the company. I worked enough homicide cases to know that hurting people strike back at those who hurt them."

Heather joined in. "At Steve's suggestion, I did some checking on Webster after you signed the contract. Do you know who he's working for now?"

Her father shook his head. It was as if the words couldn't form in his mouth.

Steve took over. "I had my suspicions of what was going on when Heather said Webster told you there was another company ready to make an offer. Has that company approached you since the story came out in the papers?"

"I've had several companies make inquiries. The numbers

they're talking about are hundreds of millions less than what we paid, but the one Webster told me about is the most attractive."

Heather leaned forward. "That's wonderful, Father."

"How could selling for less than half be wonderful?"

"Well... you don't need to sell. You can keep it a while. At least let the smoke clear before selling. If you sell now, you'll be playing into his hands. Who do you think fed the story to the newspapers?"

Steve leaned back. "Webster not only double-crossed you, I think he intends to do a triple cross. If you sell, the company that will put in the highest bid on the mine will be the one he's working with now. The other companies are a smokescreen."

"Father," said Heather. "There's nothing wrong with the mine. The original drill holes show a good supply of already discovered gold and legitimate veins of untapped ore. It's apparent Webster made a side deal with the mine owners that they'd get full price, plus save money, for slow production. The reduced mining saved them money and added validity to the newspaper stories."

Her father's eyes opened wide. "Are you sure?"

"Think about it, Father. The reduction in production didn't begin until you considered handing over the purchase of the mine to me. Webster went to the people you bought the mine from and told them how to play the deal."

A light bulb came on in her father's eyes. "Of course. It all makes sense."

"Exactly," said Steve. "Then Webster fed a false story to the press."

Heather added the final bit of information. "All the while, he gave the data my team developed to the company he's working for now. I also found out he's been going long on stock futures for his new company. In fact, he's leveraged up to his eyes."

"How do you know that?"

Heather and Steve both laughed.

"You're forgetting, Heather's the best detective I've ever worked with," said Steve.

"Speaking of," said Heather. "It appears our friends have finished their meal. I need to get them back to their room."

Heather's mother knitted her eyebrows together. "Are you two working the case now?"

"We are," said Heather. "We believe those two women to your left are in danger. We brought them to the resort so I could keep an eye on them."

"I feel like I'm in a movie."

"When they leave, I'll follow them to their room. Do you want to come with me?"

"I most certainly do."

"Now, Rebecca," said Heather's father. "Is that wise?"

"Don't be such a kill-joy. Take off that silly tie and relax."

"They'll be fine," said Steve. "Heather's an excellent shot."

Her father sat upright. "She's armed? Is that legal?"

"It is in Texas," said Heather. "Concealed carry is wonderful."

She glanced and nodded to Anna and Angelina. "Wait till I get up, Mother. We'll pretend we don't know them and follow a discrete distance behind, then close the gap at the last minute and get on the elevator with them. I'll check out their room, then you and I will come back and enjoy a nice dinner."

"Wait," said her father. "I... I don't know how to thank you."

Heather stood, went to her father and bent down to give him a kiss on his cheek and a hug. "Give me back that kiss and hug now and then. That's all I ever wanted from you."

"It's a deal."

Arm in arm, Heather walked with her mother out of the restaurant. They delivered Anna and Angelina without incident and started back toward the elevator, but Heather's mother had other ideas. "Is your room nearby?"

"Right down the hall. Why?"

"We need to have a mother-daughter talk."

"Pardon, the mess, Mother." Heather cleared a chair and sat on the side of the bed. What's on your mind?"

Her mother looked away at first, but her gaze came back, complete with cloudy eyes. "I promised myself I wouldn't cry. Now look at me."

"What's wrong, Mother? Are you ill? Is it Father?"

Her mother waved a hand to reject her guesses. "We're both fine physically, but your father made a real hash out of the gold deal. He's trying to play it off, but tonight is the first time he's relaxed since last fall."

Heather considered what had been said and what was left unsaid. "That's when he put me in charge of it."

Her mother nodded. "I need to tell you about me and your father."

Heather swallowed. "You don't have to."

"Yes, I do. Our marriage began as more of a merger than anything that resembled love. Two Boston families joined forces to make sure the collective fortunes grew to new heights. A form of love came later, but it still lacks the depth I believe you're looking for."

"What are you saying, Mother?"

She stood, walked to the window and looked out. "I'm saying, don't let your father smother you. Life is short and much of mine has passed doing things that sucked more out of me than I knew."

Heather nodded. "Does Father know you were going to have this conversation with me?"

Her mother spun around and laughed. "Heaven's no. He's only here under duress. I told him I'd demand he sell my stocks and bonds if he didn't come and apologize to you. Do you realize he never took me on a honeymoon, let alone a vacation? All the travel I did with him was on business."

Heather hung her head. "I'm sorry. I had no idea it was such an unhappy marriage."

Her mother came to her, kneeled down and took her hands. "I didn't say it was unhappy. It's different, yes, but not unhappy." She stood. "And I'm committed to making it better with the time we have left together."

"What can I do to help?"

"That's hard to answer. Your father isn't going to change all his spots, but if we work together, we can teach him there's more to living than meetings and mergers. I think he needs someone to show him how to have fun. That's why I forced him to come here."

Heather rose and smiled. "I have two men in my life that I'll enlist to help."

They hugged and Heather left the room with a new spring in her step. She had the gold crisis behind her and Jack would arrive tomorrow. Business was one thing, a romantic relationship between the heir to her father's fortune and a lowly Texas attorney was something else. How would her father react? How do you get a stodgy businessman to have fun?

26

First light brought Heather out of a deep and pleasant night's sleep. Her mind filled as a flurry of thoughts crowded each other, seeking to be the first thing for her to consider. She settled on thinking about her parents, especially her father. The only place she could remember him not wearing a dark jacket and a burgundy tie was when he went sailing. No, that wasn't right. She'd seen photos of him when he was an undergrad at Harvard, standing by his polo pony, dressed like all the other team members. He'd lost that smile in the forty-plus years of high stakes business.

Last night he rediscovered it and she saw a side of him she didn't know existed. He laughed at Steve's corny jokes and made pleasant conversation with both of them. He heeded her mother's command to remove his tie, and his coat followed. She'd never seen him so relaxed.

"Jack," she spoke his name out loud. He'd arrive today. She spoke to the air and giggled. "How will he respond when I introduce him to my parents?"

Throwing back the sheet and duvet, she pointed her toes and reached toward the ceiling with wiggling fingers. Her stretch reminded her of her cat, Max, and the way he reached with his front paws after a nap. He'd be aloof when she came home, but it wouldn't take long before he made figure eights between her legs.

"Get up," she said to herself. "To the fitness center with you."

While brushing her teeth, she considered checking in with Steve but decided against it. His sleeping patterns were haphazard. A world without light made it difficult for him to get on a schedule.

Her thoughts then went to Sue Ann and the promise to develop a financial investment plan for her and her children. She'd work on that this morning and travel to Sue Ann's home around noon for signatures. With luck, she'd score another piece of rhubarb pie and a glass of real milk.

Coming full circle, she thought again about her father and their improved relationship. She'd meet him for breakfast and ask his advice on strategies for Sue Ann. It would be just the two of them. Mother preferred to start her days slow and ordered breakfast from room service when she traveled.

The cell phone came alive. "Good morning, Steve. You're up early."

"I wanted to let you know that nothing happened at Anna and Angelina's house last night."

Heather's thoughts shifted again to the room three doors down. "Is that good or bad?"

"Neither, unless you're Marvin Goodnight or the deputies he had staked out watching the home. All it means is they'll continue surveillance all day and tonight."

"I'm going to see Sue Ann around noon. Do you want to go with me?"

The pause didn't last long. "I'll pass. Didn't sleep very well last night. I've been thinking about what could go wrong. This may be unnecessary, but why don't you trade rooms with Anna and Angelina this morning?"

"Good idea." She stepped to the mirror and put her hair in a ponytail while she continued the conversation. "I'll wait until I get back from the fitness center. It's still too early to be bothering them. Anything else?"

Steve issued a yawn before he could put words to his reply. "That's what kept me from sleeping last night. It makes me nervous when things are going the way I think they should."

"Get some sleep." She disconnected the call, grabbed her room key and stepped to the door. There was so much good going on in her life, she determined Steve's hyper-vigilance wouldn't spoil her day.

THE TRIP THROUGH THE FAST-EXPANDING CITY OF MARBLE FALLS gave Heather the opportunity to consider what she'd wear when Jack arrived. He called when she and her father were putting the finishing touches on an investment portfolio for Sue Ann. It had been another great visit with her father, and she counted it a blessing to have longstanding friction out of her life. She and Steve helped her father through a financial storm. He accepted her as a competent businesswoman and a grown daughter he wanted to spend time with. Life was good.

Still, it seemed strange not having to live up to an unspoken expectation of excellence. She put the thought aside, turned on the radio to an oldies station and sang along with tunes popular when her mother was in finishing school. Lost in pleasant thoughts, she pulled through the open gate of Sue Ann's mini-farm. The tires of the rental crunched over the gravel drive when she pulled up in front of the house. She was grateful she didn't have to worry about Grant being here.

The eldest girl met Heather with the screen door opened wide. "Hello, Ms. McBlythe. Mama's in the kitchen. Is it true we're going to be movin' and livin' with Uncle Rance?"

"That's the plan. Your grandpa left your mother and Uncle Rance well provided for."

The girl's gap-tooth smile spoke louder than words. She walked Heather through the living room and into the kitchen. The youngest girl brought her dishes to the sink. Whatever she'd eaten, there wasn't a crumb or smudge left on the plate. "That was good ham and cheese, Mama. What'd you call that fancy bread?"

"A croissant," said Sue Ann. "Rinse your plate and glass before you go play. You girls can wash and dry later. Miss Heather and I have business to tend to."

"We'll be with the boys by the river."

The back screen door slammed as the sisters ran with abandon. "They're full of energy today," said Heather.

"It's the move that's got 'em so excited. I told 'em they could have their pick of animals to raise. They all chose something different: chickens, horses, a steer for beef and the little one wants to raise a show lamb."

"You're doing a wonderful job raising them."

"It'll be easier without their father around."

Heather noticed Sue Ann had distanced herself from Grant by referring to him as the children's father. She placed her satchel on the table. "I have documents for you to sign, and I'll go over an investment portfolio with you. I need to tell you up front that all investments come with risk, but I consulted a true expert and this plan should get you off to a solid start. It's diversified into four asset classes and—"

A quick glance up from the papers connected with Sue Ann's blank stare. "You can keep talkin' if you want to, but I don't understand what you're saying. Tell me where to sign. I trust you."

Heather intended to go into detail, but closed the business by handing Sue Ann a pen and pointing to the signature line on a contract. There are times when you trust others and move on.

Heather straightened the pages and shoved them back in her satchel. She then looked at the pie safe. "Any more rhubarb?"

Sue Ann was already moving in that direction when Heather's gaze locked on the safe. "How does a slice of peach pie sound? They're fresh from the tree this morning. I hope it's cooled enough to set up."

Heather heard a floorboard squeak in the living room. Sue Ann's gaze changed from a smile to abject fear. "You're supposed to be in jail." She took steps backward until she could go no further.

"Well, I ain't," said Grant. His next words came out with a sneer. "No thanks to you."

Heather tried to rise, but Grant's meaty hand on her shoulder pushed her down.

She spun in her chair, intending to grab his finger and wrench it back if he tried to push her down again. She never got the chance. As soon as she spun, he cuffed her on the mouth with the back of his fist. Her head snapped back and her body followed all the way to the floor.

"Leave her alone!" shouted Sue Ann.

Heather saw pinpoints of light, like she was looking into a night sky. Through blurry vision she saw Grant move toward Sue Ann. "Why didn't you get me out of jail?"

Heather shook her head and wiped blood from her mouth. She tried to get up, but the force of the blow left her mind in a fog and her legs entangled in the chair.

Through the mist of semi-consciousness, she saw Grant ball a fist and bury it in Sue Ann's belly. He then grabbed her by the wrist and pulled. She stumbled but didn't fall. He let go of her wrist and grabbed a fist full of her hair.

Her breath coming in quick gasps, Sue Ann took stumbling

steps as he dragged her toward the living room. He stopped in the doorway and lifted her head by yanking upward. The sound of a fist striking flesh came next.

Heather kicked the chair out of the way and rolled over on her hands and knees. Out of the corner of her eye, she saw Grant rush toward her. She knew what was coming, but impaired reflexes wouldn't allow her to block the kick. It struck the lower part of her ribs and lifted her off the ground. The world went black.

THE SENSATION OF SOMETHING COOL ON HER FOREHEAD BROUGHT her back from wherever she'd been and into a world filled with pain. Looking down on her were all four children. She struggled to rise, but the room and the faces spun so fast she had to close her eyes. It sounded like someone else's voice when she heard herself say, "Call the police."

"We can't," said the oldest boy. "Dad pulled the phone cord out of the wall."

"Back pocket of my jeans," said Heather. "Cell phone."

He nodded.

Pain raced through her when he moved her hip to get at the phone. It subsided some when she went back to the original position. She fought to keep the world from going black again and said, "Call 911. Give them the address. Where's your mother?"

"She's gone."

"Tell them."

"I know what to do. This ain't the first time."

Heather watched the young man as he gave information in clear, crisp sentences. The eldest daughter returned with something wrapped in dish towels.

"This is going to hurt, but I'm going to put an ice pack on

your mouth and one on your ribs. He kicked you hard so you might have a busted rib or two."

The eldest boy looked down on her. "Help is on the way."

The ice packs must have numbed the pain enough for the haze to lift from Heather's brain. "Hand me my phone."

While laying on her back, she pushed Steve's name.

It rang several times. "You're spoiling my nap."

"Listen," she whispered. "I'm hurt. Grant's out of jail. He took Sue Ann."

Steve's voice took on the tone of a seasoned police officer. "Location?"

"Sue Ann's. The cops are coming. The children are taking care of me."

Steve kept his words to a minimum. "Put the oldest one on."

The conversation became one sided.

"A busted lip and maybe a broken rib or two... Her purse? Hold on." He hollered into the living room. "Anyone seen Miss Heather's purse?"

Negative answers rang from different voices.

"Her satchel is here with papers in it, but we can't find her purse... No, sir. Her car is gone... Yes, Sir. I'll tell her."

The boy placed her phone on the table. "He said he'll take care of everything and meet you at the hospital."

The first officer to arrive was a Burnet County deputy sheriff. He called the children by name as he entered. It must not have been his first time to make a house call to this residence. He came to where Heather lay and gave the standard instructions she'd given people when she was wearing a uniform, badge and gun. "Lay still, help is on the way."

"He has my purse and weapon. 9mm Sig Sauer. Two extra clips."

"The BOLO's out on your rental. They won't get far."

"Sue Ann's hurt too. She's a hostage."

The deputy depressed a microphone on his uniform's

epaulet and gave his call sign. After dispatch responded, he said, "It's confirmed. Suspect abducted his wife. She's believed to be injured. Suspect armed with 9mm Sig with two extra clips."

A tiny voice came from the youngest girl. "They went on the road that goes to the adventure park."

The deputy asked, "Are you sure?"

"I couldn't keep up with the rest. We ran to the house fast as we could when we heard Mama scream. I saw the car turn right at the main road."

"Thanks, sugar." He depressed his microphone again and went through the normal process. "Witness states suspect vehicle last seen heading east on 1431."

EMS and a sergeant from the sheriff's department arrived at almost the same time. Heather knew the procedure and didn't fight it. First the neck immobilizer, then the backboard, followed by removal from the house on a stretcher and into an ambulance. Vitals, personal data, and the insertion of an IV came next. Questions and more questions. Radio communication by the lead paramedic with the hospital. Siren and lights activated and a hurried ride to and through Marble Falls. It was all familiar, yet different at the same time. She'd never inspected the ceiling of an ambulance and didn't want to repeat the experience.

Every bounce caused her to grimace. Her lip felt like someone injected a hot dog into it. A random thought crossed her mind and her anger rose with each bump. *I haven't hugged or kissed Jack in weeks. Grant Blankenship will pay for this.*

27

After a brief time in the emergency room, a man who said he was from radiology told Heather she was going down the hall for an MRI. He wheeled her gurney into a room with a machine that looked as if it belonged in a science fiction television show. The technician shifted her onto a long, narrow slab and told her she'd need to stay perfectly still during the procedure. The headfirst advancement into the tube made her think of a pizza being shoved into an oven. Despite noise-deadening headphones, the whirling lights and high decibels sounded like a bizarre techno-disco, without the gyrations of her body. Another of life's experiences she didn't want to relive.

Then, it was off to X-ray for scientific snap shots of her brain, spine, and ribs. To complete the circuit, the same cheery attendant wheeled her back to the cold emergency room. The warm blanket the nurse draped over her drafty hospital gown was an unexpected pleasure and stopped her teeth from chattering.

It didn't take long before the emergency room doctor gave her the good news there were no signs of spinal damage or lesions in her brain. One cracked rib and severe bruising proved to be the extent of injuries to that portion of her body. He prescribed a corset-like wrap and rest. Time would heal the crack and take care of the swelling and discoloration.

Easy for him to say.

A plastic surgeon breezed in through the curtain and introduced herself. She touched Heather's face with cold, slender fingers and assessed her with keen eyes. "Not too bad," she said. "The split is on your bottom lip only, but it went almost all the way through. I'll use tiny dissolvable stitches on the inside and a special glue on the outside to minimize scarring. I recommend no lipstick until after it's completely healed. In six months, you won't know it was ever there."

Heather mumbled, "What am I supposed to do about kissing until then?"

The doctor smiled. "Sorry. Can't help you with that. As pretty as you are, he'll wait."

She said thanks, but it came out hollow.

The drug to deaden the area stung, but not for long. Her lip being tugged with no actual pain seemed like an out-of-body experience.

"It will be difficult to eat for a while," said the surgeon. "I hope you like milk shakes and Jello. You won't be on any diet restrictions, but I don't recommend nachos with jalapenos."

It amazed Heather how little time it took for the doctor to stitch her lip back together and breeze off for her next assignment.

A nurse showed up with two familiar faces. "Mother, Father. You didn't have to come. I'm fine."

Her father circled her bed and took a hand as her mother did the same on the other side.

"Don't be silly," said her father. "We had to come. Steve needed a ride."

Heather wanted to sit up, but the doctor had given instructions for her to lay flat. "Steve's here?"

"Of course," said her mother. "So is a very handsome man who's pacing a hole in the lobby's carpet."

"Jack's here, too?"

"He's first rate," said her father. "Steve recognized his voice as Jack was checking in. He left his suitcases at the front desk and insisted he come with us. I like a man who knows his mind."

Her mother winked. "I think he's dashing. Reminds me of your father when he played polo."

The nurse came in. "Your room is ready." She spoke to Heather's mother. "She'll be in room three-seventeen. Give us about twenty minutes to get her settled in."

After what seemed to be an hour, a knock on her door preceded Jack taking quick steps to her bed and taking her hand in his. "Hello, beautiful."

The shot for pain combined with the swollen lip to make her speech sound like she'd downed another bottle of champagne. "It's not so beautiful under this ice pack. Sorry about the scare. I'm all right as long as I don't take a deep breath."

"Cracked and bruised ribs are no fun." He leaned over and kissed her forehead.

"That's not the kiss I was planning on," she said.

"I take rain checks."

She knew her eyelids were drooping, but she fought to keep them open and pay attention. "Keep a running count on the missed kisses. I plan on paying them with interest."

Jack looked toward the door. "I want to keep you to myself, but Steve and your parents have other ideas."

Another kiss on her forehead and Jack's fingers slipped away.

Steve tapped his way to her bed. Heather reached over the rail and grabbed his arm. "Hey, partner."

"Hey, yourself. You sound different with a fat lip. It reminds me of a flat tire."

She chuckled, which was a serious error. "Rule number one," said Heather with a labored breath. "Don't make me laugh." She looked at the other three people in the room. "That goes for everyone. I'm not sure there's enough pain killer in this hospital if you make jokes."

Heather squeezed Steve's hand. "I made a rookie mistake. I didn't put my back to a wall when I sat at the table. A noisy fan was on in Sue Ann's living room that deadened the sound of the screen door opening. By the time I heard a floorboard squeak, he was on me. I tried to get up but..."

"It doesn't matter," said Steve. "You're all right, or at least you will be. I'm going to get out of the way now and let your parents and Jack spoil you."

A sheriff's deputy stepped into the room. "Sorry to interrupt, but I'm supposed to get a statement from Ms. McBlythe. If you're up to it, that is." He looked at those gathered around the bed. "Could you folks wait outside for a few minutes?"

Jack looked the deputy in the eye. "I'm her attorney." He pointed to her parents and identified them. "And this is Steve Smiley. He's a private detective, and he needs to be here as part of an ongoing investigation."

"Fine with me," said the deputy. He took out his phone and told her he'd be recording her statement. Before he turned it on, he said, "I hear you're a former cop, an attorney and a private detective. Normally, I ask a lot of questions, but you know what I need, so I'll let you tell what happened. Start whenever you're ready."

Heather began her tale by stating the reason she was at Sue Ann's house and the time she arrived. Every deep inhale brought a stab of pain, so she kept her sentences short and ended the tale when they loaded her into the ambulance.

Steve's question went to the deputy. "Any updates on Sue Ann and Grant?"

Before he could answer, Sheriff Blake entered the room.

Instead of addressing her, he simply nodded and took off his hat. The Burnet County deputy said he had all he needed and excused himself.

Steve played host and took care of introductions. Handshakes and names were exchanged until everyone knew each other and their reason for being in the room.

Sheriff Blake focused on Heather's mother and father. "Would you mind stepping out for a few minutes? I have some things to discuss with your daughter and Steve that are sensitive. Because Mr. Blackstock is her attorney, he can stay."

Heather's father nodded in agreement and then looked at Jack. "We'll run along. I see Heather is in excellent hands and Rebecca has a spa appointment."

Her mother smiled down on Heather and took her hand. "After your father and I take a walk in the resort's water garden. He's officially on vacation."

Heather squeezed her mother's fingers in reply.

Her father looked at Jack. "I'll arrange a rental to be delivered here for you."

"Thank you, sir," said Jack. "That would be a great help."

After hand squeezes and a kiss to her forehead by her father and one to her cheek by her mother, Heather's parents left. Her mother's voice filtered back into the room before the door clicked shut. "Can you believe it, Al? Our daughter is working a murder case, and the sheriff needs her help."

Steve moved on to business. "What's the latest on Sue Ann?"

Sheriff Blake didn't hesitate. "Lago Vista police found the car abandoned with Sue Ann in it. She's being transported to a hospital in Cedar Park. First reports on her condition are encouraging."

"Grant probably stole another car," said Steve.

Heather's mind latched on to a thought through the fog of pain medicine. "Sheriff, have you notified Rance? He needs to take care of the children."

Sheriff Blake pulled out his phone and placed a call. "Marvin, find Rance Voss and tell him to get to Sue Ann's house on the double... Yeah... tell him what happened, and that he needs to take care of the kids. She's being sent to—You already know? Good... Heather will be fine. One cracked rib, and stitches in her lip... Okay, I'll tell her."

Sheriff Blake looked down on her.

"Marvin says the word from Sue Ann's home is that the kids are worried about Miss Heather and their mom. He'll let them know that you're all right."

He raised his gaze, puffed out his cheeks and blew out a full breath of air. "The further east Grant goes, the harder it's going to be to capture him. By now he's two counties away from my jurisdiction. I'll be glad to get him back in jail, and this time he won't get out."

"Speaking of," said Steve.

The sheriff shook his head and began the explanation. "Two characters dressed as Tarrant County deputies came to the jail this morning with a bench warrant. The man said Grant was to appear before an Austin judge in the morning on another DWI charge. The woman stayed in an unmarked SUV. The deputy called the number on the paperwork and verified an Austin judge signed the warrant."

"Did your people check the deputy's identification?" asked Steve.

"He had a photo I.D." The sheriff straightened his posture. "Before anyone asks, it wasn't the first Tarrant County I.D. my officer had seen. It looked legitimate. Still, it's my department that's responsible for Grant being released."

Steve's brain must have been in overdrive. "Your deputy called the number on the bench warrant, but I'll wager it went to a burner phone held by the pretend female deputy."

The sheriff let out a huff of exasperation. "There's two murders, a jail escape, two assaults, and an abduction all tied together. The Austin press is in my parking lot, ready to ambush me if I go back to the office. A quick arrest would be welcome."

Sheriff Blake rolled the brim of his hat in his hand. "It's time for me to face the music. I need to go disturb the district attorney on his day off. He'll be glad to know he can charge Grant Blankenship with murder, escape, abduction and assault. He won't be so glad to hear we could have avoided all but one of those charges."

No one said anything except to bid the sheriff farewell.

28

The next afternoon Heather managed to dress with her mother's help. Every step she took jarred her ribs as she shuffled to the elevator with Steve by her side. She wiped a line of sweat from her top lip and put one foot in front of the next as they eased their way down the corridor that had mysteriously grown longer.

"Almost there. How are you holding up?"

"I think they gave me defective pain pills."

"Is it time to take another?"

"I'll wait until this is over. I want to have a clear head."

Steve located the door handle and opened it for her. "Sit down. I'll get you a bottle of water."

Heather knew she looked like an eighty-nine-year-old great-grandmother when she lowered herself onto the chair, but she couldn't help it. The wrap the hospital provided was a six-inch wide strip of elastic with Velcro holding it in place. It reminded her of pictures she'd seen of corsets made with whale bones. The torture device held constant pressure on the ribs, much like a boa constrictor.

Steve retrieved two bottles of water and joined her. "Did you look at the results from the DNA tests we sent off?"

"Jack read them to me."

"Were they what we thought?"

"You were right. The family has surprises in store today."

Roy entered the room, took one look at Heather and asked, "What does the other guy look like?"

Heather groaned.

Steve took over for her. "You can visit Grant in jail. I'm surprised you haven't heard about your soon-to-be former brother-in-law's crime spree."

Roy came closer to get a better look at Heather's injuries. "I thought he restricted his beatings to Sue Ann and the kids."

Heather spoke over her swollen lip. "He made an exception for me, but don't worry, he got to Sue Ann too."

Roy sat down next to her, but spoke to Steve. "Is she all right?"

"About the same as Heather."

Leaning forward, he asked through clenched teeth. "Did he hurt the kids?"

Heather put her hand on his and shook her head while Steve said, "If you draw back the blinds, you might see them in the pool. We thought they needed exercise to help them forget what they went through."

Roy was on his feet and headed to the sliding door. "I'll go say hi to them. Where's Sue Ann?"

"In the shade watching them," said Steve. "You'll recognize her by the ice pack on her eye."

The noise from the sliding door covered most of Roy's angry words, but there was no doubt about what he'd like to do to his brother-in-law.

Mae and Patrick arrived next. In keeping with her normal way of entering a room, Mae exclaimed, "I hope you brought all the property titles."

Patrick expressed more compassion. "Ms. McBlythe, did you have an accident?"

"She did," said Steve. "She forgot to duck. Grant went on a rampage yesterday. I'm surprised you haven't heard about it."

A sheepish grin crossed Patrick's face. "Honeymoons don't lend themselves to keeping up with current events."

Mae sat in the second chair on the left side of the table. "Marriage agrees with me. I haven't slept so long in years. What time was it when I woke up, darling?"

"Two-thirty this afternoon."

"I don't know what got into me," said Mae. "It was twelve thirty when we turned out the lights." She raised her chin. "That explains why we haven't heard what Sue Ann's delinquent husband has been doing."

Sue Ann, Rance, and Roy all came in through the sliding door. As usual, Mae ignored them and continued talking to Steve. "Grant must have been out on bond."

"Not exactly. Persons unknown helped him escape from jail."

"Who in their right mind would help that Neanderthal escape?"

At that moment, Sid and Sydney Walsh walked in. "I hope we haven't kept you waiting," said Sydney. "We were unavoidably detained."

It may have been the timing of their entry following Mae's question, but more than one set of eyebrows of those around the table raised. Heather could almost see the wheels turning full speed with Roy, Rance and Patrick. Did this power couple have a hand in Grant's escape?

Sydney looked at Heather and Sue Ann. "We heard police arrested Sue Ann's husband early this morning."

"That's correct," said Steve. "But that was long after he escaped jail and assaulted Heather. He stole her rental, roughed up Sue Ann and kidnapped her for insurance."

Mae stared at Jack, Anna and Angelina, as they entered the room. "Who are these people and why are they here?"

Steve lifted a hand to the door. "The gentleman is Mr. Jack Blackstock. He's an attorney and will represent me and Heather. The two ladies, some of you may recognize. This is Anna Perez and her daughter, Angelina. They're Hector DeLeon's daughter and granddaughter. His death makes them heirs to property mentioned in the will."

Jack led Anna and Angelina to seats at the far end of the table. He then moved to the head of the table and sat beside Heather.

Sheriff Blake came through the door with Marvin Good-night in his wake.

"Let's get on with this," demanded Mae.

"I agree," said Sid. "Are all the deeds in that box beside Ms. McBlythe?"

Heather spoke in a soft voice. "They're here, and so are some extra things we've discovered since we last met."

Sid narrowed his gaze. "What are you trying to pull, Smiley?"

Heather noticed the sheriff held a file folder under his left arm. He turned and took a long look at everyone in the room. "Mr. Smiley and Ms. McBlythe are here to follow the last wishes of Charley Voss. I'm here to arrest a murderer."

Gazes darted from one person to the next like pinballs. More than one person reached for their bottle of water. There seemed to be a sudden epidemic of cotton-mouth.

29

Heather continued to take shallow breaths, but the pain increased as the Tylenol with codeine wore off.

Steve leaned toward her. "Take your pain pill."

"I don't want to miss this. I'll take Motrin, but not the hard stuff."

Jack lifted her purse to the table, and she retrieved two pills from their bottle. One pill didn't make it down on the first try, causing her to cough. She gripped his hand until the squiggly lines in her vision passed.

"Jack," said Steve. "There are documents in her satchel we'll need later. Make sure she doesn't reach for them."

Steve pushed back from the table, rolling his chair, and stood. "A few weeks ago I was sitting at home minding my business when Charley Voss called me with an unusual request. He asked me to be the executor of his will. Does that strike anyone else as unusual?"

Heather watched as several heads nodded.

Mae, as usual, preferred a verbal response. "He was a crazy old man. What does this have to do with my property?"

"You don't have any idea what a profound question that

is." Steve moved to a spot behind her. "Property division is what I'm going to talk about. But first, I have to lay the groundwork. Let's start with the will." He paused. "No. I'll save that for later. Let's begin with the person not mentioned in the will but who is the descendant of Hector DeLeon, Anna Perez."

Sid interrupted. "You're wasting our time, Mr. Smiley."

"I assure you, Mr. Walsh, the story I'm about to tell will change your mind, and your life."

Steve lifted his right hand to belt level with palm open, directing people's attention to Heather. "Sitting by Ms. McBlythe is Mr. Jack Blackstock. This afternoon he escorted Anna and Angelina to their bank in Llano, where they searched Anna's safe deposit box for documents. They located the marriage license for Anna and her late husband. They also retrieved Anna and Angelina's birth certificates. Jack has those documents with him. Of particular interest is Anna's birth certificate. She was born four months after her mother, Rose, married Hector DeLeon."

"So what?" said Mae. "He knocked her up, and they had to get married. It happens all the time with those people."

Steve ignored the comment. "Jack, look in Heather's bag and find the receipt for wages paid to Hector DeLeon. Read the note at the bottom."

"The first file," said Heather.

Jack retrieved it. "It reads: *Hector DeLeon hired as ranch hand.* The note is dated and signed by Robert E. Voss."

"Who's that?" asked Sid.

"Our grandfather," said Roy. "He was a mean old cuss."

Mae and Roy didn't see eye-to-eye on much of anything, but Mae's head bobbed in agreement with his statement.

"Get to the point," said Sid.

Jack looked across the table. "The point is, Hector didn't hire on at the Rocking V until Anna's mother was four and a half months pregnant. Before that, we believe he lived in Mexico."

The room fell silent as people processed the information. A smile of enlightenment tugged at the corners of Roy's mouth, but Steve didn't make the rest of them wait long. "There's no record of Hector DeLeon's existence in the United States before he arrived at the Voss ranch. Heather, Jack and Sheriff Blake checked all available databases and came up blank, except for a work visa issued by INS. After examining other documents, we're sure of a couple of things. Hector DeLeon wasn't granted a work visa until after he was hired by Robert Voss, and he married Anna's mother the day after Robert Voss hired him."

Sidney, a seasoned attorney, was quick with an answer. "That's easily explained. She found herself in trouble and didn't want the shame of having an illegitimate child. She found an illegal, brought him up from Mexico, arranged for him to work on the ranch and married him."

"We considered that," said Steve. "But we also came up with other possibilities after Heather and I interviewed Anna. She told us her mother never lived with Hector on the ranch. He came to town every payday and left enough money for them to live a decent life."

"What else did he have to spend money on?" asked Mae. "We provided his home and food."

Roy contradicted his older sister's account. "Grandpa made him sleep in the barn until Hector could build the cabin in his spare time. As for food, he never got much more than dry beans and tortillas while Grandpa was alive. That changed after he died."

Steve took up where Roy left off. "That brings us to the next point. I found it interesting that Charley waited until after his father died before he married."

Roy issued a scoffing laugh. "Who'd want to bring a bride home with that old buzzard running the show?"

"I also found it interesting," said Steve, "that Anna's mother died a month prior to Charley Voss marrying Pearl, mother to the heirs gathered here today."

Sid slammed his hand on the table. "I'm calling a halt to this. Are you going to award the land to Mae or are we going to settle this in court?"

Steve spoke in a soft tone that required everyone to listen carefully. "Don't worry, Mr. Walsh. Your chances of going to court are getting better by the minute."

"What do you mean?"

The sheriff placed a hand on Sid's shoulder. "Sir. You're dangerously close to going to jail for disturbing the peace."

Sydney cut her eyes to her husband. The icy stare did more to end his rant than the threat from the lawman.

"Let me recap," said Steve. "Hector arrived at the ranch and the next day he married a woman he didn't know. He never lived with her, but provided for her. Four months later, Rose DeLeon gave birth to a baby girl. That child grew up and is here with us today, along with her daughter, Angelina."

Steve allowed the words to settle. Blank looks covered most faces except for Roy's. He grinned but remained quiet.

"Charley didn't marry until after Rose DeLeon died," said Steve. He paused again. "I made a mistake. I should have said Charley did not marry again until after his first wife, Rose, died."

Sid's eyebrows knit together as he put the puzzle pieces together. Sydney threw her head back in a sign of exasperation.

Mae shouted, "So what?"

Roy shook his head and said, "That old dog. He sowed his wild oats with a hot *señorita* and did the honorable thing. Grandpa found out and called in a replacement husband."

Rance sat in silence, looking down at his folded hands while Sue Ann looked out the glass door where her children played in the pool.

Sydney finally said, "You'd better have proof."

The sheriff pulled a document from the file folder and placed it in front of Sydney. "This is a certified copy of the wedding license from Bexar County. Charley and Rose slipped away to San Antonio, where a Justice of the Peace performed the ceremony."

Jack put things in legal terms. "The existence of a legitimate heir with documented preeminence will render your client's claim moot."

Sid turned a painful shade of red. He looked across the table and pointed at Patrick Shaw. "You. This is all your fault."

Sydney stared at Jack. "If all you have is a wedding license and a birth certificate, you still can't prove Anna is Charley's firstborn."

Mae cast her gaze to her husband. "What's everyone talking about? Would someone tell me what's happening? When do I get my land?"

"You're not getting the land," said Sue Ann.

Everyone looked at her.

"Haven't you been listening, Mae? You're not the oldest child. Anna is."

Steve took over. "I want Jack to read a section of the will to you again before I conclude this portion of the meeting."

Jack found the words Heather had highlighted. "Charley wrote: *The other part of me said it should go to my firstborn girl.*"

Steve took over. "Did you notice how gender specific this instruction is? Charley Voss meant for his firstborn daughter to receive an inheritance. If I'd understood this earlier, it would have been Anna playing a hand of poker with Roy, not Mae."

Steve took his time walking around his chair and rolling it back to the table. "We've offered proof today that the firstborn daughter of Charley Voss is Anna Perez. I'm awarding the titles to the land to her. All other awards will remain as previously stated."

It was Sydney's turn to speak. "You've made a grave error, Mr. Smiley. Expect a summons."

Mae was on her feet with tears making black tracks down her face. "What about me? What do I get?" She turned to Patrick, but he stood and looked to the door.

"Sit down, Mr. Shaw," said Sheriff Blake. "Steve's not finished."

"One more thing concerning family matters," said Steve.

Roy clapped his hands together. "This soap opera is getting better by the minute. Does dear-old-Dad have another ten or twelve children we don't know about?"

"Not exactly," said Steve. "But you're on the right track."

Sue Ann turned around. "Do you have to tell them, Mr. Smiley?"

"I have to. They deserve the truth."

She nodded and cast her gaze back toward the pool.

"If you remember," said Steve. "We took DNA samples from each of the Voss children. DNA results also came from the autopsies performed on Charley and Hector. The results prove that three of the four Voss children have the same father and mother: Mae, Roy and Sue Ann. Charley Voss, however, is not Rance's father."

Rance's head slowly raised. His response sounded like it came from some place of hidden knowledge. "Hector's my father?"

"Yes."

Steve's single word caused Angelina to gasp. "I'm related to Rance?"

"Not by blood."

Mae's eyes opened wide. "That means Rance isn't a Voss and shouldn't get any inheritance. I should get the million dollars from the life insurance and the cattle."

Steve shook his head. "No, Mae. Your father specifically named Rance in the will. He spelled out what he wanted him to receive. You, Roy and Sue Ann all signed away any claim to property or assets already awarded."

"It's not fair!" shouted Mae.

"This is ridiculous," said Sid. "We're leaving."

"One more thing," said Steve. "Before you consider suing, you need to know we have a DNA sample from a lock of Anna's mother's hair. Anna is the firstborn child from the union of Charley and Rose, even though Rose went by Hector's last name."

The wolves turned on each other. Sydney pointed across the table. "Mr. Shaw. You've defrauded our firm. I'll not rest until you've paid back every penny with interest." She gathered her legal pad and purse and stood.

Patrick turned away from Mae and hung his head.

"Nobody leaves," said Sheriff Blake. "We have more unfinished business."

30

After shifting in her seat, Heather wished she hadn't. Steve leaned into her and whispered. "Do you want Jack to take you to your room?"

"I'm fine. The pills are taking the edge off the pain." It was a lie, but she wouldn't miss this, even if the broken end of a rib was sticking out.

Steve repeated his action of pushing back his chair and standing.

While he made comments about moving on to the murder of Hector DeLeon, Heather took stock of those gathered. Anna and Angelina held hands, both too stunned to speak. Roy rocked in his chair, his smile signaling he approved of what had transpired. Sid and Sydney stared daggers at Patrick Shaw. Sue Ann kept her gaze fixed on the pool in the distance. The millionaire mother didn't fool Heather this time around; she tracked her brood and listened to the proceedings at the same time.

Heather shifted her gaze. Rance stole smiles and glances with Angelina and Anna. He seemed happy that Anna had won her rightful inheritance and she guessed he was even more pleased to learn his father was the man that raised him.

As for Mae, she rested her head on crossed arms folded into a makeshift pillow. Shoulders rose and fell with her sobs. Patrick kept his chair turned ninety degrees so as not to look at his wife of two days.

Steve took a swig from his bottle of water and screwed the cap back on. "Heather and I came here with no serious thoughts of working a murder case. We didn't receive an invitation to look into the murder of Charley, so we restricted our activities to things related to the will. That proved trickier than we expected. Our focus expanded when Angelina asked us to investigate the murder of her grandfather."

He walked in halting steps, circling the table. "I asked myself several questions. Why did anyone want to murder Hector? Was he a threat to someone? Did someone have a grudge against him? Was his murder related to Charley's death?"

Steve walked until he stood behind Rance. "In Hector's murder, we didn't have any witnesses and the small amount of forensic evidence we had pointed to Rance. He had access to a 30-30 rifle that went missing. We know the caliber by a round discovered by the forensics team. They found a slug embedded in the doorframe of the ranch house and a spent cartridge casing by the barn. Rance's alibi was he stayed in the travel trailer of a friend west of Llano on the night of Hector's murder. Not a great alibi, but plausible."

Steve swept a path in front of him with his cane until he stood behind Sue Ann. "I didn't seriously consider Sue Ann to be a suspect. At least not at first. As we witnessed earlier, she's smarter than most people give her credit for. I didn't realize this until Heather and I went to her home and saw how she managed it, the garden, the animals and, most of all, her children. They're bright and industrious. They didn't get that way on their own, and their father isn't the type to give them much attention. I had to reevaluate Sue Ann as a suspect."

He took a few more steps and stationed himself behind Roy. Before Steve could speak, Roy said, "Looks like it's my turn to sweat. Did you bring a rubber hose to beat a confession out of me?"

"That would be too easy. I know you cheated in the card game you played with Mae. Heather counted the cards after the game was over. There should have been fifty-four, which included the two jokers. There were the correct number of cards, but two of them were the same. You took a card off the table and replaced it with one that would give you a busted flush. You wanted to lose the hand."

Mae's head jerked up. "He cheated? That means I won. His million dollars is mine."

"Not so fast," said Roy. "There's no way you can prove I cheated. That deck may have come with two identical cards. Also, you signed a document stating you won the hand fair and square and that you'd make no claim on any of the proceeds from the will."

Rance tilted his head and asked. "Why would you cheat in order to lose?"

"*If* I cheated," said Roy, "I did so because I wanted nothing to do with the land. I'm a gambler, not a real estate developer. That would have been one headache after another." He gave his head a nod toward Sydney and Sid. "Look at the type of people I'd be dealing with. They're bigger cheats than anyone you'll find at a poker table. I'll take a million bucks and freedom any day."

The corners of Roy's mouth turned upward. "How do you think Grandpa and Great-Grandpa won all the parcels of land in the first place? I was the only one that paid attention to Grandpa when he played poker."

"We have five attorneys with us today," said Steve. "What are the odds of Mae winning a civil case against Roy if she claims he cheated?"

Sid and Sydney laughed. Heather shook her head to avoid having to speak. Patrick said nothing. Jack gave the most complete answer. "Even if you could prove cheating, which you can't, the document you signed released Roy from all liability."

Mae's head went back on her arms for another spell of crying.

Steve continued. "Roy may be a cheat, but he didn't kill Hector. His alibi of being at a poker game holds up."

"The last Voss child is Mae," said Steve.

She opened her eyes and looked around the table. No one offered a sympathetic look. "Quit looking at me like that. I didn't kill him."

Steve nodded. "Mae isn't having a good day, and it's going to get worse. But she's right, she didn't kill Hector."

After moving between Roy and Sydney, Steve stopped. "We have one family member to consider who isn't with us today." He turned to where Sheriff Blake stood. "Could you give us an update on Grant?"

The lawman spoke in a clear, even tone. "Austin Police arrested Grant this morning. They took him and a woman believed to be a female accomplice into custody at an apartment leased to the woman. Her name is Cindy King."

"Cindy?" said Sid. "She's one of our paralegals."

Sydney gave him a fist to the arm and told him to keep quiet.

Steve moved to his right. "I promised you'd go to court, Sid. You'll get to convince a jury you knew nothing about Cindy helping Grant escape or a conspiracy to commit murder."

Sydney turned to face Steve. "Be very careful, Mr. Smiley. I defy you to produce any evidence that either of us were involved in the death of Hector DeLeon or Grant Blankenship's escape."

"Not directly," said Steve. "But you knew about the ongoing relationship between Ms. King and Patrick. You were desperate to get the property, and there's every indication you supported the scheme to acquire it. Your firm bankrolled the engineers and architects to do preliminary work. You're also paying for the condo Patrick and Mae are staying in. All that smacks of a conspiracy."

Patrick turned to them and said, "It's you that needs to be careful, Sydney." His narrow-eyed gaze bore into her and then her husband.

Sydney stood and leaned on the desk with her palms flat. "Don't even think about trying to throw us under the bus. This was your idea."

The couple traded roles as Sid tugged on his wife's sleeve. "Sit down and be quiet. Remember, we have nothing to hide and nothing to say."

Patrick pointed to the couple. "Everything was their idea. They found out Mae was heiress to miles of lakefront property and thousands of acres of undeveloped land. They talked me into starting a relationship with her and then marrying this..." He gave Mae a look of utter disdain. "This plastic loser of a woman."

Heather noticed Mae's fists pull together in tight balls.

Patrick kept going. "They cooked up the scheme to get rid of everyone and everything that stood in their way. That included Hector. I tried to talk them out of it. They said they had to get rid of him because his cabin was where the front door of the new hotel would be." He looked down at Mae. "I even tried to talk them out of their plan that I marry this... thing." He looked around the room. "That's the truth. Give me a Bible and I'll swear on it."

Mae leapt from her chair. Her manicured fingernails dug into Patrick's cheeks, leaving long bloody gouges. He fell backward and she began punching his face with both fists. Curses flew as fast as her hands.

"Get her off of me," hollered Patrick.

Deputy Goodnight took his time getting to the altercation. He grabbed her around the waist and pulled her off as she screamed, "You married me while you were carrying on with some office bimbo? No wonder you insisted on waiting so long. What else did you do?"

Steve answered her question. "He drugged you when he needed to get away to kill Hector," said Steve. "Is that right, Sheriff?"

Eyes turned to the sheriff. "Deputies executed a search warrant on the condo Sid and Sydney rented for Patrick and Mae. They found a bottle of sedatives in Patrick's suitcase."

Mae stopped struggling, her eyes wide as she stared at Patrick. "You told me those pills would make me frisky. No wonder I've been sleeping so much."

Marvin directed Mae away from Patrick. "Sit by Roy and behave yourself or I'll handcuff you to a table leg."

Mae stomped to the other side of room, plopped down beside her brother and crossed her arms.

Roy gave her a pat on the arm. "Good job, sis. That creep had it coming."

"Shut up!"

He laughed. "That's the spirit. Just like old times. There's hope for you yet."

"Steve, is that all?" asked Sheriff Blake.

"We're rounding third base."

The sheriff moved to where Patrick lay on the carpet. "Get up. You ain't hurt."

Patrick rose to his feet and pulled a handkerchief out of his back pocket. He dabbed blood off his face and pinched his nose to stem the bleeding.

Steve moved to the head of the table and took his seat. "Sid, I promised you'd see me in court. I failed to mention it would be a criminal court."

"Don't be too sure of yourself, Mr. Smiley," said Sydney.

The sheriff responded, "I have sufficient grounds to arrest you, and deputies are waiting outside the door to do just that." He added, "You two aren't in Austin. I think you'll find the D.A. and judge in Llano County different from what you're used to dealing with."

Steve took his turn again. "Conspiracy to commit murder will be proven after Patrick and Cindy King tell the sheriff their side of the story."

"Don't underestimate us," said Sydney with a half-smile.

The sheriff added, "Deputies are taking files from your office as we speak. Somebody must have alerted the press. I was told film crews are there. We've already impounded your car and we'll make sure to give your home a thorough search."

Sydney lost her smile.

Heather knew the best was yet to come.

Steve turned and faced Patrick. "You overplayed your hand, Pat. That's what gave you away."

"It was Sid and Sydney. They killed Charley Voss and Hector."

Steve shook his head. "These two are big sharks. You're not in their league." Steve raised his hand and showed a quarter inch gap between his thumb and forefinger. "You're a little bitty shark who wanted to swim with the big boys."

"You'll see," said Patrick. "You'll all see."

Steve's head went side to side. "You didn't think it through, Patrick. You tried too hard. If you hadn't killed Hector, I wouldn't have dug deeper. You planted the rifle in Rance's truck, but it was too clean. If Rance had done it, the gun at least would have had some residual dust from being in the truck.

Then, you set Grant up to take the fall by placing a spent shell casing in his boat."

"He had a shell in his boat? That proves he killed Hector."

The sheriff took his turn. "Speaking of the boats. I spoke to the owner of the stolen boat. It took a little convincing for him to remember, but it seems he knows you, Patrick. What a coincidence."

"So what? I know a guy with a boat."

"I think there's a little more to it," said Steve. "That boat was payment for Grant putting the torch to the ranch house, cabin and barn. It will be up to the sheriff to prove this, but I believe you made a deal of some sort with the boat's owner. It probably had something to do with a guarantee of the boat being returned if he reported it as stolen."

Steve shrugged. "It's just a theory, but Grant will gladly plead guilty to arson in exchange for testifying against you. And he'll have the truth on his side."

All eyes focused on Patrick as Steve continued. "Hector's death was so needless. It didn't occur to me that Charley had ever married and fathered a child before he married Pearl. As far as I was concerned, Mae was the oldest Voss child. I thought the strangely worded will was just an odd way an old rancher would express himself."

Steve took a drink of water. "It was the murder, the planting of the rifle, the stealing of a boat and the burning of the buildings that told me to keep digging."

"Rance killed him with the saddle gun," said Patrick.

"A minute ago, you said it was Grant who killed Hector."

Heather asked, "How did you know it was a saddle gun?"

The question hung in the air. "You must have found the old 30-30 when you scouted the place," said Steve. "And that was easy to do. Hector and Rance are almost always out on the property working. Plenty of people pull onto the sandbar, swim and sunbathe on the bank. No one would question a boat anchored there. You broke in the main house, took the rifle, waited for Hector and killed him. But that wasn't enough. You thought you needed to frame Rance, and then frame Grant as well."

The sheriff spoke up. "It was really dumb to call 911 and leave an anonymous tip from a burner phone. We went through the motions with Rance, but that only helped to remove suspicion from him."

Steve shook his head. "Why on earth did you and Cindy King dress like Travis County deputies and use false documents to get Grant out of jail? I realize it was easy for you to put on disguises and forge a bench warrant, but how stupid can you get?"

"I'm not saying anything without an attorney present."

Steve opened up both arms. "There's four to choose from. Take your pick."

"We decline to represent him," said Sydney.

"I'm on vacation with my girlfriend," said Jack. "I have neither the time nor the inclination to represent this man and neither does she."

Heather gave Jack's hand a firm squeeze.

"Patrick," said Steve. "It looks like you're up the creek without a lawyer."

The sheriff nodded at Marvin. He moved to face Patrick. "I'm arresting you for the murder of Hector DeLeon, impersonating an officer of the law, aiding an escape and costing me two sleepless nights watching Anna and Angelina's house that never burned."

Heather couldn't help but chuckle, which caused her to pull her elbows in tight.

The sheriff had already opened the door. Two deputies entered with handcuffs at the ready and approached Sid and Sydney.

Steve leaned into Heather and whispered. "Take the pill.

Jack will take you to your room and tuck you in. I'm scheduled to have dinner with your parents and then play a round of night golf with them."

31

Heather sat in the passenger's seat of the SUV and Jack drove, while Steve and her father occupied the rear seat and jabbered about golf. Two full days of bed rest resulted in a significant reduction in pain and a desire to get up and start moving. The swelling in her lip had gone down to a point she didn't sound like she had a huge dip of snuff in her mouth.

Looking at Jack, she had a desire to apologize again for ruining their vacation. She put the thought away and reached for his hand. He'd played a couple rounds of golf and had stories to tell about how he and her father let Steve drive the golf cart. The mere thought of a blind man tearing down a fairway was enough to pull her lips into a crooked smile.

Heather pointed to the gravel road Jack was to turn on. "Anna and Angelina must already be here. They left the gate open."

Steve piped up from the back seat. "We'd better close it behind us. Rance said there are still some strays."

As Jack played rancher and shut the gate, Heather's father made a comment. "This land is much rougher than I imagined. I don't know how anyone could scratch out a living from it."

"It's all about water," said Steve. "If you have it, you can make it look like paradise."

"Like Horseshoe Bay," said Heather. "I'm still amazed they took land like this and turned it into a world class resort."

Jack climbed back in the SUV and they set off on the dusty, bumpy ride. Heather was glad she took extra strength Tylenol before she left the hotel.

The SUV eased to a stop between Angelina's car and Rance's truck. The rough road reminded her that the rib had a long way to go.

The remains of the Voss ranch house sat in a charred heap thirty yards to their right. Only the smoke-blackened stone chimney and a few cedar stumps used for floor supports remained.

Angelina kicked the dirt with a white tennis shoe and chewed on a fingernail. Her mother stood close to her and nudged her once everyone had gathered under the shade of an oak tree singed by the blaze. "Thanks for agreeing to meet with us. We want to discuss something with you, but I don't know exactly how to do it."

Rance spoke up. "They want your advice on selling the land."

"Ah," said Heather. "I was wondering what you planned to do with it. How can I help?"

Rance chuckled. "They want you to buy it from them."

Heather tried not to look startled, but sensed her eyes had widened. "How much land?"

"Well," said Angelina in a small voice. "All of it."

"Every acre," said Rance in a full voice. "All the land in Llano County and the surrounding counties."

Heather tilted her head. "Why me?"

Rance's response came with a glint of pleasure in his eye. "They trust you."

"But why not develop it yourself? It would be worth so much more."

Angelina's pony tail swung from side to side. "Mama and I paid close attention to what everyone said in the meeting Monday afternoon. Steve was right by calling Sid and Sydney sharks. Roy lost the card game to Mae so he wouldn't inherit the land. He could tell a blessing from a burden. Mama and I would worry about every decision we had to make, and we'd end up fighting."

"You could list the properties with someone local."

"Rance tells me you already know what the land is worth," said Angelina. "Mamma wants to sell everything to you at twenty percent below market value. We trust you and it's worth it to us to not have to worry."

Heather took in a breath that puffed out her cheeks as she exhaled. She looked at her father. He had on his poker face.

"I tell you what," said Heather. "You and Rance take my father down to the lake. Show him the lakefront and come back. I'll have an answer for you."

Rance led the way to the barn, down to the burned-out cabin and out of sight and earshot.

Steve asked, "Are they gone?"

"Yep," said Jack.

"No one can hear us?"

"They're long gone."

Steve reached into his pocket. He pulled out a five-dollar bill and handed it to Jack.

"What are you up to?" asked Heather.

"I'm hiring Jack as my attorney. This conversation is confidential."

Jack gave Heather a quizzical look, which she returned with a shrug of her shoulders and said, "All right, Steve. At my usual rates, this gives you less than a minute."

"You'll want to pay me for what you're about to hear. Take

me to the barn."

Heather placed his hand on her shoulder and led him to the front door of the barn.

"Have Jack help you find the place with the dent in the ground."

Heather scanned the area she remembered Steve commenting on. She found the divot and pointed it out to Jack. He ran his hand over it and his fingers went down a couple of inches. He stood up. "Found it. What does it mean?"

Steve placed both hands on the top of his cane. "We've been so busy dealing with the inheritance and Hector's killer that everyone seemed to forget about Charley and how he died."

"Blunt force trauma to the back of his head," said Heather. "I assumed it was Patrick's first murder."

"That's what the sheriff thinks, but it's not true. There was no transfer of trace material onto Charley's head. Remember?"

"That's impossible," said Jack.

"Almost impossible," said Steve. "I have a theory. I can't prove it, but I believe I know how Charley died, and it wasn't murder."

Steve pointed to the barn. "Above the open double doors, there's another opening in the loft. When they unloaded hay from a trailer, the top bales went directly through that door. They let gravity bring the bales down whenever they needed them."

"I'm not following," said Jack.

"If you read between the lines of the will, you can tell Charley grew tired of living. What if he planned and carried out his own death? That would explain why I got a phone call out of the blue, and that afternoon he took action."

"You're saying Charley Voss committed suicide?" asked Jack. "How did he hit himself in the back of his head hard enough to die and not leave a trace?"

Steve had come up with unique solutions to solving crimes

in the past, but this one stumped Heather. "There wasn't a club or a shovel or anything near him when Rance found him."

Steve pointed to the loft. "Use your imagination. Picture a board slanting downward from the loft, which was used to slide a bale of hay to the bed of a pickup truck. The plank is wide, but doesn't stick out the upper door very far. Now slide something else down the ramp. Something heavy enough to kill someone. What would happen if that object hit Charley in the back of the head?"

Jack looked up to the blackened loft and then down to the indentation in the ground. "It would kill him, but that still doesn't account for Rance not finding that object near the body."

Steve walked to the depression and felt the hole. He stood and backed one long step toward the barn. "I think the divot was a practice run. Charley needed to make sure of the trajectory so he'd know where to stand. He rigged the board, placed the object on it, and let it slide. When he was sure where to stand, he did it again. This time for real."

"But the transfer?" said Heather. "You still haven't accounted for it or how he released something heavy enough to kill him. Also, whatever it was, it wasn't anywhere near the body."

Steve allowed a few silent moments to pass before he spoke in a whisper. "Imagine a large block of ice."

Jack shook his head, but it turned into a nod. "It's possible! All he would need was some sort of trigger to release it. It could be as simple as a nail or two barely holding it in place. When the ice melted, down it came."

Heather stared at Steve, then hung her head. He'd done it again. What Jack didn't realize was that Steve, through his gift of associative chromesthesia, had known all along it wasn't a homicide because he didn't see red, only a light pink.

Steve kicked dirt in the divot. "Jack, you're a defense attorney. Poke holes in my theory."

241

"It's an unprovable crime. All the evidence melted, evapo-rated, or burned in the fire. They didn't find the body for days and it's summer in Central Texas. Fire destroyed the loft, which included the slide, or ramp, or whatever you want to call it."

"That's the same conclusion I reached. That's why I won't tell the insurance company about my theory. Roy, Rance, and Sue Ann will keep their money."

Jack took it a step further. "The D.A. will never have evidence that links Patrick or anyone else to Charley's death. It will remain an open case."

Heather dealt with her conflicted emotions as they walked back to the vehicles. On the one hand, Steve had left her in the dark on much of the case. Could she blame him? A potential financial disaster involving her father, and a romance she wanted to pursue left Steve to work on his own. A broken rib and a scar would remind her to be fully engaged the next time they set out to solve a murder. She concluded Steve had included her as much as he could.

The sound of voices coming from the lake grew louder. Heather's father continued to pepper Angelina with questions about the land and expounded on the potential it held. Soon, the group reassembled and she took her father by the hand. "Will you excuse us for a few minutes?"

In a low voice Heather whispered. "What do you think? Is it an investment worth pursuing?"

His eyes twinkled. "People are flocking to Texas in droves. There is virtually no undeveloped lakefront property in the state. This tract is a rare find." His voice dropped. "I'm not sure about the other properties, but you can't go wrong buying below market value."

Heather looked up at him and raised her eyebrows. "All the properties come with full mineral rights."

Her father winked at her. "There must be something under all the cactus that's of value. You'd be foolish not to jump on this. It will make a fine addition to McBlythe Enterprises' portfolio."

This was the part Heather dreaded but knew it had to be done. "I hope what I'm going to say won't destroy our relationship for another ten years. I was serious about striking out on my own. I can't lead the life you want me to. You're my father and I love you, but I want to chart my own course. I'll buy the land, but it will be with my company's money and in my company's name."

He nodded and looked toward the lake. His gaze shifted back to her face. "If that's the way you want it. I'll support you in whatever way I can. I've come to realize being your father means more to me than land or gold."

Heather reached up and kissed his cheek. "Thank you, Father."

She hooked her arm in his and they started walking toward the others. "I had a talk with mother. She told me you never took her on a honeymoon. Why don't you stay here a few more days and relax?"

"That's not possible. Meetings and trips are already planned and can't be cancelled."

Heather stopped. She lowered her chin and nodded. "I understand, and I'm sure Mother does too."

"It's not the way it sounds. I asked your mother if she wanted to come back in the fall when it wasn't so blasted hot." He grinned and held out his arms. "We'll expect you and Jack to join us, and I plan on beating both of you in a round of golf."

Heather buried her head in his chest. "There's hope for you yet, Father."

Ready for more Smiley and McBlythe?
Turn the page to read a preview of their next adventure.

A detective's perfect vacation: sun, sand, surf... and murder.

Escape to South Padre Island, Texas to solve the
Murder In The Dunes.

Murder In The Dunes
Excerpt

The first knock on Heather's door barely registered in her brain. Stuck in the land between dreams and awake, she struggled to determine if the noise had its origin in the here-and-now, or if it emanated from a more ethereal world. The second triplet of knocks and Kate's strained voice gave context to the situation. The door opened and Kate appeared, fully dressed.

"Steve called. He told me to wake you."

"Wh..." Her voice cracked and Heather had to take another run at asking the one-word question. "Why?"

Kate answered while wringing her hands. "Something's happened. Police are swarming the parking lot like so many ants."

Heather grabbed a light summer robe, slipped it on, and put a half hitch in the belt. "Can you see them from the balcony?"

Kate nodded a wordless reply.

Quick, barefooted steps took Heather to the sliding door that separated the living room from the balcony. It was already open a few inches, so she hooked her hand in the metal frame and gave the door a push. Once at the rail, she had a seagull's view of a scene below. Emergency lights of red, blue, orange, and white winked, blinked, and bounced off reflective surfaces, giving the scene a kaleidoscopic appearance. Crime scene tape made irregular boxes at two locations. The first was in the parking lot. It didn't rate much attention.

Heather visually followed a wooden walkway that led to the beach. Halfway down was the place of heightened activity. "Bring me the binoculars on your bookshelf."

Kate came back in seconds. Heather made the necessary adjustments to sharpen the focus. "There's a body lying face down. If there was any sign of life, they'd be working on him, or her."

"Do you think it could involve foul play?" asked Kate.

Heather kept looking. "Considering the location, and the second place that's taped off, I'd say it's almost a sure bet."

Kate jumped when she heard an insistent knock on the door. Heather lowered the binoculars. "Don't answer. I need to see who it is first."

Heather peered through the peephole. A fisheye view of Steve and Jack had a hall-of-mirrors quality to it, but caused Heather to release a tense breath. She unhooked the chain, twisted the handle of the deadbolt, and opened the door.

"I'll take the recliner," said Steve. He spoke as he walked with sure steps, his cane leading the way. "This apartment should have a better view than ours. What can you see?"

"Two crime scenes," said Heather. "One in the parking lot and one off the boardwalk in the dunes. There's a body."

"Man or woman?"

"I can't tell."

"Details." Steve made a steeple of his fingers.

Heather recounted the basics, picked up the binoculars, and said, "Come with me. I'll tell you everything I see."

All four went on the patio. Steve and Kate sat on padded patio chairs while Heather stood beside Jack at the rail. Once again, Heather gazed at the more distant scene. "The body is dressed in black or navy and is fully clothed. He or she has black hair. The face is away from us."

"Can you tell how long the hair is?"

"Not sure, but it's definitely black."

"That eliminates one possible victim," said Steve.

"Who's that?" asked Kate.

"Connie. When I heard all the sirens this morning, I thought it might be her past catching up with her."

Heather handed the binoculars to Jack and turned to see how Kate would react. Her brows were pinched together and she was dry washing her hands. "What past are you talking about?"

"It's best you don't know at this point," said Steve. He must have realized his words could have been kinder. "I counted the number of sirens. The first arrived an hour ago and continued in a steady stream. I quit counting at fifteen. Put that with a body dressed in all black inside crime scene tape and you're looking at a homicide. If so, the police will question everyone who might know something or have suspicions. I did some background checks on Connie for Heather. What I found out could have a bearing if it's a homicide on the property. The police will want to interview everyone. I don't want to tell you yet, because what you don't know, you can't tell."

"Steve's right," said Jack. "Cops can be heavy-handed if they suspect you're holding back. They won't suspect deception if you really don't know anything."

Jack put the binoculars to his eyes. "Forensics is here. They're taking photos of the body in situ."

"Once they get enough photos," said Steve, "they'll go through the pockets and try to find something to identify the victim."

Jack handed the binoculars to Heather. She stared for several seconds. "Uh-oh. They're bagging the hands."

"Does that mean what I think it does?" asked Kate.

"Standard procedure for a homicide," said Steve. "A lot of crimes are solved by what they dig out from under fingernails."

"They're bagging what looks like a wallet," said Heather.

"That could be a good break," said Steve. "It makes a positive ID easier if there's a driver's license. Anything else?"

"There's a couple of cops at the end of the boardwalk. They seem interested in an ATV parked there."

Jack tapped Heather's shoulder. "Take a look at the other crime scene. Whoever drove up has the attention of the officers standing around."

Heather pivoted and found the person Jack referred to. "Looks like a middle-age woman."

"It must be Gloria," said Steve.

"Who?" asked Kate.

"Gloria Giles, the chief of police."

Heather chuckled. "I don't know what she said, but the officers are scattering like someone set off a stink bomb."

Steve rose from his chair. "This is when things slow down. Let's have breakfast while we're waiting."

"Waiting for what?" asked Kate.

"Gloria and one of her officers. They should be here in about an hour." The certainty of Steve's words no longer came as a surprise to Heather. When murder was in the air, Steve changed into a different man, one who rarely made mistakes.

"I'll start a fresh pot of coffee," said Kate, as she bustled to the kitchen.

Heather walked to the glass door and slid it shut to prevent any accidental eavesdropping. "Spill it, Steve. Who's the dead person in the sand?"

His words came back with force. "How should I know?"

Heather took a step toward him. "I may be half-asleep, but I'm not hard of hearing. That song and dance you did for Kate about how it would be better if she didn't know about Connie had the ring of counterfeit money to it. You snapped at her out of fear. What are you afraid of?"

Steve pulled off his sunglasses and rubbed his sightless

eyes. "I may be wrong, but if that's not Connie wearing a black wig down in the sand, I think it's Kate's ex-husband, Ricardo."

Heather's stomach tightened.

"Kate's ex?" asked Jack, before he let out a low whistle. "That means Kate will be suspect number one with the cops."

"Like I said, I could be wrong. It's a good thing you were with her all night," said Steve.

"Well," said Heather. "Not exactly all night."

Murder In The Dunes is available in eBook and paperback at your favorite online retailer.

Drawing from his extensive background in criminal justice, Bruce Hammack writes contemporary, clean read detective and crime mysteries. He is the author of the Smiley and McBlythe Mystery series and the Star of Justice series. Having lived in eighteen cities around the world, he now lives in the Texas hill country with his wife of thirty-plus years.

Follow Bruce on Bookbub and Goodreads for the latest new release info and recommendations. Sign up for his newsletter at brucehammack.com and receive a free short story.

Thank you for reading one of my books. I hope the mystery satisfied your appetite for a good 'whodunit.' I would be very grateful if you would take a minute to leave a review at your favorite retail site, Bookbub or Goodreads. Reviews help authors keep churning out stories for you to enjoy.

Happy Reading!
Bruce